THE
MAP

CWC Collaborative Fiction Novel
Written by 24 International Authors

Copyright © 2017 CW Publishing House

All rights reserved.

ISBN: 1-946275-00-X
ISBN 13: 978-1-946275-00-4

ABOUT CWC

Collaborative Writing Challenge is aptly named to describe what we do. We bring aspiring writers together from all over the world to collaborate on a full-length fiction novel. We accept writers of all ages with varying degrees of experience, as we believe everyone has something to offer.

Each chapter is written by four or five different writers, and each week, one chapter is selected to form part of the ongoing novel. The experience is challenging and unique, as the writers never meet or discuss their visions for the story.

Every story is guided by a Story Coordinator, who checks names, facts, and integrity, and who works with each chapter writer to get the best results. This story has been kissed by many hands who have yet to read the completed novel.

We also introduced a new element to CWC, a short story competition, to give our writers a chance to submit a stand-alone story to be published in the novel of the same genre. At the end of this book, you will find '**Next Time'** by **M.E. Anders**. Her story was selected as the winner. Our runner-up was written by **Lorah Jaiyn**, titled '**The Swamp'**. You can read 'The Swamp' on the CWC website. Congratulations to you both.

For more information, please visit:
www.collaborativewritingchallenge.com

IBBY

This is CWC's fifth project. 10% of profits from the sales of this book will be donated to the charity IBBY. This is a wonderful organization, dedicated to providing children from all over the world with access to books.

We will be donating to the specific project called the **IBBY Fund for Children in Crisis,** which provides support for children whose lives have been disrupted through war, civil disorder, or natural disaster. The two main activities supported by the Fund are the therapeutic use of books and storytelling in the form of Bibliotherapy, and the creation or replacement of selected book collections appropriate to each situation.

Please see further details about this charity by accessing their website: **www.ibby.org**

DEDICATION

This book is dedicated to all the writers who dared to get involved in a CWC collaboration. The interest in each new project is phenomenal, allowing us to start multiple projects of varying genres. This has resulted in better-quality submissions, giving the collaborations the best chance possible at being successful.

I would also like to mention my online writing friends who have brought so much fun and inspiration into my life. This encourages me to continue growing CWC and bringing people from all walks of life together!

And, of course, our CWC Story Coordinators, who work tirelessly to make each project successful. You are all a pleasure and an inspiration.

Laura Callender - CWC Founder

THE WRITERS

We had over 70 writers sign up for The Map, and had 59 chapters submitted in total, 36 of which were selected for the story. The authors came from 5 different countries: America, Canada, UK, Greece, and Australia.

Rather than fill these pages with details about all 24 authors, all their pictures and bios can be found on the CWC Website. Please do stop by and learn more about our talented contributing writers. Some have very little writing experience, and some have reels of accomplishments under their belts. I think you would be hard-pressed to identify their individual chapters, and it's just possible that your favorite chapter could have been written by a fresh-faced, up-and-coming writer. There are certainly a few names that we will be looking out for in the future.

With CWC projects, it is inevitable that some writers will have their chapters rejected. We had some incredible submissions that we just couldn't use. These chapters are always integral to shaping the story, as the variety in chapters gave us the chance to find the best fit. These writers are as much a part of the teamwork that brought this project to completion, so to those who go unnamed: Thank you for your wonderful contributions and effort!

ACKNOWLEDGMENTS

This project has brought together so many talented people. I would like to thank **Crystal MM Burton**, who had her starter chapter 'The Map' selected by her fellow writers from 12 entries. Her work inspired so many great submissions each week, resulting in the story you are about to enjoy. Coincidentally, the voters had no idea that The Map was also written by the person coordinating this project. It gave Crystal so much excitement to continue to drive this story to a phenomenal conclusion.

As always, our Chief Editor **Kathrin Hutson** has done an outstanding job getting The Map ready for publication. It is a pleasure working with you, my friend.

I would like to take a moment to thank two wonderful ladies, **Jane Dorothy Warner & Evelyn K. Pentikis**, who kindly proofread prior to publishing.

My biggest thanks must go to **all of our writers** who agreed to participate in this project. With each new project, demand increases, but so far, we manage to find a place for everyone. Some writers are not always proficient in the genre we are writing, but often their creative minds produce work so wonderful, they surprise themselves. We are very proud of all your work.

A NOTE FROM THE STORY COORDINATOR

I had the honor of coordinating CWC's fifth collaboration, *The Map*. Though the mystery/drama/romance genre mash-up wasn't new to our veteran writers—the same genre was used in our second collaboration, *Ambition*—I was amazed by just how unique this story turned out to be. Every starter chapter we received had a perfect blend of mysterious events, dramatic shadow, and romantic tension. I was so excited for this genre that I myself even submitted a starter chapter, knowing the final choice would be made by the writers, keeping it fair. To my utter surprise, my own starter chapter was chosen as Chapter 1! I can't even begin to express how blown away I was by the direction the writers took the story. I had no set path in mind when I typed it up, just a typical waitress with a handsome new husband who is more than he seems, and the writers took it above and beyond.

Right from the start, the writers launched into a suspenseful drama that kept me begging for the following week to arrive, just so I could get more submissions and see what happened next. Whether the writers were experienced with mystery/romance or not, whether they were long-time authors or newbie writers, they all had something brilliant to offer. If only I had the time—and space—to tell you about the incredible chapters that *weren't* chosen. This tale truly could have taken a different turn. It was a fun challenge to find submissions that furthered all three aspects of the genre, though each week typically focused on a different angle.

The amount of chapters I received was always a surprise. Some weeks, I'd get a full five submissions; other weeks, I'd only get one or two. Only a single week went by without receiving any at all. Trying to choose just one chapter each week was the most difficult part of being the Coordinator. And a few times, I had to pick two because they complemented each other so perfectly and moved the story in a great direction. There were, of course, tweaks to be made along the way, which I did as carefully as I could to preserve the authors' vision. Thankfully, the writers were more than flexible, and many times we worked together to fix plot holes that marred their otherwise perfect chapters.

I have to admit, I was a bit nervous when Native American myths were brought into the mix. This was never meant to be a fantasy novel, and I was afraid the writers would lead it straight down that path. They definitely surprised me, though; each chapter walked the precarious line between magic and possibility and kept things ambiguous. Every potential fantasy element was countered with an equally potential logical explanation—to which I can only say, "Well played, writers." They crafted a legend and gave it a background as if it were a true myth. I will always be a member of the Black Coyote Project after reading this book.

I was also apprehensive about the traveling. Our characters take long road trips across the Sierra Nevadas. Travel time and distance played a big part of the consistency, and I found myself doing entirely more research than I intended, making sure the chapters stayed true to their locations. Apparently, the writers were thinking the same thing, because nearly all of them had their facts straight! It was a pleasant surprise.

When the final chapter came due, three submissions awaited me. It was among the hardest decisions I had to make as Coordinator. Each tied up the ending so wonderfully that we almost had to incorporate a temporal shift into a multiverse just so we could keep them all (which obviously didn't happen). The winning segment tugged at my heartstrings and got me all giddy for the endless possibilities that could arise if the story had continued.

For our writers, the ending of one story is only the beginning of another. Our sixth collaboration, a fantasy called *Esyld's Awakening*, began a few months into *The Map*, and our seventh collaboration, a steampunk called *Army of Brass,* came just after *The Map* ended. It won't be long now until our eighth project is underway.

I'm more than grateful and humbled by my opportunity to have been the Story Coordinator for *The Map*, and I hope to see you all writing alongside me in a future story!

Crystal MM Burton
Story Coordinator of *The Map*

CONTENTS

Short Story Winner:

CWC's Sixth Collaboration:

Chapter 1

Rain fell, heavy and cold, on the small rural town. Though it was still early autumn, a chilling breeze swept through Main Street, carrying a thick mist across the sidewalk. Only a few cars drove through the storm, rushing to get home to warmth and cover. The unkempt street went straight through what was known as "downtown," though the tallest buildings were only two stories high. Nestled beneath an abandoned apartment and tucked between an empty general store and an insurance office sat the Bridle Café. The thick drops of rain beat against the wide glass windows.

Kaitlyn Hart gazed longingly out at the dreary sky, sighing as a passing car splashed a wave of misty rain over the window she stood beside, blurring her view. The water running down the glass gave the street beyond a surreal look; everything was dark and gray, despite being almost noon. She picked up the plates and silverware left behind on the café table.

Carrying the tray of dirty dishes with one hand, she lightly touched the arm of an elderly man sitting at the bar. "Need anything else, Troy?"

"Maybe another cup of coffee would be nice," he replied. His drawn-out voice was as shaky as his hands, and he moved slowly, but Kaitlyn waited patiently for him to hand her his mug.

"No problem at all," she said kindly.

A few minutes later, she returned his mug to him filled with steaming hot coffee. She looked down the bar at the row of empty red barstools. The only other patron in the café was also an older man, who had just walked in and taken a seat in a booth by the entrance. Troy was a regular, but Kaitlyn didn't recognize this other man.

"Morning," she said with a friendly smile. "Can I get you anything?"

The burly old man unfolded a newspaper, never looking up at her. "Cuppa Joe. Black." He didn't say anything further, and his stiff demeanor suggested he wasn't interested in conversation.

Pursing her lips in confusion, she straightened her shoulders, nodded, and turned back to the kitchen. *Must be having a bad morning,* she mused.

Just after three in the afternoon, another waitress, Maya, came in for the evening rush—which didn't seem like it would be all that rushed, given the rain—and sat talking to Kaitlyn for a few minutes.

"Why don't you head home early? You have a new husband to get back to, after all."

"True." Kaitlyn grinned. "I still can't believe I'm *married*!" She looked down at her diamond ring, a line of four gems sparkling in the florescent light. "It's all moved so fast. But Brandon is just… amazing. The last three months have been incredible. I can't even remember living without him."

"You're so lucky. I wish a handsome businessman would swoop in and put a ring on my finger next."

"One just might!" Kaitlyn giggled. "You never know—if it can happen to me, I'm sure it can happen to you."

"Sure thing. I'll just keep holding out for that." Maya rolled her eyes. "Go home. Make him dinner or something. Breed some handsome babies with that eye candy of yours."

Kaitlyn's cheeks flushed a deep red, and she shrugged her shoulders. "What if the dinner rush hits and you're alone?" Both women looked out at the now-empty diner, then looked back to each other and laughed.

"Go on, honey, go home. I bet it'll be a nice surprise for him."

After a few more minutes of polite refusal, Kaitlyn finally agreed to take off early. She hung her apron on a hook in the back room and called a farewell to the chef, who sat behind the stovetops, watching a soap opera on a small TV. He stole a quick glance over his shoulder, waving back, before being sucked into his show once more.

Shaking her head with a chuckle, Kaitlyn pulled her long golden hair back into a loose ponytail at the nape of her neck, then tugged on her oversized gray sweater. Hugging her arms tightly around her waist, she went out the door into the cold, windy streets, soaked instantly by the downpour that hadn't stopped since sunrise. She tucked her head down and stayed as close to the row of buildings as possible as she followed them around to the back, where her car sat alone in the empty parking lot.

It continued to rain, and the ditches overflowed into the streets. Kaitlyn drove slowly, her windshield wipers drumming a steady beat as the raindrops played their melody. Despite the downcast grays and muddy browns, she loved the rain and enjoyed watching the wind ripple through the streams as they fell over the pastures. It was like the water danced to its own song. The imagery was enough to put her in a good mood, and by the time she pulled up into her gravel driveway, she had a content smile and a gleam in her eyes.

It had only been a week since she and Brandon had tied the

knot; the ring was still unfamiliar on her finger, the ink of her new last name still wet on the marriage license. Their relationship had indeed moved quickly. When he first walked into the diner three months ago, his suave suit and dashing smile had stolen her attention. When she walked up to take his order, his honeyed voice and smooth tongue had captured her heart. After just four dates, she had known she was in love. He had proposed, and she hadn't hesitated to say yes.

She walked into the small country house, removing her wet flats at the door. He had recently bought the home when he'd come here from the city, and she'd moved in as soon as they had said, "I do."

"Brandon, sweetie?" she called out from the short hallway. "I'm home early."

There was no answer. She strolled into the living room to check there, taking off her gray sweater and tossing it across the couch. Having seen his car in the driveway, she knew he was home; he must have been taking a nap or possibly a shower. Deciding to surprise him with dinner, Kaitlyn went into the kitchen and rummaged through the fridge. She pulled out a block of cheddar cheese and a few packages of deli meats. She set the temperature on the oven and sliced thick chunks of the cheese. Just as she turned back to the fridge to grab a can of flaky biscuits, a muffled crack rang through the house.

For a moment, she just stood there with her fingers curled around the handle of the refrigerator. She blinked and took in the silence, wondering whether or not she had actually heard anything at all. She removed the can of biscuits from the fridge and set them on the counter, then wiped her hands on a dish towel and strode into the living room.

"Brandon?" There was no one there—just the furniture and shelves full of collectable, decorative glass soda bottles. She headed into the hallway, checking the bathroom. She opened the door, but the light was off, and the room was empty.

Their bedroom door was also closed. She thought she saw a shadow move across the crack at the bottom of the door, and called out again. "Brandon, is that you?"

Turning the handle, she slowly pushed the door open. Their bed was still made, nice and neat, just the way she had left it. The curtains were open wide, offering a view of the small, barren flower garden in the backyard, flooded by the rain, with the woods in the distance. The trees were just beginning to change colors, and through the storm, she could see glimpses of reds and yellows on the tree line.

As she pushed the door open further, her eyes fell on the floor at the foot of the bed, and she froze in her tracks. Lying face-down on the hardwood floor was a middle-aged man in a black suit. His hair was short and dark, and his shoes had slipped off his feet. His head lay in a pool of deep, dark red, and his light skin was unnaturally pale. Her stomach heaved, and without hesitation, she rushed back into the bathroom and vomited into the sink.

Once she felt the nausea pass—and knew there was nothing left in her stomach to void—she rinsed out her mouth and washed her face with a towel. With shaking hands and her stomach still in the back of her throat, she forced herself to stagger back to her bedroom.

Her eyes ran over the corpse once again, but this time she was able to swallow back her nausea. She realized with relief that it wasn't Brandon. His hair was longer than that, and his suits were always well-pressed, never as wrinkled as the one on the lifeless man before her. She took a step closer and bent down, reaching out a hand. She wanted to flip him over, to see his face, but she hesitated. She had never touched a dead body before and didn't want to start now.

Behind her, the door to the master bathroom swung open, and she heard the sound of the light switch being flicked off. She leapt to her feet and spun round, coming face to face with her husband.

She couldn't manage to speak. His expression was blank, but as he looked into her eyes and saw her fear and confusion, a thin smile crossed his lips.

"Oh, Kaitlyn," he said, sounding disappointed. He shook his

head slowly, walking into the room. She backed up cautiously as he approached her, never taking her eyes off the long black pistol hanging from his hip, fastened just beneath his unbuttoned suit jacket.

She tried to ask what had happened, who the man was, why he had a gun like that… but all she managed to do was stammer, "Wh-what…" She felt her heel bump into something stiff and glanced over her shoulder to see that she had backed into the dead man's leg. She vaguely heard footsteps behind her but couldn't tear her gaze away from her husband.

"I'm so sorry, Katy." Brandon shifted his eyes to the bedroom door and gave a slight nod. "I really wish you hadn't seen this."

Before she could say a word, the burly older man from the café walked in the room. He took ahold of Kaitlyn, squeezing her arm tightly in his grasp and yanking her away from the man on the floor to bring her closer to himself.

"No!" Kaitlyn said, finally finding her voice. She tried to break free, but he was too strong. When she swung her other arm around to slap the man, he caught her wrist and spun her around, pinning her back against his chest, crossing her arms in front of her. "No, stop! Let me go! What is going on here?" She whipped her head frantically between Brandon and the older man, waiting—hoping—for an answer.

"I really wish you would have called first, Pumpkin. I could have had this whole mess straightened out. But, now… Well, I'm sure you understand that you can't be free to tell people about this little mishap." He pulled the pistol out of its holster at his side.

"Wait! What are you—"

"Now, now, don't fret. I can't very well kill my wife. Besides, I need your help. I was hoping to wait until after we had been married a month or so, but you've forced my hand."

"What do you want? Please, just let me go and I'll do whatever you ask." Tears streamed down her face as countless scenarios played out in her head, none of which answered the questions of what had happened here and what was about to happen to her. Her eyes wandered back to the corpse. "Please, just let me go."

He ran the back of his hand lightly down the side of her face, wiping away her tears. "I need your father's journal. He has a map… We'll talk about it later. I have a mess to clean and a few phone calls to make." He paused and offered a sympathetic smile. "I'm sorry, Pumpkin." Brandon raised the gun in the air and brought it down fast and hard against her temple, and with a burst of white before her eyes, Kaitlyn lost consciousness.

Chapter 2

Kaitlyn picked the lonesome dandelion from between two rocks, carefully sheltering its precious cargo with her hand to keep the wind from catching it. Her father's hands scooped her up from behind, lifting her high up into the air before cradling her in his arms.

"Ready, set," they chimed in unison before Kaitlyn gently opened her hand. The warm, dry breeze caught the white seeds and swirled them up into the air. They watched the seeds scatter out, dancing gently along the burnt orange rays of the setting sun.

"Let's head back for dinner now, sweetie," her father cooed.

Kaitlyn's bare feet touched the dry red earth. Small plumes of dust swirled around her ankles, catching the bottom of her long, white cotton dress. Raising her left hand in the air, she obediently waited for her father to take it in his. Jumping over small salt bush scrub was one of her favorite games to play with him. Tucking her knees to her chest, he hoisted her gently over each one. She could feel the top of the dry, cracked branches softly tickling her toes. She knew he would never drop her.

Her eyes traced the smile lines on his sun-browned skin. His uniform, as she liked to call it, consisted of a khaki long-sleeved shirt with matching trousers and desert boots, plus his trademark, faded blue baseball cap from his senior year of high school. The embroidered black tiger that once proudly leapt from the cap was now a faded gray kitty.

Three pens of various sizes and colors always adorned his left pocket. One pencil with an eraser at the end was tucked behind an ear, and in his free hand, he carried a small black notebook. His Canon EOS 650 hung dutifully around his neck, ready to capture a new discovery. Kaitlyn had inherited his sandy-blond hair and green eyes with small flecks of hazel. There was no doubting she was her father's daughter.

As they reached the top of the last small rise, a waft of smoke greeted them. Crouching beside the campfire, her light blue summer smock tucked between her knees, was Kaitlyn's mother. Jacqueline—or Jackie, as her father affectionately called her— turned the cooking sausages one at a time. Kaitlyn ran down the embankment, shrieking with delight. Jackie rose to embrace her daughter, kissing her on both cheeks, then lay one on her forehead for good luck.

Her father playfully planted a kiss on Jackie's lips before taking the tongs from her. Childhood sweethearts, the only time they spent apart was when Kaitlyn's father was off on one of his research assignments. Kaitlyn and her mother had spent two days driving from their home near Cannon Beach—two hours northwest of Portland, Oregon—to the edges of Owens Lake in Sierra Nevada, California.

Kaitlyn didn't mind the long journey. Her mother's yellow Yukon Combi van camper was entertainment in itself. Everywhere they stopped, people instantly fell in love with her pride and joy, curious to see what a compact van like this could offer inside. Parked beside two cottonwood trees and the small log cabin her father had been lodging in, it looked as much at home there as it was in her small, coastal hometown.

Buttered hotdog buns and ketchup were fetched from the van, and together with apple juice, dinner was served. Even though she was only seven, Kaitlyn longed to find a man who cared for her as much as her father cared for her mother. As she wiped the ketchup from the corners of her mouth, she declared to herself that day that she wouldn't settle for anything less.

The next morning, the sun rose over the Inyo Ranges. Kaitlyn could feel the warm beams on her face as they peeked through the small cracks on either side of the yellow-and-green-striped curtains. She unzipped her sleeping bag, too excited to sleep any longer. Today, her father was going to show her what he had been working on. The van door creaked open; she winced as her feet touched the thawing, thin layer of frost that had collected on the ground overnight.

Her father had already risen and was seated by the fire, writing in his journal—something she saw him do often.

"Morning, sweetie. How did you sleep?" he said, kissing her on the cheek.

Kaitlyn smiled, taking in the vista before her. Owens Lake shimmered in the morning light, the sun reflecting off the salt pans reminding her of a million pink diamonds. It was breathtakingly beautiful, even to her young self.

"What are you writing?" Kaitlyn grabbed a warm scone her father had just made.

His eyes lit up as he added tea leaves to the simmering water inside the camp coffee pot. "Well, my darling child, it is a book of secrets and mysteries." He chuckled.

Kaitlyn pouted at him.

"Okay, okay." He held his hands up in surrender. "I am writing a book… an adventure story. It's about a young boy who is given a map. He must then follow the map to find the treasure."

Kaitlyn's eyes lit up.

"I mean, that's the general outline, but it could all change in the flick of a page." He mimicked the action with a flurry of hands.

Kaitlyn watched him pour the steaming tea into her red camping cup. Her mother had joined them at the fire, still in her floral-print dressing gown, carrying the milk.

"Perfect timing as always, my dear." He reached for the milk, took her wrist instead, and pulled her into his lap.

Mimicking her father, Kaitlyn pulled the pink handkerchief from her pocket and wiped her brow. Trekking around the shore line and up into the foothills had been thirsty work. Under a rocky outcrop, they briefly paused for a water break. The morning had been one of exploration, her father showing her many of the birds which still called the lake home. As they peered through their binoculars, her father talked her through the different types, where they migrated to and from, and how they survived in such a harsh environment. Hanging on his every word, she felt herself falling into his world.

Breathing in the salty air, she relished the world of nature and the challenges it overcame. Hopefully, she could follow in her father's footsteps and make a difference one day.

"Ready, kiddo?" He screwed the top back on the water bottle. "One last stop before we head back?" he queried.

Wrapping her handkerchief around her wrist, she held it up for him to tie. "I am now," replied Kaitlyn, surveying his knotting skills.

Three pieces of decaying timber precariously held up the entrance to the old silver mine. The narrow railway tracks, enveloped by dust from the salt pans over the years, were now two hardened ridges of dirt. Kaitlyn steadied herself between them and held onto her father's hand. He tapped the flashlight on his thigh, and it finally snapped into action.

The dank smell of dust hit Kaitlyn's nostrils, causing her to sharply exhale. Bringing her wrist up to her nose, she let her breath come in and out through her mouth. Her father turned and laughed a little.

"You will get used to it. Imagine this place smelled like your favorite flowers, then surround yourself with them."

Kaitlyn recalled the Chinese jasmine winding its way up the trellis outside her bedroom window. Its sweet, exotic aroma would lull her to sleep at night. She lowered her wrist a little. *It's not as bad as before,* she thought, smiling to herself.

The flashlight exposed an old mining cart. Once the workhorse of the mine, its rusted wheels now barely held together the last pieces of its rotting wooden body. The shaft steadily sloped the farther down they went, until a large area of water now blocked their path.

"Not sure how deep this is, partner," her father said in his best Clint Eastwood impression.

Kaitlyn couldn't contain her laughter. Soon, they were both laughing then ducking as a few annoyed bats decided to see what all the noise was about. Kaitlyn squealed as they flew around their heads, and her father dipped down, allowing her to climb onto his back. They continued laughing back up the shaft, Kaitlyn already eager to relay the story to her mother.

Suddenly, her father stopped. Putting his finger to his lips, he turned so Kaitlyn could see, then shut off the flashlight. She buried her head into the top of his neck, listening for what her father had heard—muffled voices. As they inched their way along, she could now make out men's voices arguing.

Kaitlyn couldn't understand what they were saying. Their accents were not American; they were from another country. It seemed one man yelled more than the others. One of them kicked the old mining cart in frustration, then there was silence.

Kaitlyn's father slowly lowered her down and grabbed her hand. One foot in front of the other, they gradually made their way back, feeling along the wall until they could see the light of the entrance. Pausing by the thick beams of wood, her father tucked her in behind him and craned his neck around to see if the strangers had gone.

She felt her heart beating in her chest. It was the first time she had ever felt this scared. She wasn't even sure what to be scared of. Ten minutes ago, it was the cave; now it seemed that had been their savior.

Her eyes watered as they darted out into the midday sun. When they followed the same path they had come up, there appeared to be no sign of the men they had just heard arguing in the cave. Her father piggy-backed her down until they hit flat ground again.

"Are you okay?" He knelt and took the water bottle from his canvas side-bag.

Kaitlyn gulped from the flask. Half of it missed her mouth and soaked the front of her denim overalls. She nodded, unable to really comprehend what had just happened.

Her father's eyes darted nervously around. "Let's get you back to camp. I think it may just be lunchtime."

Kaitlyn ate her baked beans in silence, looking over the rim of her bowl as her father paced up and down the side of the cabin. One hand on his hip, the other waved wildly around in front of him, as if he were conducting an orchestra. Her mother occasionally nodded, her arms crossed, making circles in the dirt with her sandal.

Kaitlyn was confused; they were leaving early. Both her mother and father assured her they needed to make a start home, and to make up for it, Kaitlyn could pick a town they would be passing through and they would spend a night there. Her father still had a month left of his assignment, so he would not be joining them on the journey home.

His last big bearhug had almost squeezed the life out of her. When he stood back up, Kaitlyn was certain she saw a tear roll down his cheek.

The Combi van spluttered then roared into life, eager to eat up the miles of road which lay before it. Kaitlyn did not stop waving until her father was completely out of view. Sitting back on her booster seat, she unbuckled it to take her pencil from the glove compartment, unfolded the map, and started looking at all the towns along US-395.

The edges of the map flickered in the breeze. Kaitlyn wrestled with it a little, trying to tuck the corners under her legs to keep it from escaping out the window. Her mother fiddled with the radio, turning the knob left and right, trying to decide what she wanted to listen to.

Kaitlyn circled the town she had picked with the pencil. She turned and beamed at her mother. "Okay, I have the town. Are you ready?"

"Ready as I'll ever be." Her mother smiled.

"The town is—"

A truck horn blasted from behind them. Kaitlyn's eyes darted to the front windshield. A black pickup truck in front had suddenly slammed on its brakes. Black smoke billowed from behind it, enveloping them, obstructing their view of the highway. Kaitlyn hit the dashboard with her chest, her forehead hitting the windshield. Her mother gripped the wheel as the van slid from one side of the road to the other, throwing Kaitlyn against the door.

The van careened sideways. When she looked up at her screaming mother, time seemed to stand still as the van slowly tilted before slamming down on its side onto the highway. Rocks and shards of glass whipped her face.

***

Kaitlyn awoke screaming, pulling viciously at the ropes binding her arms and legs to the bed. Tears ran down her face as she choked on her own exploding sobs.

Brandon ran into the room, grabbed a washcloth from the bathroom, and stuffed it in her mouth. "There, there, Pumpkin," he soothed. "Did you have a bad dream?"

27

Chapter 3

Kaitlyn stared up at her husband, unable to comprehend what was happening. She couldn't breathe. She spat the washcloth out of her mouth, drew in a quavering breath, and sobbed again.

"Control yourself, Pumpkin. Any more noise, and I'll have to gag you with duct tape."

Tears leaked silently down her face, but she stopped sobbing. He used what had previously been an endearing term with such spite and anger, she hardly recognized the man she had vowed to love forever.

She squinted through the pain searing across her head from the earlier blow, trying to find something familiar about Brandon. He had never spoken so roughly to her before or looked so distracted. She could tell he no longer listened to her, not the way he used to when rubbing her feet after a long day. She would tell him all about the café patrons, the different characters who came in, and he would genuinely seem interested. He was now set on weeding out the information he wanted, seeking out certain words that would help him with his objective.

"Where is your father's journal?"

"What journal? I don't know anything about it. Both of my parents died when I was seven. There was a car accident. I barely survived myself. I was raised by my aunt until she died last month. You know that. I told you all about it."

"Your mother died in that accident. Your father's body was never found. Pieces of his research have been cropping up here and there long after he disappeared. You're getting a reasonable allowance every month. Where does that come from, do you think? Don't tell me it's your inheritance, because there was barely enough to bury your mother, and your aunt didn't leave much either."

Kaitlyn's eyes opened wide despite the throbbing pain in her brow. She hadn't known any of that. Her aunt's lawyer had told her the allowance was her inheritance. She had never questioned it; she'd had no reason to.

"I… I don't know," she whispered; her voice cracked. She looked away to a distant blank spot on the wall, trying to consider if Brandon's suggestion was possible.

"Don't lie to me!" He raised his hand as if to strike her, and she shrank back against the pillow.

A fresh wave of tears obscured her view, and her gasp opened the way for another hard sob, making it difficult to speak. "I'm not! I don't know anything, I really don't. Aunt Louise never talked about my dad at all. Even when I asked her about him, she said they weren't that close—that the last time she saw him was at his wedding, then he and Mom went off on Dad's research adventures." Spittle flew from her mouth as she spoke hurriedly, angry and desperate and quickly losing hope that anything good remained in the man she married.

"Research adventures?"

"Yes. That's what she called his trips away from home."

"Do you remember any of those trips? Do you remember a journal, or a map?"

Kaitlyn sniffed hard, trying to clear the free-flowing mucus that made breathing difficult. "Everything before the accident is gone. Aunt Louise said it was amnesia caused by trauma. My mind couldn't accept what had happened, so it blocked out everything before I was seven."

Her aunt had also told her it might come back some day, but she didn't tell him that. She'd been getting back snippets over the years, but nothing cohesive. Nothing she could understand. Her recent dream was the most she had remembered since the accident. It was probably brought on by the trauma of seeing the dead body and Brandon knocking her out cold. She didn't tell him that, either. All the trust she'd had in him was now gone.

He bent down and stared her full in the face for several minutes, then straightened up. Apparently satisfied she was telling the truth, he turned around and left the room.

After a few minutes, she heard voices on the other side of the wall beside the bed. *The walls must be very thin in this house*, she thought. She rolled over as close to the wall as her restraints would let her and listened intently. Brandon's voice mixed with the voices of two other men, but they were much softer than Brandon. Their words rushed and slurred, clearly frustrated by Brandon's inquisition—or perhaps frustrated with her.

"You had one thing to do, Mettinger. One thing. You had to keep her in the café, and you couldn't even do that!"

A sickening crack sounded, like a fist colliding with a skull, ending in a series of thuds as someone hit the floor. Brandon clearly resorted to violence when he didn't get what he wanted. *That's good to know.* He had called one of the other men Mettinger. That must be the unfriendly, burly old man from the diner.

"What about the aunt's house? Anything we can use?" someone else said. It was a voice Kaitlyn didn't recognize at all.

"Nothing. I went through it attic to basement," Brandon said.

"There's lots of stuff about Kaitlyn, and even some old stuff about her mother, but nothing about her father at all. The aunt didn't keep anything of his. Maybe she hated him."

Kaitlyn's eyes stung at the suggestion. She knew her aunt cared for her father. Despite her own predicament, she felt the need to protect her aunt's good name. Besides, she might have still had some of his things somewhere else. Aunt Louise's estate lawyer had mentioned a storage unit somewhere, and he said he would give her the key, but not until he explained some stuff to her. That had been two days before her wedding, and she had forgotten all about it. She also wondered when Brandon had gone through her aunt's house. She'd had put it on the market right after her aunt's death, and it had sold just a few weeks later—a week before her wedding.

A sudden urge hit and she yelled as loud as she could, because she didn't want him to know she knew he was right on the other side of the wall. "Brandon, I have to pee. Unless you want to change the bedding, you better let me up!" she shouted. As expected, in five short seconds, he was back in the room. His presence suffocated her like a heavy fog.

"You better not try anything smart, or I'll lay you out cold," Brandon growled.

Yesterday, she would never have believed he would do that. Now, she realized he really would knock her out in a heartbeat. He was capable of murder, after all.

He approached her and loosened her restraints. As she lifted her legs down, every inch of her ached. She felt a little lightheaded and took her time before heading to the bathroom. Rubbing her wrists as she walked, she thought of what she could do next if she were to gain any advantage in this mess.

She paused at the mirror, one eye already blue and puffy on the side where Brandon had hit her. Her sturdy mascara had no chance against the cascades of tears; she gently wiped away the dark streaks, then washed her hands. With so few ideas, she limply reached under the vanity for her cordless curling iron. It was almost laughable to attempt using it as a weapon, but the fighter in her urged her to at least try. She let it get good and hot before going back into the bedroom, holding it behind her back as she stepped through the doorway.

Brandon waited for her, so she knew she had to act fast if this had any chance of working. He pulled her left arm to direct her back to the bed. She swung her right arm around fast, smacking him in the face, her fist balled tightly around the plastic handle. He pulled away, staggering. She held the weapon with a shaky hand, appalled by her own behavior. Instinct kicked in, and she reached out again, pressing the hot metal rod against his ear and shoving him hard against the side table, causing him to fall back on top of the strewn laundry basket.

He howled a string of profanities as she ran for the bedroom door, hoping his two henchmen weren't out there. They were nowhere in sight, and she hurried down the stairs, knowing Brandon would soon be in hot pursuit. A big, overstuffed chair came into view; she pushed it in front of the bottom step, then ran toward the front door. She heard Brandon screaming and swearing as he fell over the chair, giving her the two-second gap she needed.

Her purse sat on a small table by the door; she grabbed it and ran out, leaving the door ajar behind her. Closing it was just another obstacle between her and her car, which she was relieved to see exactly where she had left it.

The sun was just coming up over the horizon. It was still raining, but not as hard as it had before. She jumped in her car and floored it in reverse. As she backed out of the gravel driveway, small stones flew out onto the manicured lawn. Without a second glance back, she headed to the police station—the only place she thought would make her feel safe. Kaitlyn felt a degree of guilt for causing pain to the man she had so passionately loved, wondering if that man had ever truly existed.

Chapter 4

"Kaitlyn!" James screamed at the top of his lungs, sitting bolt upright in bed. The covers fell off as his arm shot out, reaching for her. Sweat dripped down his torso, soaking his sheets with a dark, human outline.

Dim rays of mid-morning sun sliced through the darkness of his room as he stared at the old Bruce Springsteen poster hanging on his wall. His heart hammered against his ribs, and he gulped a lungful of hot, stuffy air. Burning tears rolled down his cheeks while he choked back a sob.

James had seen her in his dream; the image of her pale, freckle-dotted skin, decorated with her beautiful smile, seemed to hang in the air before his eyes. But she had cried out, she was in pain, she was in trouble, she was … she was … what? The dream was fading. Like mist under the morning sun, reality burned away the important details of the dream.

He leapt from his bed and frantically searched for something to write on—*anything* to write on. Finally, he found a pen and snatched an old pizza box from the pile in the corner. He clicked the pen, and her name flowed from its tip, but then it stopped. He forced his brain to recall what he had seen in his dream. With all his will, he tried to focus on what he had been shown. But it was hopeless; the dream was gone. All James could remember was the sound of her crying out, "Please, just let me go!" as someone hit her.

A sigh escaped his lips before the pizza box slipped from his fingers and back to the garbage-littered floor. He didn't have to be at work until six tonight and normally slept until noon. He felt like he had let her down; his little *Gule* needed him, and he couldn't help. Maybe he would go down the street and use the payphone at his uncle's store to call her. He still had her number where she was staying. Yeah … he would call her before going to work, she would laugh at him for being so silly, and they would chat for a few minutes.

These thoughts danced through his mind as he shuffled into the kitchen and started some coffee. But before he could open the coffee tin, a thought struck him. His grandfather's books—the ones about spirits, dreams, and such. It had been his present for his twenty-first birthday. His dad had frowned and called them a waste of paper, but his grandfather still believed in the tribe's old ways.

The old, handwritten book was heavy, its uneven pages rough under his fingertips. James dropped down on the couch and thumbed through the book, looking for some kind of help. He became aware of scratching at the back door; his dog, Bullet, wanted in. He closed the book and dropped it on the couch as he walked through his cramped little house. As soon as he opened the door, the large German Shepherd shoved his way past James and shot toward the front door. Before the dog had made it through, someone knocked loudly. It wasn't a polite knock but a machine-gun shower of blows. Still spinning from Bullet's charge, James reversed and went to answer it.

The door opened, revealing his grandfather, Thomas. "What's wrong, *Ganodo*?" the old, leather-faced man asked. His gray eyes, crowned by worn wrinkles, shone intently.

"Hey, wow. I was just—"

"What's wrong?" his grandfather asked again.

"Nothing, I'm okay. I was just—"

"What's wrong?"

"I had a dream about Kaitlyn. It's nothing," James assured him.

"Bull," the old man said, forcing his way inside. He took James by the arm and pulled him onto the couch. "Sit. I'll finish the coffee. You need to tell me what you saw."

James heard his grandfather rummaging through his cabinets, and his mind turned once again to Kaitlyn and the day he met her.

***

James sat with his numb legs crossed in front of the spirit-fire. He had been truly trying to follow his grandfather's instructions, but this was boring. His dad had agreed to let his grandfather take him "camping," but this was not how James understood camping should be.

The old man had told him about spirits and the flow of energy they followed. He had told his grandson stories about the old warriors of their tribe and their amazing adventures. James had really enjoyed the ones about the hero called Fire Dancer and how he tamed the golden sky bird.

But now they attempted to talk to the spirits of the desert— which meant sitting and staring into the fire until they showed themselves. His grandfather had been humming a low, repeating song over and over. It was putting James to sleep, and he had really been looking forward to roasting marshmallows before bed.

"You're not concentrating, *Ganodo*," Thomas said. He had

one eye open, looking at his grandson.

James had just managed to stifle a yawn, but his efforts were in vain. "No, Grandpa. I am. Really, I am. It's just…" James shifted to get some feeling back into his legs.

"Just what?" his elder asked. His sun-bronzed skin was decorated with waves of wrinkles that seem to somehow enhance his frown.

"Well, I wanted to do some marshmallows, and was wondering…"

His grandfather's scowl ended his sentence. "Grandson, you need to take this seriously. When I'm gone, who will follow in my footsteps? Our ways need to live on, and you are their keeper."

"I know. Sorry," the boy said, ashamed.

"Now, pay attention. If you don't, we could attract a wendigo or some other evil spirit."

James was confused. "What's a Winnebago?"

Thomas gave him a serious look from across the flickering fire. "A wendigo is a spirit of the dead. They died hungry, cold, and alone. So they rise up from their graves and wander around at night looking for someone to eat. They look like normal people, but they have blood on their faces, and are very pale. They trick you into coming close by saying they are lost, but when you do get close, they have long, sharp claws that can slice you up." The old man watched his grandson's eyes get bigger and bigger as he told him about the monster. Thomas had always been good at ghost stories and smiled as he watched the color drain from the boy's face.

James had been listening to his grandfather with little interest, but then he saw it. Slowly, the ghostly-pale figure stumbled out of the desert behind the old man. It had blood smeared across its face, and it was white as freshly fallen snow. It wore a ragged, torn dress covered in more blood. The monster's hands were tucked under its arms, and James knew at any second it would pull them out, revealing long, dark, black, blood-caked claws. No one would find their bodies because the monster would gobble them up, bones and all. James screamed.

The next morning, James sat on the tailgate of his grandfather's truck next to the strange girl as they munched on egg sandwiches. He kept glancing over at her to make sure she didn't have monster claws and wouldn't suddenly jump up to eat him. Even though she had scared him silly the night before, he couldn't stop thinking how beautiful she was. The way her hair was blown by the desert breeze, and the freckles across her nose made his stomach feel funny. She had a bandage on her forehead that his grandfather had put there after he had cleaned her up.

The old man called her *Gule*, and when she asked what that meant, Thomas had smiled a warm smile and told her it meant *hard nut*—because her head must be a hard nut to crack. They had laughed as James' grandfather finished putting the bandage on her head.

The old man had asked her where her parents were, but all she could tell him was that she didn't know. She told him her address, but that was in another state. It seemed she had been in a car accident, and maybe there were some men chasing her. He had scratched his head and told her they would take her to the sheriff's office back in town.

Before they packed up camp, Thomas took his grandson aside for a private chat. "*Ganodo*, this is important. The spirits have guided this girl to you. Your fates have been joined, and I think they mean for you to watch after her."

"Yes, sir." The boy nodded. The old man smiled affectionately at his grandson; maybe he would be a good warrior after all.

They took Kaitlyn back to town, and she stayed with James for a week until her aunt arrived to get her. Not once had he left her side; he was like her shadow the whole time. Even after she had returned home, he wrote her letters, telling her all about his family, friends, and adventures. She wrote back, telling him about her school, her music recitals, and her pet cat.

The state police opened an investigation surrounding the death of her parents. Her mother's body was found at the scene and the accident classified as a hit-and-run, but her father's body was never found. After six months, there was no progress, and so it was labeled an unsolved mystery. James wrote her a letter saying how he wouldn't stop looking for answers for her. But he was just as fruitless as the police. The only thing he had ever managed to dig up was something called the Black Coyote project. But besides the name, he couldn't find any more information. He had gone to his grandfather for advice, and the old man's eyes had grown wide, yet he had shaken his head and denied knowing what it meant. After a month of hounding him for more details, James finally accepted that his grandfather didn't know anything.

Slowly, over the years, the letters dried up until finally they only sent each other birthday cards. Still, James kept a picture of her in his wallet and would pull it out occasionally to look at it. She had still been in his thoughts until he had gotten the wedding invitation in the mail. When he opened the envelope, his heart dropped.

He went home that night and nursed a beer as he watched the old cartoons on the busted black and white TV. The shows were the same ones they had watched together when they were kids. Why had he waited? Why hadn't he asked her? Hell, why hadn't he gone to visit her? Thoughts and regrets circled each other like angry dogs, until finally he pitched the half-drunk beer bottle into the screen. The TV had been fine, but his heart was broken.

So, that night before lying down to sleep, James opened his wallet and took out her picture. He watched it slip from his fingers and into the trashcan. When he let his foot off the little paddle, the lid slammed shut. She was now gone forever … or so he thought.

***

James finished telling his grandfather about what he could remember of his dream. Thomas took the dream book in his leathery hands and flipped the rough pages, contemplating the dream's meaning and wondering if James' vision of Kaitlyn had anything to do with the Black Coyote project. It was the only reason he could think of that Kaitlyn would be in such deep trouble that it would affect James outside of waking hours. Thomas had been more than a little shocked the day his grandson had asked him if he knew what the Black Coyote project was. When he himself had looked up her parents later that evening, the recognition hit him instantly. They were the same couple from his past, from the project. *Fate works in mysterious ways*, he thought.

Thomas occasionally stopped on a page, his eyes moving back and forth as he read, then he turned some more pages. Finally, when he decided what he'd say, he snapped the book shut.

"Grandson, listen to me," Thomas said in a somber voice. "Your father never put stock in our ways, but I hope you do. I had a dream too. In this dream, I was standing in the desert. There were bones everywhere, bones of all peoples of the world. Above me was a giant black coyote, whose eyes seemed to glow with the strangest green light, and I saw you hanging from its jaws. But I also saw *Gule*—she was riding on its back. I think our dreams are telling us the same thing."

"What should I do, Grandpa?" James asked with a concerned frown.

The old man reached into his pocket and pulled out the keys to the same old, beaten-up truck he had taken James camping in all those years ago. "I think you got a long drive ahead of you, *Ganodo*."

Chapter 5

It was the most action the sleepy little police station in Cannon Beach had seen in three years, since that time the mayor's niece got a little tipsy and drove her daddy's station wagon into the ditch at the town line. Mostly, the orders of the day for the officers in town were the usual small-town dilemmas—cats stuck in trees and old ladies to help across the street. The only real crimes tended to be the victimless sort—people doing drugs or drinking too much because there was nothing else to do and they needed a way to kill the boredom. Occasionally, there was a bust for disturbing the peace on a Friday night when the bars let out. Every once in a blue moon, there was a call for a domestic disturbance … but murder? Never. The station had retired two police chiefs without a murder on the books. That was why it was hard for Detective Stacy Logan to swallow Kaitlyn's story.

"Okay, Mrs. Hart. I appreciate your details and I have your statement, but I need you to try to help me understand this thing. Normally, we don't have a murder without a motive. You are sure this wasn't a burglary gone wrong or something like that?" Detective Logan asked as she sipped her lukewarm coffee and scratched at her notepad with her blue ballpoint pen.

"No! No, no. I told you this was *not* a robbery. Brandon killed a man in our bedroom. Or he had one of his men do it," Kaitlyn said in frustration.

"Right, your husband," Logan said as she flipped the pages on her notepad. "And how many men did you say were in your home?"

"I don't know. Three, maybe four? What does it matter? They killed someone!" Kaitlyn yelled. She felt like she had not been taken seriously from the moment she'd walked into the police station. At first, they listened to her, but once she laid out the whole story, Kaitlyn quickly saw the skepticism forming on the faces of the officers in the station. When the police had asked her to take a field sobriety and drug test under the guise of standard procedure, Kaitlyn knew she was in for a fight to convince them of the truth.

Logan put her hands up in a calming motion. "Hey, it's okay. Just stay calm. I believe you. I don't think you're lying to me. It's just that what you're telling me doesn't sound like a normal, textbook kind of crime," the detective continued with what sounded like forced empathy.

"I know. I know it all sounds…" Kaitlyn stopped herself before she said the word 'crazy'. She didn't want to help put that notion into the detective's head. It was probably there already. "…a little farfetched, but I swear to you this is what happened. I have never been so afraid before in my life," Kaitlyn continued. She fought to keep calm. She wanted to scream and hit the walls. The bruising on her temple was clear as day, but it might as well have been invisible to the detective.

"Look, you are perfectly safe here, okay? Nobody is going to hurt you. We have officers at your home right now looking into it. We have your husband. He's not under arrest, but he has agreed to come in for questioning and to give a statement," Logan said after putting the Styrofoam cup back on the table and swishing the dark drink around in her mouth.

"I don't want that man anywhere near me," Kaitlyn said defensively. Her eyes went wide when confronted with the image of being face to face with the man she had allowed herself to marry. It hit her hard how fast her feelings for him had gone from hopelessly, deeply, and profoundly in love with him to utterly horrified of the man.

"He won't be in the same room with you. Promise. He won't even know where you are, okay? You'll be able to see and hear him, but he won't know you're listening," Logan said confidently as she pointed to the large two-way mirror showing into the adjacent interview room. "I'm sure you can understand that we need to get his side of the story."

"Yes, I understand that," Kaitlyn said. She scratched her head roughly enough that it pulled out several strands of her long golden hair. It was not easy for her to endure this kind of apathy and neglect. She knew what she was saying was fanciful, but she had no criminal record, and everyone she met told her she was an honest person. It infuriated her to see just how little the police believed what she told them. She felt as if they were treating her like a little girl who had just woken from a bad dream.

Logan's phone vibrated as it notified her there was a new text message. The detective picked up the device and read the text. "That's my partner. He has your husband with him, and he's going to bring him into the next room right now. You're okay, and I'm going to stay with you the whole time," Logan said in a mostly reassuring tone.

"Okay," Kaitlyn agreed reluctantly.

The door to the other interview room opened, and another detective led in Brandon. The detective was a middle-aged, slightly overweight, and slightly bald man with large framed glasses and a dour expression. Kaitlyn felt her heart skip a beat when she saw Brandon again. In that moment, she knew she did

45

not love him anymore and never could love him again. The detective indicated for Brandon to sit, which he did, and the detective sat down in the seat across from him.

"I want to thank you for coming down to the station so we could all get this cleared up, Mr. Hart," said the detective as he opened a manila folder and took out a notepad from his brown suit jacket pocket.

"It's no trouble at all, Detective. I just want to make sure my wife is okay. I'm very worried about her," Brandon said with all the conviction of a perfectly innocent child.

When she heard Brandon speak, Kaitlyn's stomach churned with bile. She nearly retched as she thought of all the times she had allowed that man to touch her. Her hand went to her lips as she remembered what it felt like to kiss him. A sour, metallic taste filled her mouth, and her head felt light. What had been love not even a few hours ago was now replaced with fear and hatred.

"You understand that she's made some very serious claims, Mr. Hart? She said you've murdered a man."

"Well, clearly, that's not the case. Your officers even said there was nothing out of the ordinary at the house, let alone evidence of a man shot to death in our bedroom," Brandon said with feigned vulnerability.

"She also said you and several other men assaulted and forcibly detained her," the older detective pressed.

"Yes, I know she said that. It's hard when she has one of her episodes. I've only been there for two of them before this one." Brandon's voice echoed nothing but mercy and compassion, but his eyes held a predatory and malevolent glint only Kaitlyn could see.

"Episodes?" The detective adjusted the glasses that had slipped down his nose and shuffled some papers around in the file envelope.

"Yes," Brandon said before his eyes flicked to the mirror for a moment. Kaitlyn felt like he stabbed through the glass and into her heart with that glance. "Kaitlyn suffers from bipolar disorder and… and one other condition I can never pronounce correctly.

Normally, the medication keeps it under control." Brandon lied as convincingly as the devil himself.

"What? That is *not* true. I'm not bipolar or unstable!" Kaitlyn objected, speaking to Detective Logan as she nearly jumped out of her chair.

"It's okay. Just let my partner keep on asking the questions. If your husband is telling a lie like that, it will be easy to catch him in it," Logan said supportively.

"Your wife is in treatment?" The detective seemed caught off guard by the revelation.

"Yes, she told me she has been seeing a doctor in Portland for about the last nine years, once a month," Brandon said matter-of-factly.

Behind the glass of the two-way mirror, Kaitlyn's mouth hung wide open in stunned disbelief.

"Really… and the name of this doctor?" The detective clicked his pen and flipped to a clean sheet of paper in his notepad.

"Dr. Portsmyth. I called him the second it happened. She had never been violent before during one of her outbursts." Brandon turned his head to show the detective the burn from the curling iron on the side of his head. "He told me he was on his way as soon as he got off the phone. I'm sure he'll be happy to clear all this up and get Kaitlyn the help she needs…" Brandon stopped as he checked his phone, then showed it to the detective. "It looks like he just got into town. Should I have him come to the station?"

"Yeah, have him come down," the detective said warily as he shifted in his seat and turned to look at the glass of the two-way mirror. "Just wait here. I need to talk to my partner for a minute."

"Absolutely, sir, whatever you need," Brandon agreed.

Kaitlyn gave Logan a panicked look. "Everything he says is a lie. I am not in treatment. I don't have bipolar disorder. He's lying!" She could see the doubt in the detective's eyes.

"I believe you—just stay calm. I need to step out and talk with Detective Payton for just a little bit," Logan said as she stood and headed for the door to the interview room. "Can I get you anything while you wait? Water… coffee?" she asked passively.

"No, I don't need anything to drink. I need you people to listen to me!" Kaitlyn nearly screamed at the other woman.

"Just wait. I'll be back in a few minutes," Detective Logan said in a dismissive fashion before the door closed behind her.

It was not a few minutes. Kaitlyn waited in the interview room for nearly an hour. The whole time, she kept her eyes fixed on Brandon on the other side of the mirror. He sat calmly in his seat, looking as relaxed and picturesque as he had the first day Kaitlyn laid eyes on him. He seemed in total control of the entire situation.

Kaitlyn inhaled sharply in surprise when the doors opened in tandem. Detective Logan returned, and in the next room, Brandon stood as Detective Payton entered, leading the heavyset man Kaitlyn had seen earlier at the diner and then again at her house. She went cold as Brandon extended his hand and greeted the other man.

"Thank you for coming on such a short notice, Doctor," Brandon said.

"I'm here for a patient in need. I'm concerned for Kaitlyn just as much as everyone else," said the man posing as a doctor.

"Please sit down, Dr. Portsmyth," said Detective Payton.

Kaitlyn turned to Logan and started to get out of her seat. She stopped when Logan put her hands up and signaled for her to remain sitting. "That man is not a doctor. He is one of Brandon's men. He is part of this. I have never seen him before today. He is not my doctor," Kaitlyn protested.

"Thank you, Detective. I don't like breaking doctor-patient confidentiality, but when someone under my care becomes a danger to themselves or others, I have to. I brought Kaitlyn's case file with me," said the man as he sat next to Brandon. He handed a large file folder to the detective. "As you can see, she has done a lot of hard work to battle her condition."

Detective Payton flipped through the files. "What are you proposing, Doctor?"

"I work predominantly out of the mental health ward of Cedar Hills Hospital in Portland. We have an excellent inpatient facility there. I would like to have Mrs. Hart remanded into my custody to continue her treatment at Cedar Hills, where she can have round-the-clock care."

"No! I'm not crazy! They're both lying... it's not true. He is not a doctor. He helped Brandon kill a man in my home today!" Kaitlyn feebly protested.

Detective Logan crossed her arms and sighed pitifully. "Come on, Kaitlyn. Why don't we go talk to Dr. Portsmyth, get you some help?" she said gently.

**

James' eyes flew open as he felt the rumble of grooved pavement beneath the tires of his grandfather's rusty pickup truck. This was the third time he had dozed off behind the wheel. It had been a long, hard trip from Reno. If he had left earlier in the day, he would not have been so tired.

He thought maybe he could pull off to the side of the road and rest for even half an hour, but he didn't allow himself to entertain that thought for longer than a few moments. If he stopped now, he would not reach Kaitlyn in time. She needed him; he sensed she was in danger.

James saw the sign that read 'Oregon Welcomes You' and was renewed in purpose. He pressed on into the night.

Chapter 6

The moon shone full and bright that evening. High above the dark spires of the majestic pines and distant mountain peaks, its magnificence was in union with Mother Earth. Its radiant glow, keeping at bay the deep darkness of night, illuminated the two-lane road on which James traveled. Purposeful in funneling him to Kaitlyn, the night exhibited many of the same traits as the night he'd first met her. Just like tonight, there had been a full moon, and it had also been the night of a total lunar eclipse. He believed Kaitlyn was in much the same trouble as before, both lost and scared. This coincidence startled James. He believed everything had meaning.

Strange, he thought, that after the passage of almost two

decades having not physically seen her, he would lay eyes on her again under that same fading light. He wished their friendship could have been closer in nature, but their monthly correspondence had seemed enough for Kaitlyn. From the childish letters she sent as a kid to the electronic messages that had buzzed his phone of late, she always had something to share with him, be it a funny joke she thought he would enjoy or a picture of her in some exotic location with her girlfriends. The two communicated quite often, but James had frequently regretted not having the nerve to invite himself to come see her or tell her how he felt. He had grown to love her but knew she never felt the same, and since meeting and falling for Brandon, she had become quite distant.

***

Kaitlyn sat with her arms folded in front of her, nervous and guarded. The so-called Dr. Portsmyth sat directly across from her, legs crossed with his hands folded on his lap. They sat front and center before Detective Logan's solid wood desk. Both of them were in the detective's danger zone. She had broken down many a witness and petty criminal in those chairs, drilling them until the truth oozed from them. She sat behind the desk, in command, jotting down both random, superfluous information that came to mind and the smallest of details that triggered her well-developed senses. Detective Payton sat comfortably in the corner, sunken deeply into an old, worn leather couch.

"You surely remember your monthly sessions?" asked Dr. Portsmyth. He bent over to retrieve his briefcase from the floor, then laid it across his lap and thumbed through the mess of paperwork. "I have your file folder in here somewhere, chronicling your monthly visits, notes, and so forth. You certainly remember your drawings," he continued.

Kaitlyn explosively uncrossed her arms and grabbed both sides of the armchair, raising herself up off the seat. She leaned in toward the doctor. "I certainly do not, since I have never met you before! And I don't care to see anything you have on me, because it too is a damn lie!"

Detective Logan snapped her reclined chair forward. She readied herself as if she'd jump into the middle of a fight should the cornered Kaitlyn feel threatened enough to lash out. Detective Payton attempted to react to the exploding situation as well, but the worn couch prevented him from making any real progress from its embrace.

"Try to calm yourself, Kaitlyn. We're just talking. No one is accusing you of anything, and I haven't made up my mind in regards to any of this," cautioned Detective Logan. "Sit, please," she continued with a raised voice.

"But this is all lies. I don't know what's going on here." Kaitlyn brought her hand to her face, obscuring the view of the others should she begin to cry.

"Yes, I realize your position, and I'm trying to help. But I have a duty to hear all sides and any information that may be relevant. Detective Payton and myself will decide what's true or not." Detective Logan flipped her spiral-bound notebook to a clean page and titled it *He said* and *She said*. "Doctor Portsmyth. We'll look at your files later. But for now, I would like to know what her diagnosis is. If that's okay with you, Kaitlyn."

Kaitlyn rolled her eyes and shook her head in astonishment. "Fine, whatever."

"Why is she seeing you on a monthly basis, as you and her husband claim?" Detective Logan continued.

The doctor shut the briefcase and set it on the floor. "It's a dissociative disorder brought on by a childhood trauma. Namely the death of her parents, due to a car accident in the Sierra Nevadas when she was just a small girl. She confided that she feels responsible for their deaths. Now, when anything in her life happens that reminds her, on a subconscious level, of any suppressed memories which occurred before that event, she slips into a depressive state. She imagines what life would have been like had they survived. Depending on the importance of the memory, the triggering of the mind's response is in direct proportion."

"I don't feel responsible for my parents' death. I was a child. I had no control over what happened. I hardly even remember it!" Kaitlyn exclaimed.

"You told me that, had you not been there on that fateful day with your father at the mineshaft, he wouldn't have been so concerned with your safety and wanted to drive you and your mother back home. Your father would have been up there doing his research as he did often, and you and your mother would have been home."

Kaitlyn paused in her chair, bewildered, contemplating how this stranger knew the details of that night when she herself had only just come to realize much of it.

"But I never told anyone… I didn't remember much of it. I don't understand." Her speech was uneasy and hesitant. Had she expressed these feelings to this man? Was she having some type of breakdown?

"Could you have told Dr. Portsmyth?" asked Detective Logan.

A knock on the detective's door interrupted the tension in the room. Kaitlyn's stiffness relaxed, and she slumped back into the office chair, exhausted. Detective Logan motioned for her receptionist to enter.

"Mr. Hart has finished with his paperwork. He's ready to leave." The receptionist glanced at Detective Payton, waiting for a response.

"Yup, I'm coming," responded Detective Payton. He tried to get himself out of the cushy chair but struggled with being sunk in too far. Whether it was the squishy condition of the couch or the squishy condition of the man, his attempts were yet again unsuccessful.

Detective Logan stood from behind her desk. "Tell Mr. Hart I'll be there to walk him out in a moment," she interrupted, motioning for Payton to stay put.

"Yes, Detective," the clerk responded, judging Detective Payton with his eyes as he exited.

"Excuse me, Dr. Portsmyth… Kaitlyn. I'll be right back."

She walked over to Kaitlyn and placed her hand on Kaitlyn's shoulder. "I have to walk Brandon by these windows on the way out. Would you prefer that I pull the blinds?" Detective Logan whispered.

"Please. Thank you for that."

The detective pulled down the blinds and switched on the overhead lamps. "When I get back, we'll take a look at those files and session transcripts. Will that be okay, Kaitlyn?"

"I don't know," Kaitlyn replied.

Detective Logan left the room, shutting the door behind her. Kaitlyn was relieved she wouldn't have to see Brandon. She couldn't handle an altercation with him right now.

Dr. Portsmyth retrieved his briefcase from the floor again and sat it on his lap. He popped the latches and opened it. "You see, Kaitlyn, your condition is somewhat normal. Many people who go through an ordeal as you did often forget vast chunks of their memory. They repress the memories, but the feelings never quite go away. You may not know why you're feeling as you do, because you can't remember the underlying emotional or mental trauma that caused it. See? You most certainly do have repressed memories, because you don't remember me, do you?"

"No, I really don't," she replied.

"Well, I'm not referring to me being your psychotherapist, because we both know that's bullshit," Dr. Portsmyth exclaimed in a smug tone.

Kaitlyn tried to rise from her chair to turn to Payton, but the detective already had his big, meaty hands on her shoulders and forced her back into the chair. He took a free hand and covered her mouth before she could scream for help.

"You don't remember me from the night your parents were killed, do you? Shake your head for me, darling."

She shook her head from side to side, acknowledging she didn't recall.

"That night, I ran you off the road. Your mom died instantly, I would suspect, but you survived. You hit your pretty little head quite hard. My guess is that's the cause of your fleeting memory.

I'm really sorry about that. You were all supposed to die that night. Your father, however, I couldn't find at the crash site. He must have run off into the woods and left you to die." His voice trembled as he recalled the exciting events of that night nearly twenty years ago.

From his briefcase, Dr. Portsmyth pulled out a syringe with a yellow, cloudy fluid inside. Kaitlyn panicked and struggled under Detective Payton's restricting embrace.

"My name is Mettinger," the doctor said. "I'm no doctor, and I work with your husband. I always have." He stabbed her in the thigh with the syringe, injecting the fluid.

"In about sixty seconds, you'll go into shock and pass out after a fit of convulsions. My men will whisk you away in an ambulance to a private facility so we can see what you really know about your father's whereabouts. Unless you can tell me where the notebook containing the map is right now. Then we can forgo the unpleasantness that's bound to occur, and you'll wake in a hospital with a severe headache."

Kaitlyn's eyes widened, and she looked up to see Detective Payton smiling above her. She tried to focus on Mettinger, but a bright light flooded her vision. She could only hear the sound of his shrill voice and the heavy breathing of the portly detective.

"He left you to die! I let you live. Granted, I knew he would contact you eventually, to my benefit. I didn't think it would take nineteen years, but I'm a patient man, and I always get what I want, one way or another. You owe *me*, not him. Now where's the damn notebook?"

Kaitlyn went into convulsions. Detective Payton pulled the chair from under her and gently helped her to the ground, where she flopped around uncontrollably. Mettinger tossed the used syringe into his briefcase, thumbed through a few loose papers, and retrieved a drawing. He set it on Logan's desk, then locked up the case. He then knelt beside her body, trying to ease her through the seizure, placing himself in an inconspicuous position before help arrived.

Motioning to Payton, he said, "Now. Get some help. She

can't talk anymore."

The detective walked to the office door and threw it open. "Get some help! Call an ambulance. We have an incident here," he yelled to the staff. "Johnson?" he said to a nearby officer. "Get Logan here, and Mr. Hart."

Detective Logan appeared from around the corner with Brandon Hart immediately behind. They both moved past Payton as they entered the room.

"What happened here?" she asked emphatically.

"I'm not sure," Payton responded, shrugging.

"Can you help her, Dr. Portsmyth?"

"I'm not a medical doctor, but I do have some training. I think she's coming out of the seizure. Has an ambulance been called?" he asked.

"Yes, I believe so," she responded. "Payton?"

"They're on their way now," he replied.

Kaitlyn slowly came out of her seizure and normalized. Though her breathing was sporadic and heavy, the convulsions stopped, and her body relaxed. Drenched in sweat, she passed out.

"What in the hell happened?" asked Brandon, who stood behind Mettinger, looking down at his new bride as she lay on the floor. He cupped his mouth with his hand, as if in shock. He portrayed an anxious husband with as much believability as any Shakespearean actor.

"When Detective Logan had stepped out of the room, I proceeded to remove my file folder from my briefcase, as the detective had discussed. I pulled out this drawing Kaitlyn had done in one of our sessions a few years prior. She took a look at it and went into this fit on the floor. The picture is there on your desk." Mettinger pointed to a very childish drawing of a black coyote with glowing green eyes.

"She drew this?" asked Logan.

"A few years back. Yes," Portsmyth replied.

"It looks as if a child did it."

"I agree," he confirmed.

The blaring siren and colorful, dancing lights of the ambulance filled the lobby of the sheriff's office. Under different circumstances, Kaitlyn would have been very cordial with the young, handsome EMTs. But these were Mettinger's men—hired killers, no doubt—and she would be waking from her stupor and meeting them soon enough.

***

The night seemed unyielding. James had been driving for hours, and still the clock on his dashboard read 9:30 pm. He anticipated arriving in town just before midnight. His plan was to call or message Kaitlyn when he arrived to see if she would meet with him. He feared if he had called while he was still far off, she would tell him to turn back. How he planned to explain why he needed to see her in the middle of the night would have to come to him in the spur of the moment. He was often better able to express himself to her when he didn't overthink things too much. She had that effect on him. He missed her.

Chapter 7

While James waited for the light to turn green at a quiet intersection, he looked up through the clear windshield. The moon shined its bright white light all over the street ahead and over the nearby stores, which were closed for the day.

What if I make a fool out of myself? Should I call or text? Which one would be the least harmful so late at night? he thought, nervously tapping his fingers on the steering wheel. *What was his name, again? Oh, they'll both kick me out of their house before I say anything, that's what's going to happen…*

In an effort to stop trying to guess the future, James switched on the radio, and lively saxophone music immediately filled the truck. He had attended a couple jazz performances in his life and had once bought a CD or two. Even though he wasn't crazy about the genre, he decided to leave it on and told himself it would always remind him of the day he went back to her.

The light turned green, and James stepped on the gas. Opposite him, on the other side of the road, the glimmering lights of a lone ambulance shone under the full moon.

"Hope it's nothing serious," he said aloud.

***

At the Cannon Beach police station, a perplexed Detective Logan looked at various reports spread all over her desk. Her officers had found nothing noteworthy at the scene. Her shift had ended hours earlier, and another officer had already been placed in charge, but she couldn't make herself go home. She had never dealt with a complex and exciting case before. What if this was *the one*?

Detective Payton sat casually on the squishy couch, keeping his partner company by biting loudly on a juicy, sour green apple. He felt it was his duty to stay at the station for as long as Logan did. When Logan picked up the drawing of the black coyote with the green eyes, Payton got up and stood over her desk to examine it.

"What's that, Logan? Your niece draw it?"

"Dr. Portsmyth must have forgotten it here. Ugly, isn't it?"

Payton shrugged.

"Let me check something…" Logan flipped the pages of her notebook in a hurry, then stopped once something significant caught her eye. "Tell me, did we ever see any of that doctor's ID?"

"He was … very professional." Payton had finished his apple and now looked for a place to throw the core. Not finding an appropriate spot, he chose to discreetly leave it at the corner of Logan's desk.

"Well, *sure*, but did we actually *see* an ID? Did we ever confirm any of the information he gave us?"

"It didn't seem necessary at the time."

After a short pause, Logan continued. "Where was the ambulance heading, again?"

"Um…"

"You're kidding me, right?" She was the closest anyone had ever been at stabbing another person with her eyes.

"I thought… you said… we agreed that—"

"For Christ's sake, Payton! Grab the keys to the cruiser. We're going looking for that ambulance!"

***

James had reached his destination and admired the dark, daunting woods in the distance from the warmth and safety of his driver's seat. He had parked right at the edge of the gravel driveway, not daring to drive any farther.

He hadn't imagined her living in such a remarkable house … but then again, he thought it was what she deserved. None of the lights inside the small country house were on, with the exception of the garden lighting along a stone path leading from the sidewalk to the front door. He clenched his cell phone as he had done so many times that evening during his journey. No matter how many times he had tried, he couldn't find the courage to text or call her. What would he say? Instead, he had chosen to drive all the way up to the address he had learned by heart.

In one breath, determined not to give himself any time to change his mind, James got out of the truck and reached the house with long, quick steps. He would explain himself if he had to, but all that mattered was to see her again. Just talking to her from a distance was no longer enough.

Standing on the large, square welcome mat, he first checked the doorbell to make sure the name was indeed *Hart*, then put the phone back into his pocket, glimpsed up at the sky, and gently tapped on the door. As soon as his finger came in contact with the sturdy wooden panel, the door offered no resistance and moved inwards at the touch, taking James by surprise. After superficially examining the lock, he could find no signs of forced entry, but clearly someone had left the front door open.

James stepped inside carefully, worried he was trespassing. "Hello?" he asked, too quietly to be heard by anyone.

He trod slowly in search of a light switch. In the dark, the house smelled incredibly clean, almost like a hospital. Losing his footing, he stumbled on a piece of furniture that sounded like it supported several glass objects, which—had he not regained his balance and stepped away—would have effortlessly broken.

As his eyes adjusted in the dark, he spotted a table lamp and felt for the switch. Now he could see most of the living room. Out of place in an otherwise neat and tidy room, an oversized gray sweater lay on the couch, giving James the impression it had been thrown there in a hurry.

Minding his every step, James went upstairs and stepped inside the bedroom, where the door was open wide. The smell of chemicals and cleanliness was even stronger in that room. He proceeded to switch on a table lamp on one of the nightstands. The curtains were open, but it was too dark to see anything outside. The comfortable and lavish king-sized bed had not been slept in, and a wide area on the hardwood floor at the foot of the bed was discolored.

James thought something very wrong had recently happened in that house, but before panic could set in, he heard a toilet flush and a voice coming from the master bathroom. Instinctively, he hid behind the thick curtain and listened as the man slowly approached.

"...done. Yes. That too. Look, it wasn't our first scene, all right? When I tell you it's done, it's done. We're not gonna babysit an empty house. Hey, Terry, turn off the damn light!" The man directed the command inside the bedroom. "Anyway, I'll call you back from the safe house." James heard the man walk up to the table lamp and switch it off. "Terry? Come on, we're out of here!" he yelled with his back to the curtain.

At that moment, James wondered whether to attack him and demand an explanation or remain there, hiding.

***

In Reno, Thomas rested in his worn leather chair in the center of the living room, smoking his pipe with a blanket on his legs. He couldn't get the image of the coyote out of his head. It could not have been a coincidence that James had had that dream about the girl. He did not regret giving him the keys and telling him to drive to her; he could not help but feel restless, either.

Bullet, sad that his master was gone, slept at Thomas' feet. It was best for both James and Bullet that the German Shepherd stayed with a familiar face.

"He'll be back, don't you worry," Thomas had said as he patted the whimpering dog's back when James left.

Before Thomas was done with his pipe, a knock on the door interrupted the still silence of the night. Bullet woke up, wagging his tail and letting out a single loud, playful bark.

Chapter 8

Her head hung low, her body slumped over. If it weren't for the rope binding her to the chair, she would've flopped onto the floor the second she came to. Kaitlyn wiggled her feet slightly, dragging them against the chilly concrete floor. They had taken her shoes.

She was afraid to open her eyes for fear of what she might see. Maybe if she kept pretending to be asleep, she could buy herself some time. Time for what, she didn't know. She didn't see how she could get herself out of this situation. Her fight-or-flight response was out of commission. She couldn't flee, and all fight had left her the moment they shoved that damn syringe into her.

Her body felt weak, as if she had run a marathon for which she hadn't trained. Her mouth was dry and her tongue thick. She suddenly realized how incredibly thirsty she was. It wouldn't be long before she would have to beg them for a drink. She wondered how much she would come to trade and submit just to get a swallow of water. Her arms were stiff, and she wasn't sure how much she could move her fingers. The rope grated against her skin, making every shift of her hands incredibly painful.

She jolted slightly as a hand caressed her cheek. Her head snapped up and back. She cringed, trying to shy as far away from that hand as she could. What a fool she had been, believing he loved her. Letting herself get swept up in the fleeting promise of love. He had been such a fantastic liar.

"Don't touch me," she sneered, hoping she sounded more threatening than afraid. Inside, she shook like a leaf, but she'd be damned if she showed him that.

"Katy, Katy, Katy." His honeyed voice was both mocking and scolding.

She tilted her head as far as it would go, willing herself not to cry. How could she have been so blind?

"Look at me," he growled, grabbing her face, his fingers digging into her cheek just enough to get her attention. He crouched in front of her, his gun in his other hand across her lap.

Kaitlyn's eyes bored into his. She would not back down. Before she could think about what she was going to do, she took what little saliva she had and hocked it right between his eyes. She felt victorious. She may not have had the upper hand, but she was still in the game. They needed her; they could hurt her, sure, but they wouldn't kill her.

Brandon growled, letting go of her face. He wiped the spit with his hand and flicked it off as best he could.

Kaitlyn smiled, smug and proud of herself.

"Can't say I saw that coming." He chuckled and wiped his hand on a towel. "You sure are a spitfire… but then again, I already knew that, didn't I?" He ran his finger down her neck, and Kaitlyn shivered.

"You're disgusting."

He waved his hand, and Mettinger came out along with three other men dressed in EMT uniforms. The men were tall and muscular, giving off a vibe that would make anyone want to give them a wide berth.

Kaitlyn may have stood a chance if it were just Brandon. She did spend the last few months with him, after all—not all of it could've been a lie. There had to have been some truth in his words or actions; she just had to figure out his weakness. There was no way she was going to make it past those henchmen, though.

"Take a look around, Katy. Drink it all in."

She did as he commanded. She looked up to see rows and rows of fluorescent lighting as far as she could see. They crackled slightly, as if running out of power. There were no windows and only one steel door to her right. The room was completely concrete and consisted only of a few chairs and a table. It was colder than she realized. They must be somewhere farther north.

"What do you hear?" he asked.

Her face fell as she listened, closing her eyes to open her hearing more. It wasn't what she heard, but what she didn't. She didn't hear anything at all. "We're underground," she plainly stated. Brandon didn't need to reply or say anything. Kaitlyn knew all she needed to, and the threat had been conveyed efficiently.

"I'm going to send them away now so we can talk, if that will be all right."

Kaitlyn narrowed her eyes at him. What kind of game was he trying to play now? She nodded amid Mettinger's protests, and the four men grudgingly exited through the steel door.

Brandon put his gun down on the table and lifted his hands slightly as if calling for a truce. "I'm going to untie your arms, Katy, but be warned. Nobody will hear you way out here, and if you try anything, you're outnumbered. You're going to want to hear what I have to say."

Kaitlyn scoffed audibly. "I highly doubt that."

Brandon knelt before her and wrapped his arms around her waist, his hands moving about the rope. He brought her hands to her front, and she almost cried with relief. "You'll want to massage them out," he instructed and sat backwards in one of the other chairs, resting his hands on the back of the chair. "What if I told you we aren't the bad guys?"

"Is this a joke? You killed people."

"I killed one man who wanted to kill you."

"You hit me with your gun," she argued.

"I didn't have time for your questions. You messed up the plan. I needed you down for the count for a little while."

"You aren't the good guys."

Brandon laughed loudly, and it reminded Kaitlyn of when they first met, his laughter carefree and infectious. She felt as if he had been laughing just for her, and it made her feel special and wonderful. "Well, you're right about that. We aren't the good guys. However, we aren't the bad guys, either. Shades of gray, Katy. Shades of gray. Better the bad guys you know than the bad guys you don't."

"He tried to kill me. He killed my mother." She motioned toward where Mettinger and his henchmen had disappeared.

"Yes. That he did. I had nothing to do with that. I have aligned myself with them as a means to an end."

"I don't believe you."

"Believe this, Katy. I am all you have. I'm the best chance you have of getting out of this alive. You need me just as much as I need you. I'm the only thing standing between you and Mettinger."

Damn him, Kaitlyn thought to herself. He was right. She didn't have another choice.

"We can work together, you know. You need things, I need things. Isn't marriage all about compromise?" he teased, shrugging.

"I don't need anything from you," Kaitlyn snapped.

"But you do. You need your memories, you need your father. We can help you with that as long as you help us."

Kaitlyn wasn't sure what to do.

"Admit it, Katy. Some small part of you is excited by this.

You have your father's blood—you can't help wanting to go on an adventure. To dive in headfirst and figure the rest out later. It's the same reason you married a man on a whirlwind."

Damn him! Kaitlyn thought again. He knew her. She didn't know how he did, but he was right. She was intrigued. She needed to find her father, needed the answers. Kaitlyn thrust her hand out, ready to make a deal with the devil.

Chapter 9

Brandon left the room, shutting off the light before he did so to give Kaitlyn time to mull over his proposal. Her freedom— her *life*—in exchange for cooperation in helping them find her father's journal. Not seeing any viable alternatives, she went along with it, even though she wasn't sure she had anything they needed. She was in the dark, figuratively and literally. Her only edge, the only piece of information she could think of that gave her a piece of the puzzle they didn't have, was Hugh McGraff.

McGraff, her aunt's attorney, had told Kaitlyn he held a key to a storage unit he'd been holding for her, waiting for the right time to hand it over. And he had passed along the cryptic message that he had some information to share with her too. Kaitlyn was now convinced that McGraff and the key were somehow related to whatever Brandon and Mettinger were after. It was the reason her life had been turned upside down. It was the reason she was in danger. And it held the answer to the three most important questions. Where was her father's journal? What did the map lead to? And the biggest question of all, the one that mattered most— was her father still alive?

After an hour of being alone with nothing but her thoughts, fear made a comeback. Her resolute promise to remain strong faltered. She hoped Brandon would come back soon, bring her something to drink, and lead her away from her windowless, cement prison.

She heard the door open and saw someone standing in the doorway, silhouetted against the backlight. The shape was wrong; it was too tall, too bulky.

Hope vanished, and reality set in. It wasn't Brandon.

Mettinger.

He hit a switch on the wall, and bright light assaulted her eyes, causing her lids to flutter as they made the slow adjustment. "Coffee?" he said. He handed her a cup.

Thirst-quenching water would have been her preference, but she was in no position to be choosy. She wondered if the drink might be spiked, something to knock her out, but the dryness in her throat was almost choking her, so she lifted the cup to her parched lips and took in just a taste of the liquid.

As he watched her sip it, Mettinger grinned. A Cheshire-Cat-like evil grimace spread across his face, adding to her paranoia that maybe there was something in the cup besides coffee.

His next words gave her pause and made her wonder if he could read her mind. "How's the coffee, Kaitlyn? It doesn't taste funny, does it?"

He toyed with her like a mouse swatted back and forth between a cat's paws. It was then she noticed a slight change in the air—he even *smelled* evil. She resolved to stay strong, to not let him know he was getting to her, but the truth of the matter was, she was terrified.

"I know Brandon had a nice chat with you, made you certain promises. I'm here to tell you he means to keep that promise. He's an honest man."

Kaitlyn felt momentarily relieved. Then Mettinger completed his statement.

"His honesty and good nature are his weakness. I, on the other hand, suffer from no such handicap." He pulled up the still-backwards chair before her, straddling it while facing her. He leaned forward until his face was just inches from hers, their noses almost touching. He pressed his point and stated his desires. "Myself? I don't care if you tell us what we want to know. Truth be told, I'll have more fun if you refuse to cooperate. After all, your resistance would only be temporary."

Kaitlyn wondered if they were playing "good cop, bad cop"—Brandon playing the part of her friend, Mettinger taking the opposite role. Then Mettinger spoke again and removed all doubt of playing any role.

"Some people use torture as a means to an end… to get information, for example. But some people torture because they like to. I'm in camp B."

He pushed his chair back abruptly, the legs scraping against the floor, knowing the screech and sudden motion after a sustained stillness would serve to startle her. He was correct; she flinched. "I'll leave you now. Brandon will be back to talk to you. If you tell him what we want to know, you won't see me again. I won't be back. And Kaitlyn… you don't want me to come back. Me? I'd love to see *you* again." He touched his pointer finger to her forehead and gave a slight push, an odd gesture but frightening nonetheless. It conveyed his message—he was in total control. And she was powerless.

She knew he was sincere. He would hurt her without hesitation. In fact, quite the opposite. He would relish it. And then it hit her—McGraff, her only bargaining chip. If she gave him up, they would get the key to the storage locker from him, extract whatever information he had for her, and then they would kill him.

If she didn't give him up, they would kill her.

Mettinger paused as he turned to leave. He grinned at her again, as if to tell her he knew she had just fully realized her deadly quandary. Once again, she wondered if he could read minds. He closed the door.

She thought back over the last twenty-four hours—finding a dead body in her home, the husband who betrayed her love, the gun butt to the head, the injection, the kidnapping. The cumulative weight overwhelmed her. She would never let them know they were getting to her, but right now, she was alone, and no one could see if she let it all out and cried.

She broke.

***

The search for Kaitlyn proved fruitless. Detective Stacy Logan and her partner Detective Payton trailed the ambulance all the way to Cedar Hills hospital. Hospital Admissions had no record of a Kaitlyn coming in that day, nor had they ever heard of a Dr. Portsmyth.

Logan decided to head over to the Bridle Café. After a long, hard day, she was running low on energy and wanted to fortify herself with caffeine. It would also give her the chance to question Kaitlyn's coworkers for some background or a clue as to where the missing woman had been taken.

First, though, she wanted to ditch her partner. Detective Payton was starting to rub her the wrong way. At first, he seemed totally uninterested in looking for Kaitlyn, but then he wanted to tag along on the search anyway. Payton was more hindrance than help, continually advising his partner she was making much ado about nothing, stating the doctor had probably just checked the girl into a different hospital. Logan was amped by the sequence of events, while Payton downplayed them, so she decided to jettison him.

Something about the whole situation bothered her. And the feeling grew. First, Kaitlyn showed up at the station. Despite her story sounding fantastical, Logan read her as sincere. Though she didn't know Kaitlyn that well, she had spoken to her at the café a few times, and she seemed normal. Then her husband, Brandon, came in to tell the police his wife suffered from mental conditions and was seeing a psychiatrist in Portland. Why would she see a psychiatrist in a city an hour and a half away from Cannon Beach? That seemed inconvenient. Then the psychiatrist showed up at the station—a doctor who made house calls, in this day and age? And a house call an hour and a half away?

Niggling little details were adding up, and she didn't like the sum of the equation. Something was wrong, maybe dangerously so, and she kicked herself for not paying closer attention to detail and asking more questions while Kaitlyn had still been at the station.

At the café, she took a stool at the counter. The waitress, Maya, came over to take her order. "What'll it be, Stacy? The usual—grilled cheese and a cup of joe?"

"You know, Maya, to me and you, a cup of joe means a cup of coffee. But to Jeffrey Dahmer, a cup of joe means, well… a cup of Joe."

Maya frowned at Logan and held onto the world-weary, deadpan look to make sure her annoyance sunk in.

Logan thought she didn't get it and needed an explanation. "It's cop humor. You see, Dahmer was a serial killer, and he liked to—"

"I *get* it," Maya interrupted. "I just don't *want* it. You need some new material, Detective."

Logan had her comeback ready. "Congratulations on your raise."

Maya was confused. "What raise? I didn't get a raise."

"Well, based on the service you provide, I thought for sure you're not working for tips."

"Okay, that was a good one," Maya admitted, licking her finger and pantomiming a checkmark in the air, signaling a point scored for Logan. It was the usual, good-natured, cop-and-waitress banter the two had enjoyed for years.

"Seriously, Maya, I have a bit of a situation on my hands." She wasn't sure how much of the story she should tell. Kaitlyn's medical condition, if she even had one, might be confidential, and Logan didn't want to make it public. Rather than divulge anything, she opted to just probe. "Has Kaitlyn ever been sick? She have any health problems you know of?"

"Never misses a shift. Why're you asking?"

"Any marital problems?"

"None that I know of, and you didn't answer my question. What's going on?"

Logan was spared from having to answer when her cell phone chimed in with the opening bars of a Muzak version of *I Fought the Law and the Law Won*. It was the ringtone she had assigned the station house. "Logan, here."

The officer on duty advised her to head back to the station pronto. Logan excused herself, told Maya she'd be back later, and ran to her car.

Back at the station, the duty officer pointed to an agitated man standing at the counter and said, "I think you might want to talk to this gentleman."

He was young, about twenty-five years old, Logan guessed. Black hair, a slightly dark complexion, and prominent cheekbones. She put him at maybe one or two generations away from pure Native American.

"I'm Detective Logan. How can I help you?"

"I think a friend of mine is in danger. I went to her house, knocked, no answer. The door was open, so I went in." The man introduced himself as James and went on to explain about the two men he heard in the house, the strong smell of disinfectant, and their mention of going back to a safe house. "I was going to confront them, but it would have been two on one, and I thought that would be a mistake. I hid until they left the house. Then I came here."

Logan digested what she heard and thought he was likely a jealous boyfriend overreacting. "What's your friend's name?"

"Kaitlyn Hart."

Logan was stunned. She made him repeat his story again, hoping for a new detail that might help them figure out where Kaitlyn had been taken, but nothing stood out.

"I believe you, and I want to help. Fact is, I've been looking for Kaitlyn myself today. But I'm at a dead-end. I don't know where to look next."

"I know where," James said. "Before the two guys drove off, I got their license plate number."

Logan pumped her fist. Suddenly, there was life in the dead-end. "Great! Let's run it through the computer and see what we get."

***

Thomas made his way over to the door and opened it without hesitation. If it was danger, Bullet would have let out a low growl instead of wagging his tail. He had a sense for such things. Plus, the old man was pretty sure he knew who was knocking on his door so late at night. Thomas and the visitor locked eyes for a moment, no words spoken. The man had skin like a saddle, leathery and tanned from years of exposure to the sun. Under the ragged old baseball cap on his head, traces of sandy brown were still visible in his hair but mixed now with strands of gray. His eyes had the twinkle of an adventurer, a wanderer, a free spirit who loved life and lived it to the fullest.

He smiled at Thomas and broke the silence. "*Osiyo.*"

"*Osiyo,*" Thomas replied, exchanging the familiar Cherokee greeting.

"It's been a long time, *Adawehi*," the visitor said, calling Thomas a wise elder.

"You got my message. Thank you for coming." Thomas paused before stating his purpose in summoning his old friend. "I think the circle is about to be completed."

"The Black Coyote project?" the visitor asked, though he already knew the answer.

77

"Yes, Black Coyote."

"We always knew this day would come. Not all secrets stay hidden forever. Are you ready?"

"Yes. I'm ready. James and Kaitlyn are going to need us now."

The two men embraced. Thomas stepped aside to let the man enter his home.

Kaitlyn's father, Daniel, leaned down and scratched Bullet behind his ears while the dog's tail rhythmically thumped the floor.

Chapter 10

"Here, honey. Let me show you how to do it."

Kaitlyn looked up to see her father smiling down at her.

He had trouble sitting and ended up just flopping back onto the sand, eliciting a laugh from his daughter. He wriggled around until he lay on his stomach next to her, then took hold of the shovel in her hand and helped her scoop out some sand.

"Is there going to be anything in this one, Dad?" Kaitlyn asked. "You made finding things sound so much fun, but this is dumb."

Her father laughed. "I'll admit, it's a bit more fun when you're actually finding things. But patience is the name of the game." He guided Kaitlyn's hand to a sifter, where they dumped the sand, and he shook it. A jagged green shark tooth bounced on the top of the sifter. Kaitlyn squealed with excitement. "See what I mean?"

She snatched the tooth and held it against her chest. "I *found* something. What did I find, Daddy?"

"You found something really cool, sweetie. You found a shark tooth."

"What kind? Is it a big shark? I hope it was a big shark," she said as she jumped up and down.

"Well, ease up for a second. Let me take a quick peek at it. I'm no encyclopedia on sharks, but I know a thing or two." He took a quick look at the tooth. It was asymmetrical with a slight tilt to the left, like the tip was just pulled off-center. "If I had to guess, I would say a bull shark. It's a really cool shark, Kaitlyn. It can actually live in freshwater *and* saltwater."

"Cool! I have a bull shark tooth. Why is it green? I thought shark teeth were white."

"See, here's what's cool about shark teeth—when a shark tooth is buried, it's protected from decomposition from oxygen or bacteria. However, they tend to absorb surrounding minerals when they're buried in sediments. Their color is entirely dependent on the sediments around them when they're buried. Green is an unusual color, but then again, we're in an unusual place," he said.

"So you brought us here because the shark teeth are green here?" Kaitlyn asked.

"Hardly. It'll make sense later, Kaitlyn. I brought you here because this place is full of interesting things. I'll show you all of them at some point." Her dad hugged her and looked over the horizon toward the entrance of the old silver mine.

***

"Mettinger is an antsy type of person, Kaitlyn. When he found out you had no memory of anything before the accident, it took me a full hour to convince him that you were still useful enough to keep alive," Brandon said. He sat on the floor against the wall, looking at Kaitlyn, who still sat in the chair to which she had been tied.

"Am I?" Kaitlyn said in a tone a shade too confrontational given her current predicament.

"You are. You're going to remember what happened. You're going to help us get your father's notebook. And then you're going to help us find what we're looking for." He stood and walked toward her.

"And what if I can't? What if I won't?" Kaitlyn asked, testing him. This person calling himself Brandon wasn't the man she'd married; she needed to re-acclimate to him. She also needed him to show her just how important she actually was to the operation.

"I thought you were on board. We're going to get you the answers and closure you want." Brandon rubbed his head and sighed.

"Don't get me wrong, Brandon. I want my answers. But you're still the man who helped kidnap me and who murdered a man in the home we shared. Now, you say you're not the bad guy, and that's good enough for now, because I can't disprove that. But I'm going through all this *among* you all, not *with* you. Keep that in mind." Kaitlyn waited for his response, and Brandon dropped his shoulders and nodded. If he conceded that quickly, she must be a crucial piece.

"Okay, and I get that. I'm going to spend this whole trip trying to make everything up to you. I want to show you that I'm not the bad guy. I'm not going to let anything happen to you," Brandon said.

"What happened with my aunt's lawyer?"

"That's why Mettinger's antsy right now. I can't find him. His office is closed. None of his numbers or accounts led anywhere, and his condo is totally empty. He's gone. Now, lawyers make a lot of enemies, so I first thought he might have been scared. But maybe he took a look inside that storage unit you told me about. Maybe he just figured out what it all means. Maybe he's already out with that map."

"He wouldn't…" Kaitlyn said.

"He might," Brandon replied. "Now, listen. I don't expect memories to just pop into your head whenever we ask you about them. That's unrealistic. However, you need to know that we need something from you soon. Because it's very possible your aunt's lawyer is out looking for what we want, and he has something better than memories… he has the real thing."

Brandon walked to the door and knocked two times. The door opened, and a large box was handed to him. He walked back over to Kaitlyn and placed the box on the concrete in front of her. "When we searched through your aunt's house, we found a bunch of your old stuff. We packed some up for you. Hopefully, something in there will remind you of something. Oh, and I brought you your shoes." Brandon walked back to the door and knocked three times. The door opened again and Brandon walked through it. Kaitlyn heard the door locked behind him.

She opened the box, and the first thing she did was pull out her shoes from the top of the pile and slip them onto her feet. Then she found a bunch of things from her childhood—pictures, books, stuffed animals. She tried to look through without getting distracted by nostalgia but stopped when she found a necklace. She pulled it out. It was adorned with several small stones and cheap gems. Hanging at the bottom was a green shark tooth.

* * *

On the other side of the door, Mettinger waited for Brandon. "Feisty little thing. I can see why you went for her," he said with a dry chuckle.

"Save it. She knows the stakes now. She won't be pushed around. She just needs to think she's pushing us where she wants to go, and we'll be fine." Brandon walked around the corner to another heavily locked metal door. "Once she realizes that it's really where *we* want to be, we'll already be there."

"Oh, Brandon. This is why I need you. It's hard to be anxious when someone has every detail ironed out to perfection," Mettinger said.

"Don't I know it. Now, if you'll excuse me for a moment, I have another patient to check in on." Brandon unlocked the door as Mettinger gestured for him to go. He walked into a room very similar to the one in which he held Kaitlyn. In the center, a well-dressed man sat chained to a chair, duct tape strapped across his mouth. Brandon closed the door and heard Mettinger lock it behind him.

Brandon strolled over to the chair and lightly slapped the man, who awoke instantly. Eyes wide, he cried and whimpered under the duct tape. Brandon grabbed the man's chin and shushed him. The man calmed down for a moment until Brandon violently ripped the tape off his mouth. Half a scream escaped before Brandon's hand on his mouth shut him up.

"Shh! What did I say? We have other guests here. Don't want to upset them, do we? Now just relax a minute. We're going to have a conversation."

The man nodded and slowed his breathing. When Brandon felt the man was calm enough, he removed his hand.

Brandon grabbed a chair for himself and faced his captive. "Now Hugh. Let's talk about one of your clients."

Chapter 11

Detective Logan strode purposefully to her computer and typed in the license plate James had given her. It came up immediately as the property of an office-cleaning business out of Portland, Oregon. She turned around to gaze up at James, who had been trying to look casual as he snuck a peek at the computer screen. Normally, she would be annoyed by a civilian looking at official police business, but she would need James' help, so she kept her irritation down.

"Why don't you go have a seat in the waiting area while I research this?" she said calmly.

He nodded and approached the chairs on the other side of the sergeant's desk. She did a thorough search on the cleaning company and found it was legitimate. That didn't mean whoever owned it didn't use the two goons James had seen to clean up the occasional crime scene. She yawned and stretched. Her shift had been over hours ago, but the only clue they had was the cleaning crew address. She wanted to investigate it before the two guys disappeared and the trail went completely cold. Shutting down the computer, she walked toward James.

"I'm going to change out of my uniform, then we're going to Portland—incognito. I'm assuming you have a vehicle."

"Yeah, a truck. But I just spent eight hours driving here from Nevada. I'm beat. I don't want to fall asleep on the road, so you'll have to drive," James told her.

"Okay. It's only an hour and a half." James gave her the keys and led her out to the truck.

When they got in, Detective Logan handed him the drawing of the coyote. "You've been friends with Kaitlyn for a long time. Apparently, this image triggered one of her seizures. Does it mean anything to you?"

"Yeah. Katy's dad was a research scientist. He was working on the Black Coyote project when he died. I think my grandfather had something to do with the project, but he would never tell me anything about it."

"The license plate is registered to a legitimate office-cleaning company. I grew up in Portland. I know the area very well. There's a wide alley right down the street from there, and it should be within viewing distance. We'll go in there and watch for that vehicle. It's a long shot, but my gut tells me the guys you saw in Kaitlyn's house are directly involved with her abduction. If they are, they might lead us to her."

After ten minutes on the road, James texted his grandfather.

'Kaitlyn is missing. Her new husband Brandon is involved. Detective Logan from the Cannon Beach Police and I are on the way to Portland to look for her. She might be in danger.'

***

Thomas picked up his phone as soon as it buzzed and read the message twice before answering. *'Be careful. Let me know what you find out.'*

He handed Daniel the phone. "It has begun."

***

When they reached Portland, Detective Logan drove straight downtown. Halfway down the main street, she pulled into a long alley that curved the farther they went. By the time they got to the end of it, the main street was no longer visible. She parked, then picked up the leather satchel she had carried to the truck. She pulled out a pair of high-powered binoculars and scanned the parking lot directly across the street.

"Can they see us from there?" James asked nervously. They were Kaitlyn's only hope. They couldn't risk being spotted.

"Not likely. This alley is known as Lover's Lane. It's not uncommon to see a vehicle parked at the end. My dad was a cop here when I was growing up. He used to tell me and my brother some of the funniest stories about this alley. One time, he and his partner snuck down it from the main street with the lights out on their cruiser. When they got behind the vehicle parked at the end, my dad put on the siren and the lights. The car in front started up so fast it nearly stalled, then raced out of there like a bat out of hell. Dad never told us who was in the car, but years later, I heard it had been the mayor and the fire chief's wife." She laughed.

"Is your dad still a cop here, Detective?"

"Please, call me Stacy. And yeah. He's the chief of police now. If we find anything at all worth investigating, I'll call him." She paused. "I'm starving. There's a burger joint on the corner, right across from the office we're watching. Get me a burger, fries, and a root beer... and whatever you want. Watch the front of the cleaners' for those two guys you saw. I'll watch from here. What did they look like?"

"I only saw one from the back. Shorter, with a thick neck and short black hair," he said. "I saw the other's face when they got into their car. He's tall and muscular, like a wrestler, maybe. He had short, sandy-blonde hair in a military cut. Looked mean."

Stacy went into her satchel again and brought out a dark green leather wallet. She pulled out a crisp twenty and handed it to James, who took it with a grin and a thanks, then climbed out of the truck. He loped down the alley like a lithe young animal. Stacy zoomed in her binoculars on the parking lot behind the cleaners'. There were only three vehicles there, two of them company vans. The third was a sedan with the license plate James had given her. She pumped a fist in triumph, then focused on the car. James returned minutes later with a takeout bag of food and a couple cans of soda.

After a few bites, he turned to her. "I didn't see anything unusual. Customers came and went. I didn't see the two guys we're looking for."

"They're not in the front of the building, then. It's dusk now. By the time we finish eating, it'll be full dark. If there's no action before then, we'll go peek in some windows in the back and hope for the best," Stacy said.

They munched away for a while without speaking. They were still eating when the back door of the cleaning shop opened, and the two men they were looking for came out.

Stacy leaned over and spoke quietly to James, even though there was no way they could be heard from that distance. She had gone into cop mode, her playfulness giving way to a no-nonsense demeanor. "I recognize the one with the black hair. His name is Gordon Sleavey. He's a drunken thug. Beats his mother. Of course, she never presses charges. I'd love to get something on him that'll stick. My dad hates him. I don't know the other guy. You should drive, in case he recognizes me. Here, climb over me. Don't pull out until I tell you to."

Without wasting any time, she scooted over to the passenger side of the bench seat, and James crawled over her knees. There wasn't time to feel awkward. They had to be in position before Sleavey and his cohort left. Stacy scrunched down under the dashboard, facing the seat, then reached into her satchel and pulled out her own personal weapon. She was off duty; any time her service pistol was fired, it had to be reported. She shouldn't even be there, doing what she was doing, and she didn't want to add a possible weapons charge to the mix. Her father being who he was felt more of a liability than an advantage. Even when he'd caught her drinking underage, he had threatened to throw her in jail if she ever did it again. She never did. The chief of police was never one for empty threats.

The cleaning business faced the main street, but the parking lot faced Dibble. The sedan pulled out of the parking lot and turned left, away from the main street. Stacy knew that if they kept going, the street would take them right out of town and out to the highway. She put her elbows up on the seat and turned her head toward James.

"You can go now. You won't have to follow close. Just keep his taillights in view. Please let me know if he pulls off anywhere," she said.

James started the truck and did as Stacy instructed. After a mile or so, she got back on the seat and buckled her seatbelt. It was now dark, with substantial cloud cover. That could be to their advantage. They were well out of town when James saw the car ahead take a left onto a side road.

"Drive on past and pull off into the bushes about a mile down the road. I know where they're going. There's nothing on it but a bomb shelter built during the Cold War. It used to be attached by a tunnel to an old stone farmhouse, but the house was blown down by a tornado in 1972. The family survived by hiding in the shelter, then they moved away. My dad knew them. My friends and I used to explore down there when we were kids. Nothing much except cement walls and steel doors, in case of fire. There's an entrance from the farmhouse and a hidden escape hatch out the other end in the woods. We'll have to walk from here."

When they got out of the truck, James climbed up into the bed and unlocked a wooden tool chest, pulling out a tire iron and a long, heavy-duty flashlight. He handed it down to Stacy and dug out one of his own, then jumped down and stood beside her.

"What's with the tire iron?" she asked.

"You never know when you'll have to pry something open or defend yourself."

They made their way through the woods until they found the stone rubble of the house. The sedan was parked in a machine shed still more or less intact. They had their flashlights turned on low-beam as they crawled around the footing. Stacy led James down wide cement steps to a part of the basement that still had some of its ceiling, thanks to reinforced floor beams. They went down and entered a tunnel built with cement blocks. At the end was a locked steel door, and they had to turn around.

"We'll have to try the back way in, through the woods. It's accessed by a trap door. I don't think anyone knew about it besides my friends and I… and the family who built it. We explored every inch of this place."

They trekked through the bushes for half a mile, then Stacy stopped and trained her flashlight on the ground. She walked several paces in a circle, dragging her feet. Her toes caught on something under the leaves, and she knelt. She scrabbled away the thick layer of undergrowth and dead leaves until she found a steel ring attached to a steel hatch cover.

"I could use that tire iron right about now." She grinned up at James. He handed it to her, and she used it to clear away the earth and leaves around the hatch, then inserted it through the ring. Standing, she brushed off her knees. "Your turn," she said.

He knelt to pry the edges of the hatch cover. It took some doing, but finally managed to open the hatch. Shining his flashlight down into the space, he revealed stainless steel ladder rungs going down a hole lined in cement.

Stacy swallowed back a jolt of anxiety. She'd failed to mention that her childhood friends had to dare her to go down in the tunnels in the first place; she never was one for small, dark places. For Kaitlyn, though, she'd suck it up.

James went down first while Stacy lit the way from above, then he returned the favor when she descended. The hole only went down about eight feet, then made a turn to the right to become a fairly high tunnel, also lined in cement. The floor tilted down gradually, then came to a set of cement steps ending at a steel door at least twenty feet down. It was locked, but Stacy dug around in the dirt directly below the threshold and unearthed a key. She lowered the beam of her flashlight and kept it trained on the ground, bringing her finger to her lips. They would have to go in quietly.

Chapter 12

S tacy yanked the door, but it was lighter than she remembered from her childhood, and she almost overbalanced. James steadied her with a hand on her shoulder. She took a calming breath and carefully pulled the door open the rest of the way. It squeaked as she did so, and they winced at the noise, holding their breath and hoping anyone inside hadn't heard.

The area on the other side of the door was dark, and Stacy slowly raised her flashlight, illuminating a short hallway framed by doors and ending in another steel door.

"Let's go," she whispered and led the way.

"What's in these rooms?" James asked. "Do you remember?"

Stacy shrugged. The doors had always been locked, and her younger self had been more focused on getting in and out than on exploring. She tried the door on the left, but it would not open. She turned to see James reaching for the door on the right. It was slightly ajar and gave way with a loud screech. Again, they turned to look at the steel door at the hall's end and froze.

After a few seconds with no sound, James stuck his head in the door's opening and shined his light inside. Metal shelving lined the walls, bare except for cobwebs and a dusty oil lantern. A glass jar lay shattered on the floor, the shards too dull to reflect his light.

"Storage," he whispered as he stepped away.

Stacy nodded and crept forward until her toes nearly touched the door at the hall's end. She pulled the handle, but it was secure. Leaning in, she pressed her ear against it, listening.

***

"Why did you become a lawyer, Hugh?" Brandon asked, throwing an arm over the back of his chair. The man irritated him with his refusals. When asked about Louise Gilman's estate, he had repeatedly said he couldn't discuss his clients' business and that there was nothing of interest about any of them anyway.

"I don't know, sir," Hugh said, sweat dripping from his forehead despite the chill in the room. "I suppose I wanted to help families."

Brandon nodded. "Because you're a nice guy. You like to help people, and that's noble." He leaned forward, arms on his knees. "An estate lawyer can be a nice guy. You know, trial lawyers aren't nice guys. They're tough. You're not tough, are you, Hugh?" Brandon smiled at the bound man like one might smile at a dog that had just run into a screen door. Hugh shook his head. "You're nice. I can be nice, Hugh. I'm a lot like you." Brandon paused to clear his throat and sit upright. "But Mettinger out there, remember him?"

Hugh nodded, his expression changing as he began to understand the tone of the conversation.

"He's more like a trial lawyer. He's mean. Cutthroat."

Hugh swallowed audibly, the gulping sound loud in the quiet of the bunker.

"Wouldn't you rather just deal with me? I mean, Louise is dead. What you tell me won't hurt her, but what you keep from me... Well, that just might hurt you."

Hugh McGraff cast his eyes down at the floor and shut them. He took a deep breath and nodded. "You want to know about the storage unit," he said.

Brandon's slow grin was interrupted by a knock on the door. He gritted his teeth but reached forward and patted Hugh on the knee. "You're a smart man, Hugh," he said. "Hold that thought while I hold Mettinger off." He stood and strode across the room, then opened the door and fixed Mettinger with a hard stare. "What?" he said coldly.

"Sorry to interrupt," Mettinger said. "The boys and I heard a noise. Like a door opening. Through there." He gestured to the steel door at the back of the outer room.

Following Mettinger's pointing hand, Brandon saw that all five of his guard team milled about the room, waiting for his response. His frown turned to a scowl and he stepped through the door, pulling pulled it shut behind him. "Why the hell are you standing here, then? Why is no one guarding the entrance or the driveway? What are we paying these idiots for? Go check it out!"

"The door's locked," one man protested, looking up from fiddling with the EMT insignia on his jacket as it peeled away from the fabric.

"There must be a back way in," Brandon said. "Go find it."

The men bustled about for a moment, shrugging on coats and grabbing weapons. Mettinger shouted a few more orders at them and turned back to Brandon. "Where do you want me?" he asked.

"Guarding my wife's door," Brandon said. He passed back into the lawyer's room and slammed the door in Mettinger's face. Smoothing back his hair, he crossed to his chair at a brisk pace. "Sorry about that, Hugh," he said. "We were chatting about the storage unit, right? What's in there, do you suppose?"

Hugh's shoulders had slumped, and he refused eye contact. "I don't know what's in it. I only know that I'm supposed to give Louise's niece a letter when I deliver the key."

"What's in the letter?"

"I don't know."

Brandon clicked his tongue. "Now, Hugh. You knew exactly what part of Louise's estate I wanted to know about when I said her name. You must know something more."

Hugh let out a shuddering sigh. "She said it could lead to great wealth, so it was a matter of life and death. She was very cryptic and obviously scared. I think it was the reason she hired me, really. She had very little to settle other than that." The man looked up at Brandon, his eyes full of disgust. "That's all I know."

Brandon's hand slid beneath his jacket and closed around the cool steel silencer on the end of his gun. "So where's this letter? And the key?"

***

Kaitlyn stared at the necklace in her palm, fingering each small gem in turn. She frowned as she tried to remember where they'd all come from. The pink one had been her favorite, and she knew it had come out of a cheap cereal box ring. Some of the others she and her father had plucked from piles of rock or sifted out of dirt.

But the two on either side of the fossilized shark tooth had drawn her attention. She didn't remember them. They were similar in size, and both appeared to be mere rocks, but one seemed broken. She ran her thumb over it, drawing it closer to her face. No, she realized, a piece of the rock had simply been chipped away to reveal something smooth and fine underneath.

She turned the small stone into the light, and it shone a dark green. It looked like an emerald, though surely not real, she thought. The stone reflected the light until it seemed to glow like the eyes of an animal in the dark. Her father's smiling face flashed before her eyes, and she remembered that day, sifting through dirt with him. She remembered him tilting his head down. She'd always loved the battered baseball cap he wore. A black animal staring at her with embroidered green eyes.

"Black Coyote," she said quietly.

Her head whipped up as she heard the muffled sounds of feet running past her door. She squeezed her fingers tightly around the necklace and scrambled to her feet. Moving cautiously toward the door, she stared at it, unsure what to do. She knew it was locked, but she tested it anyway.

Struggling to hear something—anything that might give her a clue as to what was happening—she froze and held her breath. She heard a shout—just an echo through the bunker. There was a dull clank like metal against concrete, and then silence again.

***

"I sent someone to Kaitlyn," Daniel said, taking a sip of the cool water Thomas had offered him. "A friend. To warn her and make sure she got the key to the storage unit. I haven't heard from him."

Thomas pushed aside a Styrofoam container to make space for their glasses on the table, then seated himself across from Daniel. "How far will your friend go to look for her?" he asked.

Daniel shook his head. "He was only supposed to deliver a message. If he doesn't find her, he won't go looking. I didn't want to involve him any deeper than necessary." There was a stretch of heavy silence between them. "I should've sent him sooner."

This time it was Thomas' turn to shake his head. "We had no way of knowing when this would happen. Or that she wouldn't have received the key yet."

"I should've told her," he said.

"No." Thomas set his now empty glass down with an authoritative thud. "You were trying to protect her."

"Thomas, she married one of them," Daniel said. "She got married. There was no wedding announcement. I was watching the paper. And with Louise dead, I didn't know. I had no way of knowing. I couldn't see her on her wedding day." Daniel put his head in his hands.

"You were being watched," Thomas reminded him. "It was risky enough when you visited me here."

"I've missed so much," Daniel said, his voice muffled by his hands.

Thomas frowned as he watched his friend. "Daniel," he said, his voice harsh now. "You haven't buried her. You could still know her. But we need to make a plan to put this to an end."

Daniel nodded and sat up straighter. "We'll have to go to the mine, Thomas. There's no way around it."

***

James watched Stacy lean into the door, wondering what she might be hearing. Was Kaitlyn on the other side somewhere? Was she safe?

Stacy jerked away from the door, nearly smashing the back of her head into his face.

"What is it?" he asked.

"Oh, God, James," she said. "They heard us. They're coming!"

"How many?" James asked, his heart pounding in his chest. He gripped his tire iron tighter.

"I dunno. More than I thought," Stacy said. She knelt and frantically brushed away the dust at the bottom of the door, looking for another key. But James knew they wouldn't get so lucky twice. Stacy cursed and stood. "Run," she said.

James turned and pounded down the short hallway toward the first door they'd come through. He reached to open it when Stacy grabbed his arm and yanked backwards.

"They're already here," she whispered. James set his jaw, prepared to fight his way past the coming threat, but Stacy shoved him back toward the storage room door. "Get in there," she said. "Hide behind the door."

James braced his feet. He had no intention of leaving her to face this alone. "No, Detective. I'm not hiding."

"We're no good to Kaitlyn if we're both dead. I have a plan. Just hide!" She shoved him against the door, which gave way behind his back.

He scowled but darted inside and pushed the door mostly closed before flattening himself against the wall behind it. He held his breath as he heard the hall door burst open, followed by the sounds of scrabbling feet and yelling.

"Don't shoot," Stacy said. "I've dropped my weapon. Don't shoot!"

A raspy voice said, "That's the detective from Cannon Beach."

"Ours?" another voice asked.

"No."

Stacy gasped, and there was a sound of scuffling before a gun went off. The pinging of a ricochet echoed through the space.

"Are you crazy?" the raspy voice shouted. "We can't kill a cop."

James' heart thudded in his chest, and he had just lifted a foot to step out when he heard Stacy's voice.

"I have a proposition for Brandon Hart," she said, her voice clear and unwavering. James relaxed a bit. She didn't sound as if she'd been hit.

"I'll bet you do," said the raspy voice. "Keep your hands up."

James heard heavy footsteps approaching. The man was much closer this time when he spoke. "Do you have your handcuffs?"

"No." Stacy's voice wavered a bit as she spoke. There was more scuffling and the sound of a zip tie being tightened.

"Let's go see Brandon," the raspy voice said. The footsteps withdrew, and James let out a shaky breath. He could hear shoes climbing the metal ladder down the hall.

He was just beginning to think of his next move when another voice boomed a command. "Terry. Search those rooms before you come back."

Chapter 13

Daniel picked up a magazine from the coffee table and raised his eyebrows. *"Lost Treasures?"*

Thomas shrugged. "It's *Ganodo's*. He's obsessed with finding buried Cherokee fortunes lost in the Civil War. He believes if he reclaims some of the lost money, the tribal elders will exonerate his father and welcome him back into the Cherokee Nation."

Daniel sighed. "It's not that simple, is it?"

"No. But the boy is determined."

"How much does he know about the Black Coyote project?"

"I have kept it from him. But now, with the others closing in and Kaitlyn in trouble, I fear he will have to know it all. It is just a matter of time before they connect him to me and thus to the map."

Daniel strode toward a painting on the wall—a depiction of the massacre of Wounded Knee. A lone Native American stood holding a rifle, surrounded by US Army soldiers with raised arms. Dead Native Americans were strewn across a battlefield. It was a bloody, startling painting.

"We do not want to be like the Black Coyote shown in this painting, Thomas."

"He was an uneducated Lakota Sioux. He should have given up his weapon, prevented bloodshed. We are smarter—stronger. Though our enemy is not as visible now as the White Man was then. I've learned something since you last visited. I fear the timing of the prophecy."

Thomas pulled at the bottom corner of the painting to reveal a hidden panel behind it. He pressed a code on the keypad. It opened. Then he pulled out a heavy, leather book from the chamber with a zodiac insignia on the cover. He brought it to the table and opened it carefully, trying not to harm the yellowed parchment paper.

"I came across this book. It begins with the same Cherokee legend mentioned in the letter you were given. The myth that the Great Spirit spoke of another attempt to make a circle of the four parts of this world—earth, water, wind, and fire—together combining to create an all-powerful, indestructible, and magical stone. The same one you've been searching for. The constellations point to this happening during the year of three celestial events. The solar eclipse, the great comet, and the alignment of the four stars. You already know all this, except… it says here its creation will happen on the winter solstice."

He consulted a calendar, then looked at Daniel. It was October. Winter solstice was December twenty-first. "The mountain passes will be deep in snowfall if it is a bad winter, as they have predicted."

Daniel considered this. "Well, legend or not, we'll find out. You assume the location is in the mountains? The map in the journal is incomplete, though I suspect you're right. But whoever finds my journal will know all I know. That I think the missing piece is in the cave behind the mine… the piece that, if this legend is true, shows exactly where the event will occur." Daniel looked up through a skylight in the ceiling. "The circle is closing. Two of the prophecy's events have already occurred. I should have found the piece of the map earlier, but when Kaitlyn and I went to the mine… we had to flee. And then the accident…" His voice trailed off.

"You had no control over that, Daniel," Thomas said, pressing a palm to Daniel's shoulder. "The Bratvas would have killed you and Kaitlyn if they'd found you. They have probably scoured the mine over the last decade and still come up empty."

"Probably. But if they're coming after me now, after all these years, it means they've also noticed the events occurring. The third one grows closer each day as the stars align. If what you say is true, their alignment will be complete at the solstice. They'll be in the same position as the year Kaitlyn was born."

Thomas smiled thinly, not meeting his friend's eyes. "You know what this means, don't you?"

Daniel nodded sadly. "It means Kaitlyn may be the key. We can't let them know that. We'll go to the mine, complete the map, then bargain for Kaitlyn's life. The stone doesn't matter to me anymore."

Thomas stood still. "The stone is everything, Daniel. But we'll take care of Kaitlyn." He took out his cell phone and dialed.

"Good evening, Chooli. It's Thomas. It's time to make the journey," he said. He listened, then said in reply, "I understand. I need at least two, so bring someone with you. We leave at dawn tomorrow."

Chapter 14

James looked down to see his hand on the doorknob. He eased it away, careful not to jostle the knob, as he listened for footsteps approaching the other side of the door. There was the sound of shoes scraping against the floor in the hall.

He took up a position to the right of the door, holding his crowbar tight to his chest. His heart hammered against his ribs, and he reminded himself to breathe. The footsteps in the hallway were louder now, as if the man, Terry, was across the hallway. Hinges creaked, and low muttering reached James' ears. He couldn't make out the words themselves.

When the footsteps made their way toward him, he hefted his tire iron up and over his shoulder. His arms shook. Sweat slicked the metal bar.

Terry jiggled the doorknob, and the internal mechanism clicked. James watched the door open and Terry's head appear. He didn't have time to question what he was about to do. Aiming for the man's head, he landed a glancing blow right above the temple before hitting him square in the shoulder. Terry let out a pained grunt, then toppled to the ground. His head caught an edge on the bottom shelf of a metal shelving unit, and he stilled completely.

The crowbar almost slipped from James' hand, but he readjusted his grip just in time. He started for the door but stopped before he could step over the threshold and returned to the depths of the storage room. After further inspecting the mostly-bare shelves, he pocketed a handful of dusty nuts and bolts, along with a pair of slightly rusty wire cutters and a flathead screwdriver. He almost left then, but he stopped one last time to rifle through Terry's pockets, digging out a gun from a holster beneath his arm.

Satisfied, he shut the storage room door. It was only a matter of time before Brandon and his men started missing Terry. James could not afford to waste another second.

***

Brandon tapped a finger on the table in front of him while his other hand squeezed the gun silencer beneath his jacket. If the silencer had been made of anything other than steel, his vice-like grip would have dented it.

"Well?" he asked impatiently. "I'm waiting. Where's the key? And where's the letter?"

Hugh McGraff glared across at Brandon—not the glare of a man who would launch himself across the room if he were not tied to the chair, but the look of a man angry and yet resigned to his fate. "In my office," he said. "I secure clients' paperwork and effects in a lockbox hidden under my desk."

Brandon forced his hand away from his gun, sighed, then stood. His chair scraped against the concrete floor. "I'm disappointed, Hugh," he said. "Very disappointed. I thought you and I understood each other, but I see I was mistaken. Your office has been searched, and we found your lockbox."

He paused to watch Hugh shift against his bonds.

A thin smile crossed Brandon's lips. "You and I both know what we didn't find," he continued. "A single file for Louise. Not one. Now, I'm afraid you've left me no other options." He sighed again and strode toward the door. "Mettinger will be most effective in getting the answers you've been unwilling to give me."

"Wait," Hugh shouted. Panic rode his voice. "Wait."

Brandon paused at the door, his hands at his sides. He looked pointedly at his watch and then expectantly at the bound man. He didn't say a word.

"They're in my condo," Hugh said. "In the safe bolted to the floor underneath my bed. The combination's sixty-one, seventeen, three."

"Thank you," Brandon said coolly. He walked out of the room, shutting the door firmly.

Down the hall marched Gordon Sleavey and Detective Stacy Logan. Stacy's hands were secured at the small of her back, and she struggled to keep up with the man shoving her along. He yanked her to a standstill. Stacy let out a yelp and favored her left shoulder.

Brandon's eyes narrowed.

"I found the detective here at the other end of the bunker," Gordon said. "And she says she has a proposition for you."

"I see." Brandon studied Stacy. "I'm afraid you have me mistaken, Detective. I am a married man."

"I spoke with the dispatcher at the Portland PD when I parked my car," Stacy said. "He's sending a couple squad cars this way, and they should be here any minute." She saw Brandon open his mouth to speak, but she didn't let him get a word out. "In exchange for calling them off, I want a piece of the action."

"What action?" Brandon asked, suspicion dripping on the two words.

"The inheritance," she said. "Kaitlyn's inheritance."

Brandon pinched the bridge of his nose between his thumb

and forefinger. Then he looked beyond Stacy to Gordon Sleavey. "Have you received a call from our man at the Portland Police?" he asked.

"No," Gordon replied. "No calls."

"There you have it," Brandon said. He adjusted the cuffs of his shirt. "The lawyer gave me the location of the letter and the key, and we're going to need him to get past the doorman at his condo. Grab him, then lock the detective in that room. We'll deal with her later." He surveyed the hallway behind the man. "Where's Terry?"

"Searching the other rooms," Gordon said. "To make sure she's alone. He should be finished soon."

"Mettinger," Brandon said over his shoulder. Mettinger leaned against the wall next to the door of the room where Kaitlyn was secured. "When Terry gets back, send him back down there to figure out how she got in and station a guard."

Mettinger pushed himself away from the wall. "You want me to stay here?"

"Yes," Brandon said. "Have one of the other men find her car and get rid of it. We don't have time to deal with anyone who might see it. When we come back, we'll deal with the detective and my wife."

***

James inched down the hallway. He retrieved the gun from his pocket and meticulously fiddled with the safety until he switched it off. He wasn't sure if he was prepared to actually pull the trigger, but he had no intention of letting Brandon know that— or whoever he came face to face with next.

Counting to fifteen, James turned a slight corner and flattened himself against the inside wall. There wasn't the sound of an alarm suddenly being raised, no loud voices carrying through the hall, and no footsteps. So he figured so far, so good.

The next few minutes passed by in an eternity. Getting down the hallway, making the least amount of noise possible, caused

James to break out in a full sweat. His shirt clung to his chest, and he stopped to dry his hands on his jeans more than once.

The wall bent at a ninety-degree angle where the hallway took a right turn. James sucked in a breath until his lungs filled with air. He slipped around the corner with his arms and the gun stretched out in front of him. There was a pair of doors along the wall about thirty yards down, and a man stood between them.

The man noticed James a fraction of a second before he saw the gun. He didn't move from his position between the two doors, but his arm moved at his side.

"Don't even think about it!" James shouted. "Nice and slow, now. Remove your weapon and slide it across the floor."

The man sneered but did as he was told. Slowly, without breaking eye contact with James, he removed his pistol from his side and bent forward to set it on the floor, then leaned back up and kicked the gun toward James.

James kept his own gun trained on the man and kicked the abandoned weapon farther down the hall, then stepped closer and aimed for the space between the man's eyes. "Where's Kaitlyn?" he asked.

The man didn't say anything.

"Where's Stacy?" James asked. His hands twitched around the gun.

Again, the man was silent.

James ground his teeth in frustration. "Open the door, now," he ordered.

The man opened the door on his left. There was shuffling inside, but James kept his eyes on the stranger. He used the gun to motion him through the doorway. They both walked into the small concrete room with fluorescent lights flickering at the ceiling. A table and two chairs sat in the middle of the room.

Stacy perched on the edge of a chair. She wobbled to a standing position, bending forward to keep her balance.

"Are you okay?" James asked.

"I'm fine," she said. Her voice trembled ever so slightly. "The door—the door locks from the outside."

"You're going to stay here," James said to the man. He opened his mouth to urge Stacy out the door, but she was already in the hallway. He backed out of the room, keeping the gun trained on the other man. James used his free hand to pull the door shut. It locked automatically.

Eventually, James realized that his index finger was dangerously close to squeezing the trigger. He willed it to unbend and slipped it from the space between the trigger and trigger guard.

"The safety," Stacy reminded him.

He nodded, flipping the safety on the gun.

"You don't happen to have anything that can cut this zip tie?" She wiggled her hands behind her back.

"Wire cutters should do the trick." He instructed Stacy to turn around and went to work on the plastic tie. It took a few seconds of cautious maneuvering to get the tie without scraping her skin. Then, with a bit of pressure, the plastic snapped and tumbled to the ground.

Stacy rubbed the matching red welts on her wrists, rolling her shoulders in their sockets. "Kaitlyn's nearby," she said as she took the gun from James. "I overheard Brandon talking about his wife."

James's heart fluttered against his ribs, and his eyes fell on the second door. It made sense that Kaitlyn would be on the other side. Easier to have a single person guarding two rooms side by side than two people guarding two rooms at opposite ends of the bunker.

He strode over to the second door and yanked on the handle. It didn't budge. He tried again with the same result. Panic set into his throat. "Kaitlyn," he shouted.

"Wait," Stacy hushed. She undid the deadbolt on the outside of the door. "There."

James flung open the door. The crack from it smacking the wall echoed in the hallway.

Kaitlyn stood behind the table. Her chair had fallen on its side and lay on the ground behind her. She gripped a necklace in her hand, the cord dangling from her fist. "James?" she asked, as if she couldn't believe her own eyes.

"It's me, Kaitlyn." He crossed the room to embrace her, and she buried her head in the crook of his neck. Tears dampened the collar of his shirt. They were the only ones in the room—in the world—in that moment.

"I hate to break up the reunion," Stacy said, "but we need to get going. Brandon probably left some of his men behind to make sure this place stays secure."

Kaitlyn eyed Stacy over James's shoulder, trying to place the familiar woman. James saw her struggling.

"Stacy Logan from Cannon Beach helped me find you," he said. "She's on our side."

"I apologize for not believing you at the station," Stacy told Kaitlyn. "We might still be in a mess, but it probably wouldn't have gotten to this point."

"It's okay," Kaitlyn said. "And you're right, we need to get out of here."

***

Brandon Hart stood in the middle of Hugh McGraff's bedroom. The immaculate hardwood floors beneath his feet were quickly drenched in Hugh's blood. Hugh himself lay face-down at the foot of the bed. He was dead; the bullet Brandon had put in his brain pretty much guaranteed that.

In Brandon's hand was a crisp white envelope with the name Kaitlyn Hart neatly printed across the front. A small silver key was taped to the front of the envelope with the number 7410 etched into the metal.

"Clean up the body and make sure this place is spotless before you leave," he instructed Gordon.

"Are you going to open that here?" Gordon nodded toward the envelope.

"No," Brandon said. "There's someone else who deserves that honor."

Chapter 15

B rows pulled together in frustration, Maya mindlessly wiped the counter. It had been two days since she had last seen or heard from Kaitlyn. Despite being newly married, her friend was not the type to skip out on work unless encouraged to do so by the rest of the staff; she was punctual, diligent, and dedicated, so the fact that she had not so much as received a text message from the other girl had her on edge.

The visit from Detective Logan had thrown her off a bit, too, and for a while there, she had even begun to worry about Kaitlyn.

But an hour after the detective had left the café, Brandon had called, claiming that Kaitlyn was sick and was resting at home. Maya had thought nothing of it, only grumbled under her breath about having to either pick up more tables or be forced to call in and work with Jennifer; both were less than appealing options. But regardless, if Kaitlyn were truly sick, Maya was more than willing, beneath all her reluctance, to pick up the slack. They were not the best of friends, as they had only met through working together, but she had a pretty good grasp of the other girl's character. Plus, her grandmother had said she had a knack for reading people, a fact she found had proved itself true over the years.

She couldn't read minds or anything, but her gut would wrench when talking to some people, and in situations such as those, she didn't need telepathy to feel uncomfortable.

Which was why, shortly after Maya had received that call from Kaitlyn's husband and the middle-aged balding man had walked in, she found herself suddenly more cautious—not that she did anything of interest in the first place.

When she had taken the man's order, she caught a glimpse of an ID—Detective R. Payton. Part of her whispered that she should have found comfort in the fact that there was law enforcement there—for whatever reason she would ever need to be protected—but her intuition screamed at her to stay away from him. And it wasn't just his aura. It was in the way she felt his eyes bore into her when she talked to other customers, in the way he stared at her when she checked her phone—in the way that, for two days straight, he was the first to come and the last to leave. He had told her that this area was his new beat assignment, and with his partner gone for the week, he figured he'd play it safe and sit in a central location. She had nodded and smiled, only to turn her back to him and hold down the shudder threatening to wrack her body.

The second time Brandon had called, she made eye contact with Detective Payton. It had been a horrible feeling, trapped in that man's stare, and for the first time since she had ever spoken to Brandon, it had also been a horrible feeling hearing the man's voice.

Hugging her arms around her waist, Maya stared outside at the setting sun. It must have been a coincidence, that suffocating sensation, a result of the detective's stomach-twisting look.

It *had* to have been.

When Brandon had first walked through the doors those few months ago, she thought he was the most charming man she had ever laid eyes on. She could not have helped the envy she had felt toward Kaitlyn when the businessman had courted her. She could only think of how attractive a couple they were and how lucky they were to have coincidentally stumbled upon each other—serendipity or some such shit.

She thought he was a catch, bringing Kaitlyn flowers and chocolates.

Her gut had said so.

Anxiously wringing her hands on her apron, Maya closed her eyes, praying she hadn't been wrong.

***

Humming along to the car radio, Chooli tapped his thumb against the wheel. It was a sad attempt, truly, to calm his nerves, but it was the only option he had at that moment. He and his friend Russ had left the minute the call with Thomas ended. They quickly packed their bags and hopped in Chooli's truck. He took over the driving while Russ sat in the back seat, restlessly looking out the window and napping. They had been on the road for six hours, and it would be another one before they arrived.

He trusted Thomas unconditionally, for it had been Thomas who had saved him and his brothers when they were children during a hunt gone wrong. He was a respected man, and Chooli was honored to serve under him. However, he couldn't shake the feeling of impending doom that seemed to overtake them the closer they got to their destination.

He did not know much about the Black Coyote project; it had been agreed upon years ago that it was for the best if each person involved only knew bits and pieces of information in case of capture. Thomas of course, and Daniel, knew the most, but Chooli was sure that even between the two of them, there were secrets on each of their ends. It was impossible to get oneself wrapped into something as extensive, consuming, and convoluted as this and come out still trusting others the way he did Thomas.

But what went on between the two of them was really none of his business. His task had been to be ready to go whenever the call from Thomas came.

He had been briefed years ago as to what his specific job was, and he was sure he would hear it again. From what he understood, he was to protect Daniel's daughter—a task he accepted with the utmost gravity. The girl was certainly confused beyond her wits at this point, for even he was unsure exactly what was happening to her and why. He understood that everyone involved in the Black Coyote project, whether or not they were on their side—whatever side that was—was involved for a certain reason. A lot of the players who had been active years ago were resurfacing for reasons only they knew.

He had heard whispers in his time waiting to be summoned to action, that Tarren had been killed in the girl's house. Clicking his tongue, he sighed. He had not known much about the man, only that he had been on their side and had worked closely with Daniel at one point before the accident. In all reality, it was terrifying what was happening. Chooli often tried to take a step back and look at the situation objectively, but when he thought it through deeply, he found himself questioning things he had never questioned before. He would quickly put a cap on those ideas and re-immerse himself in his role.

It was best not to question everything.

Chapter 16

K aitlyn sat quietly, pretending not to notice James' furtive glances at her as he drove. She recalled his rugged face, framed by a sweep of dark, ruffled hair as he stepped through the gloom to save her from that torturous cell. It had been a long time since she had seen him in person, the boy now grown into this tall, handsome man. She turned her head slightly and studied him in her peripheral vision, searching for the boy she once knew. She caught traces of him in the curve of his lips and the lines on his brow—lines which had made him appear such a serious child at times. Every fiber of her body twitched at his slightest movement like the passing of an electrical charge through her.

Kaitlyn shook herself, dispelling the feeling, and concentrated on the passing countryside from the passenger window. She remembered what had happened the last time she'd allowed herself to entertain feelings for a man—the man who had betrayed her. She wouldn't be doing that again.

"Are you okay?" James asked, quickly glancing at her.

She nodded silently, the flash of his concerned green eyes momentarily catching her off guard. "Yes, I'm okay." She broke his gaze. The silence returned. Absently, she turned the green shark's tooth repeatedly between her fingers, her mind trailing back to the bunker.

They had escaped quickly, slinking through the darkened corridors and ducking into shadows to avoid patrolling guards. All the way, Kaitlyn had tightly gripped James' hand. She still felt his enveloping warmth now. When they had escaped and reached a safe distance, Detective Logan told them to get somewhere safer while she called into the station for backup. She had promised Kaitlyn she would find Brandon. James told her he knew a place and gave Detective Logan his number as he dropped her off in town. He would take Kaitlyn to his grandfather's in the country. They should be safe there.

"Do you want the radio on?" James asked, bringing Kaitlyn back to the present. She sensed he was trying to get her to talk about things, but she didn't know how to start. In truth, she didn't know what to say.

"I'm fine," she said after a short pause. "Thank you for saving me. How did you know anything was wrong?"

James tapped his thumbs on the steering wheel. "Do you remember when we were children and we talked about my dreams that sometimes came true?"

Kaitlyn giggled softly at the memory. "Yes. It was never the dreams about finding gold, was it?"

James laughed. "Yes, more's the pity. I had a dream the other night. I don't remember the details, but I just had this overwhelming sense that something was wrong. That you were in danger. It was so strong that I had to come see that you were all right."

"And so you got on your horse and charged over."

"Something like that."

Kaitlyn looked at him, the prickles of electric static returning once again. "Thank you," she said softly.

James curtly nodded. "Are you going to tell me what this is all about? What's going on?"

Kaitlyn sighed. She couldn't avoid it any more despite how much she wanted to. "It was Brandon." She hesitated, blinking back the tears and rage suddenly consuming her.

James reached over and squeezed her hand reassuringly. "You're away from him now. I've got you."

She wiped the tears away with the heel of her hand and let out a groan, marginally relieving the twisted knot of fear in her chest. She leaned her head back against the rest and closed her eyes. "I should have known from the start that something was wrong. It was all just too quick. He was too charming, I was too naïve," she began.

She recounted how she came home early to find a body in the bedroom with her husband holding the gun. How Brandon had incarcerated her, pushing her to tell him where her father's map was. Her escape and subsequent recapture through his lies, and how she was dragged to the bunker and threatened if she didn't start remembering soon.

"Surely he knew about your amnesia?"

"Yes, he knew. He had some of my father's things to try to shake my memory." Kaitlyn held the green shark tooth up to the light between her thumb and index finger.

"Did it work?"

"Not really. Nothing came back to me that was of interest to them." She closed the tooth back in her palm and put it in her pocket.

"So what's this map they're after?"

119

She shook her head. "I have no idea, but they're desperate to get hold of it. They also mentioned something about… oh, what was it? Black… Black Coyote project. Ever heard of it?"

James's brow furrowed. "Nope, never heard of it."

He swung the car right; the smooth tarmac transitioned into a dirt road, tossing them around. He pulled into his grandfather's drive and noted two other cars already parked.

"It seems we're crashing a party." He winked at her before turning the engine off and stepping out.

Kaitlyn followed James into the living room. Bullet bounced up into James' arms with a wide grin and wagging tail; he then cautiously sniffed at Kaitlyn before returning his attention to his master.

"Come on, you. Out the way." James gently herded the dog as he pushed past the door. Kaitlyn stepped through, closely following him.

To her left, on a worn leather couch, sat two men. One leaned forward, elbows on his knees, a beer cradled between his hands, staring up at them inquisitively. The other sat back in the couch, nonchalantly stubbing out a cigarette into a clay ashtray on the armrest.

"Grandpa." James walked to the far right corner and gave his grandfather a bear hug. All the while, Kaitlyn noticed that his grandfather did not take his eyes off her. There was something in his look. She didn't know what it was, but it made her uneasy.

"Kaitlyn," he greeted her.

"Grandpa Thomas," she replied warmly.

Behind her, she sensed movement, and then heard him—a half-forgotten memory from her childhood that crept up and chilled her spine.

"Katy."

Chapter 17

Brandon fished around through the takeout bags between the driver and passenger seats for his cell phone. He kept his eyes glued to the road as he leaned a little more, his fingers barely brushing against it, pushing it farther away. He looked over at Gordon sleeping in the passenger seat with his hat pulled down over his eyes. He considered waking him up but figured it would be easier to grab it himself.

He quickly glanced down but couldn't see the phone in the pile. The sun had just barely cleared the horizon and spread an orange light across the white bags, almost camouflaging them, but he spotted it after a second glance and leaned deeper, grabbing the phone.

Sitting back up, he recoiled, jerking on the wheel to get back into his lane. A car was headed straight for him, horn blasting. He swerved to the right just in time, skidding to a stop in the gravel on the side of the road.

"Shit," he said on a loud exhale. He rubbed his face, trying to calm his heartbeat.

"What the hell, man?" Gordon said from the passenger seat, now wide awake.

"I needed my phone."

"Why didn't you ask me to get it?" Gordon leaned forward and picked up his hat from the footwell.

Brandon ignored the question as he dialed Payton's number. "Come on, pick up," he murmured, listening to the shrill ring.

Just as Brandon was about to hang up, he heard a groggy voice grunt into the phone.

"Payton, it's me. Shouldn't you be up already? The diner opens in fifteen minutes."

"Are you forgetting that I don't work for you?" Payton said, his voice crackling with sleep and oozing with annoyance.

"You do if you want that cut," Brandon said condescendingly. "Anything at the diner? Does it seem like she knows anything?"

"Nothing so far. I think if Kaitlyn was going to call the diner, it would have happened already. We're wasting our time sitting around waiting for a trace."

"You're the detective. I don't care how you do it, but you'll find out who took Kaitlyn and where they went." Brandon ended the call before Detective Payton could answer and tossed his phone onto the dashboard. He punched the steering wheel before pulling back onto the road, gravel spraying behind him as he slammed his foot on the gas.

He racked his brain, trying to think of who would come after Kaitlyn. Who knew she was missing? The only real friend she had was Maya. They had already ruled her out. There was no way she had been unfaithful; not only did Brandon make sure their relationship was utopian, he had his men watching her whenever she was out of his sight. There was only one place he could think of to find any answers—Kaitlyn's apartment.

"I can't believe someone outsmarted the guys," Gordon said with a chuckle.

"Yeah, except it ain't funny." Brandon had been in a bad mood since he got the call about Kaitlyn being gone. "We still need Kaitlyn to figure out where this damned unit is."

"Wouldn't her father have told her in that letter?" Gordon asked.

"No, I know how he works. It's probably a letter filled with countless memories and personal information that hints to her where the unit is. There's no way around it. We need her."

He parked on the corner and jogged into the building, putting his head down and avoiding passersby, Gordon following right behind. In the elevator, he pulled out Kaitlyn's set of keys, jangling them as the elevator dinged for her floor. Glancing over his shoulder, he slipped the key into the lock and stood in the middle of the living room.

"All right, Kaitlyn. Where would you keep your most personal information?" he mumbled before turning to Gordon. "Go check the dresser and the closet. Make sure there are no hiding spots."

"What exactly are we looking for?" Gordon raised an eyebrow skeptically.

"Anything that would tell us where she'd go if she were in trouble."

After Gordon left the room, Brandon surveyed the large boxes that hadn't been moved over to the house yet, considering each as a possibility. Kitchen, no. Bathroom, not likely. Books, doubtful. Bedroom closet, maybe. Just as he was about to rip the tape off the cardboard box, his phone rang, vibrating in his pocket. It was Detective Payton.

"You didn't tell me about your boy Mettinger's run-in with the guy," Payton said, chewing into the phone.

Brandon had no idea what he was talking about.

"Mettinger got locked in one of the rooms. Got a description out of him too."

"What are you waiting for, a gold medal? What did he look like?" Brandon couldn't wait to be finished working this closely with Payton, but he couldn't burn the bridge, no matter how irritating the man was.

"Green eyes, tan skin, long black hair. Said he got the distinct impression he was some sort of—"

"Native American." How could he forget her father's Native American ties? She had mentioned James before. It still didn't explain how he knew where to find Kaitlyn, but that didn't matter right now. He just needed an address. "Let me call you back, I think I might have a lead."

Pushing the bedroom closet box to the side, he ripped the tape off the books box. He vaguely remembered seeing a little wooden box on her bookshelf with the initials K and J etched into the front. He took out a full layer of books, tossing them onto the floor beside him before seeing it. It was small and shabby; Brandon had always assumed it was for jewelry. Inside was a dreamcatcher with a small stack of letters.

"Mettinger," he said into the phone, holding up a weathered envelope. "Get the guys together. I think I know where they are."

***

"Dad?" Kaitlyn half whispered before turning around. How could this be possible? She put a hand over her quivering lip, afraid to turn around and find out it was just another dream. Had Brandon been telling the truth for once? She turned with her eyes squeezed shut.

"Baby." His voice shook with emotion. "I thought I'd never see you again."

She opened her eyes when she heard the footsteps come closer. Looking up into the face she'd longed to see since she was seven years old and throwing herself forward into his open arms, she sobbed against his chest.

As he closed his arms around her, he laid his head on top of hers. "Shh. It's okay, now," he said comfortingly.

She felt like a little girl again. Her mind raced with questions, but she couldn't seem to get them out. Part of her didn't care about anything else now that she had her father back. A rough voice interrupted the reunion.

"Not to dampen the mood, but we really need to get started." The man sitting on the couch put down his half-empty beer and stood, focusing on Kaitlyn. "Where is it?"

"Where is what?" Kaitlyn asked, looking back and forth between the men and her father.

"The key," he said impatiently.

"All right, Russ. Just calm down," Kaitlyn's father said, narrowing his eyes at the man.

"I think Kaitlyn needs some rest," James interrupted, stepping beside her and putting his hand on her shoulder.

"She has been put under a lot of stress with these events," Thomas agreed from the corner.

"The unit is only three hours from here," Daniel said, running his hand through his hair. "There's no way anyone else would know where it is. I didn't even tell Hugh or Louise. I think we can wait a few more hours."

Kaitlyn barely slept. Every time she closed her eyes, she saw Brandon's face. It kept flashing between his charming smile and his cruel grimace. The few times she did drift off to sleep, she jolted awake, sitting up so fast she almost got dizzy. It took a few minutes of her squinting in the dark and seeing James sleeping in the chair near the door for her to get ahold of her bearings. Once the sun came up, she knew it would be useless to try anymore.

She lay in bed, waiting for either James to stir or to hear other people getting up. Lying on her side, she studied James' face as the morning light danced across it. She couldn't help but wonder what he'd been up to in the years since they stopped writing. Almost as if he heard her thoughts, his eyes snapped open, meeting her gaze. He immediately sat up, clearing his throat.

"You're awake. Did you sleep okay?" he asked, his

eyebrows furrowed.

"Better than recently, I suppose."

There was an awkward pause. "I'll go start breakfast," he said.

Kaitlyn took her time getting out of bed and freshening up. When she came to the dining room, all the men sat around the table, deep in serious conversation. They stopped talking when they noticed her enter.

"Sit and eat, Katy," her father said, pulling out the chair beside him.

Before she took her first bite, Russ was back to business. "So, when you saw Hugh, he didn't give you the key?"

"I…" Kaitlyn stammered, looking at her father, wide-eyed. "I haven't seen Hugh at all. Maybe Brandon was right. Maybe Hugh did take the stuff and run." She frowned as she tried to sort through what was truth and what was a lie. She couldn't be sure about anything anymore, it seemed.

"Brandon?" her father asked.

"My husband," Kaitlyn said, her eyes dropping to the floor. "Well, that was before he murdered someone in our house and kidnapped me and tried to torture information out of me."

Her father's hands clenched into fists, his grim expression not revealing his thoughts. The lines in his face deepened as he stared into Kaitlyn's eyes. He took a shaky breath. "Do you have anything from when you were a child?"

"Nothing from you. Aunt Louise said she wanted to keep it safe." She paused, her hand going into her pocket, fingers running over the shark tooth. "But Brandon somehow got this." She held the tooth up toward her father.

The deep lines in his face softened as his lips turned up into a half-smile. "You did good." Daniel kissed the top of Kaitlyn's forehead.

"What is it?" Russ asked.

Daniel tossed the tooth to Russ, who examined it briefly, then promptly shoved it into his pocket. Daniel looked back at Kaitlyn, his eyes glistening. "You turned out to be so strong, baby girl."

"What are we going to do without the key?" Russ said, swallowing a mouthful of beer. "How are we going to get into that storage unit?"

"Looks like I'll have to pull out my old lock-picking kit." Daniel scratched the back of his head. "Things have definitely gotten more complicated, but not impossible. Has anything ever been impossible for us?" He flashed a smile at Thomas, who sat quietly in the corner.

"Never impossible for us," Thomas said, letting out a small laugh. "*Ganodo*, come help me bring Daniel's box up from the basement."

"Go get the car ready," Kaitlyn's father said to Russ and Chooli. "And make sure we have all the supplies in the trunk. I have a feeling we're going to run into some trouble."

Just as Russ and Chooli stood, the front door swung open. Kaitlyn's whole body went numb as she stared with a slack jaw.

"Thought I'd find you here," Brandon said with a grin. Mettinger stood behind him, arms crossed at his chest, looking just as intimidating as ever.

Her father put his arm up protectively toward Kaitlyn as he stood, putting himself directly between her and Brandon.

"Daniel," Brandon said, as if speaking to an old friend.

"It's been a while, Brandon," Kaitlyn's father replied. "I hear you're my son-in-law now. You always did fancy me a father figure, didn't you?"

Brandon chuckled. "Well, now that the family's all together, let's get this over with, shall we? I'll drive so no one tries to pull anything funny."

Chapter 18

"We'll have to split up," Daniel said, still standing in front of Kaitlyn, staring Brandon dead in the eyes. "There's too many of us to go in just one car."

"Perhaps," Brandon replied, staring back at him, unmoved. "But we know what happened the last time I trusted you. So this time, we do what *I* say." He moved closer to Daniel, the two now standing face-to-face.

"No, *Ganodo*," Thomas yelled as James threw himself at Brandon, heated from Brandon's fearlessly bold and disrespectful behavior toward Kaitlyn's father.

Before he reached him, however, Daniel put out his arm and stopped James in his tracks, shaking his head. "It's not worth it, son."

"Yeah, listen to him if you know what's good for you," Brandon said condescendingly. "Who knows? Maybe I'll let you and Grandpa live a few days longer." He flashed the famous, million-dollar smile that had made Kaitlyn fall for him at first sight; except this time, she saw a flash of evil in his eyes. She realized that whatever he was looking for, her father had been working his entire life to protect, though Brandon was more than willing to kill for it.

Kaitlyn's thoughts were interrupted by her father's smooth and steady voice, unaffected by Brandon's intimidation. "You're not hurting anyone. Regardless of whether you trust me or not, you're going to need all the help you can get when you finally open that storage unit. So *trust* me when I say everyone needs to go together." Brandon said nothing. "Either we all go, or none of us go."

Brandon stared at Daniel for a long while, as if trying to figure out if he was telling the truth. "And what if I say no?" he said, trying to call Daniel's bluff.

Kaitlyn's father smiled a smile she had never seen before. "Suit yourself," he answered. "But if you want to get any closer to what you're looking for, we'll need to do what *I* say." There was complete silence in the room as the two men stared each other down, Brandon still trying to figure out his next move. The tension was so thick she could've bitten it.

"Okay, fine," Brandon finally said after a long pause. "But you're all going to be separated." He smiled as he regained control of the situation, then turned to his partner in crime. "Mettinger, take the old man, the boy, and that one there"—he gestured to Russ—"and I'll take this one." He glared at Chooli, but only briefly. "And you," he said, smirking directly into Kaitlyn's green, speckled eyes as she hid behind the protection of her father's back. "You and Daddy are coming with me."

***

James's patience had pretty much worn completely thin. He sat in the back seat of his own truck, being driven by Russ.

Mettinger, who seemed to be in a good mood, sat in the passenger seat with his gun aimed at Russ' head, blasting classic rock on the radio. It only got worse when his favorite AC/DC song played, his loud, off-key voice making the entire experience even more agonizing. "*...No stop signs, speed limit. Nobody's gonna slow me downnnn...*"

James clenched his fists so tight his knuckles turned white and the blood slowly drained from his hands.

Thomas sat in the back with James, humming an old Native American hymn James faintly recalled from his childhood. "Easy, *Ganodo*," he said, putting his hand on James' shoulder. "Don't let your anger get in the way of your focus."

James unclenched his fists. "I'm trying, Grandpa. I just feel so helpless. Katy's in the car with that monster, and I can't even help her." He felt his anger stirring up again. This time, his entire body heated and he started to shake.

"Breathe," Thomas said in his soothing voice. "A man's anger is his worst enemy. It distracts him from his goal and causes him to make irrational decisions."

James truly had admired his grandfather for always managing to stay calm even in the most unnerving situations. This attitude of his was something James always strived to achieve, especially in his darkest times.

He decided to listen to Thomas and take a deep breath, letting go of all the negative energy he harbored. He immediately felt more at ease. "Thanks."

"Once you learn to control your breath," Thomas said, "you can control your entire body."

For James, his grandfather's teachings were like a law carved in stone. He held heavily onto each of Thomas' words. So he sat there, in the back seat of his truck, practicing his breathing. He closed his eyes and thought of Kaitlyn. He smiled. She had been so beautiful as a child and was even more so now as a woman. He allowed images of Katy to flash through his mind like a slideshow while he inhaled and exhaled. He felt the calmness take over his body and started to feel much better until his thoughts were interrupted again by Mettinger's out-of-tune singing.

"*...I'm on the hiiiiighway to hell. Hiiiiighway to hell...*"

"Oh, is that where we're going?" Thomas said sarcastically to James, trying hard not to laugh at Mettinger's horrible voice.

"It sure feels like it."

***

Brandon drove with the speed of a racecar driver, constantly glancing in his rearview mirror at Kaitlyn, who sat in the back seat. His smile was as sinister as a villain who looked forward to the hero's demise. Kaitlyn stared back at him in the mirror, her gaze unmoved so that, whenever he glanced up to intimidate her, her eyes were already drilling a hole into his head.

She found the fear of her husband slowly diminishing, replaced with a different feeling. Was it courage? Perhaps, but she wasn't quite sure. Nonetheless, she still felt helpless and knew the only thing she could do right now was trust her loved ones.

Kaitlyn looked down at the envelope Brandon had handed her before they got in the car. Inside was a letter addressed to her from her father and a silver key inscribed with the number 7410. Although the letter was of no use anymore since they knew where they were going, he gave the envelope to her anyway so she could "do the honors" and open the storage unit when they arrived at its location in Vallejo, California.

Something told her to hold on to the letter, however. She knew it contained clues that would point her to the storage unit; although she didn't remember ever going to Vallejo, by now she pretty much knew her father. She knew there would not only be clues to point her in the right direction, but something that would also tell her *what* information to look for. Something the bad guys wouldn't be able to solve if they got their hands on that letter.

Kaitlyn looked down again. The letter rested on her lap, and her sweaty hands shook at the thought of opening it and reading it. Daniel, sitting next to her, put his hand on hers and gave her a soft, encouraging nod. "It's okay, baby. This was going to happen sooner or later."

"What if I can't figure it out?" she said, worried.

"Just breathe, and everything will be okay."

Her father always had a way of making her feel safe. Even now, after all these years, she still felt the same security with him as she had when she was a child. Kaitlyn flipped over the envelope and removed the single piece of tape sealing it shut. She glanced at her father once more before pulling the letter out. Daniel patted her knee gently, which gave her the confidence she needed. She took a breath and looked at the piece of paper.

When you wish upon a star,
The answer surely can't be far.
As the sun meets with the moon,
What is missing uncovers soon.
Plant your feet, relax your jaws,
Take a breath and take a pause.
When the earth and sky align,
There you'll find this secret of 'mine'.

Kaitlyn read the letter over and over. Something about the riddle seemed familiar, as if she should know the answer. She wasn't surprised that her father had disguised the clues in such an intricate way; she had the impression he was always well-versed in poetry and rhyme. In fact, she recalled, he had a habit of leaving clues for her and sending her on a scavenger hunt every year on her birthday. She used to love figuring them out, even if he *did* give her a few hints to make it easier. This time, however, Daddy couldn't help her. They couldn't risk the bad guys finding out his secret. She had to figure this one out on her own.

She stared at the piece of paper, wracking her brain for something—*anything*—but she couldn't come up with a single clue. She glanced at her father, who gave her a sweet smile.

"You got this, baby."

Before she accepted her defeat, she decided to do what her father had instructed in the letter. She planted her feet on the floor of the car, relaxed her jaw, and took a breath. She closed her eyes and played the riddle over and over in her head until she finally drifted off to sleep.

***

It was December, the morning of Kaitlyn's seventh birthday. She opened her eyes and jumped out of bed before her mom had a chance to wake her. It was the same thing every year; she liked to rummage through her closet for her favorite princess dress, put it on along with all of her accessories and tiara, then snuggle back into bed and close her eyes.

Her mother Jackie came into the room with her first present—an elaborate breakfast in bed with all her favorite breakfast items, including chocolate chip pancakes. Her mom quietly walked into the room, chuckled at the sight of her dolled-up daughter, who she knew full well was pretending to be asleep, and gave Kaitlyn a kiss on the forehead before she sang "Happy Birthday" to her.

Kaitlyn jumped up as soon as she heard the song and could smell the butter and chocolate chips melting into her pancakes. Jackie set the breakfast down in front of her, gave her a big bear hug, and handed her an envelope with her father's handwriting on it. "Hurry and eat your breakfast, then open up your first clue. Daddy's waiting for you downstairs."

As soon as she finished her breakfast, Kaitlyn ran down to find Daniel sitting in his study, scribbling in his notebook. When he heard her footsteps, he dropped what he was doing, turned around, and stretched his arms wide. "Happy birthday, big girl.

Bring it in." She ran into her daddy's arms and squeezed him as hard as a seven-year-old could.

She loved her dad so much. She buried her face in his chest and took in his scent, memorizing the moment. As they pulled away, Daniel asked, "Did you get your present?"

Kaitlyn proudly waved the envelope in her hand. "I didn't open it yet," she said as she looked for her father's confirmation.

"Well, what're you waiting for? Open it!"

As she got ready to tear through the envelope, something caught her eye on her father's desk. His journal was wide open, and on it lay a tattered and torn paper, seemingly held together with tape, that appeared to have a map drawn on it. Next to his journal on the desk was another piece of paper that looked very similar, except it was in one whole piece and had dots and lines all over it.

"Hey, Daddy, what's that?" Kaitlyn said, pointing at the paper on the desk. "Are you playing connect the dots?"

Daniel chuckled and said, "These right here are constellations."

She gave him a confused look.

"Constellations are maps of the stars, but these are no ordinary stars. This is a map of the stars that were directly on top of us when you were born, so they're *very* special. Just like you, sweetheart."

Kaitlyn giggled at the idea and hugged her father one more time before he smiled and reminded her again, "Now, open up that envelope and go look for your present."

***

Kaitlyn jerked out of sleep as Brandon roughly slammed on the brakes of the car. "Huh?" she croaked, still groggy and confused from the crazy dream.

"All right, wakey-wakey, sunshine," Brandon called mockingly from the driver's seat. "We're here. Let's get things moving, shall we?"

Kaitlyn glanced out the window as they rolled through the gates of the storage center, reading the wide blue sign overhead. Wishing Star Storage. She furrowed her brow. Wishing star… *When you wish upon a star*… Just as the letter had said. Well. That was one puzzle solved easily enough, though she hadn't had to do much solving. She had a feeling the rest wouldn't be so simple.

Daniel smoothed the top of Kaitlyn's hair and ushered her to follow the others, who had already gotten out of their respective cars and now made their way down the row of storage units.

When they arrived at the right unit, Daniel stood by her side and squeezed her shoulder as she stared at the door before her, the reflective 7410 stickers in the center peeling away at their edges. Brandon looked at the two and scoffed. "Okay, enough waiting, Pumpkin. Hurry up and get this thing open. I don't have all day."

James clenched his jaw and balled up his fists. Thomas rested a hand on his shoulder, and James turned to see his grandpa shaking his head in discouragement. James took a deep breath and stepped back.

Katy put the key in the door and prayed for a moment that it wouldn't work. She nervously turned and—*click*—it unlocked. A few quiet sighs of relief scattered throughout the group; she could practically hear some pulses starting to race. The door slowly creaked open, and everyone peered inside. A single table sat in the center of the room with a lone file lying on top.

"That's it?" Mettinger laughed. "All this protection for a *file?*"

Brandon glared at Mettinger, who immediately shut up. They all entered the unit, Brandon and Mettinger still aiming their weapons at the rest of the group, and Brandon picked up the file. He broke the seal, took out the contents, and spread them out on the table. Among the papers were photographs of Kaitlyn as a little girl with her mother and father in her childhood home, and notes and diagrams in her father's handwriting from his research projects.

Brandon went through the papers, his brow furrowing, looking angrier and angrier as he repeatedly searched. "What is *this*?" he yelled. "Is this some kind of joke? Where's the map?" He threw the papers in the air and slammed his fists down on the table. Kaitlyn caught a glimpse of something among the papers—something familiar.

She bent down and moved some of the papers aside to see the constellation map that had been on her father's desk on her seventh birthday. The same one that looked like the map in her father's journal. Her eyes widened. What could this mean? What was the significance of these stars? She thought of the letter and her father's riddle again. Some things must be kept secret. Some things were finally starting to make sense.

Chapter 19

Detective Stacy Logan tried to contact her father at the Portland PD when she first got back into town but got no answer. She jogged the ten blocks over to her parents' house and found that her father and mother were not there. Deciding to wait just a few minutes for them to return, she used her spare key to get in, then lay down on the couch and fell asleep.

Stacy woke with a start hours later, the tail end of a bad dream lingering in her memory. Still, there was no sign of her parents and no return call from her father. This wasn't a surprise. True empty-nesters, her parents were spontaneous and traveled as much as her father's job allowed. After a quick shower, she was back on the street, driving her mother's Impala and mulling over every detail.

"We aren't the bad guys." Kaitlyn had quoted what Brandon told her in the bunker. Stacy thought about that. If a guy like Brandon—a murderer and a kidnapper—was not one of the bad guys, then the real bad guys had to be even worse. The real bad guys had to be more ruthless, more cunning, more persuasive, and crueler than even Brandon. Crueler than a handsome man who swept a beautiful young girl off her feet, making her fall hopelessly in love with him only as a means to a greedy end.

Her thoughts turned from Brandon to Payton. She used to think Payton could be a great detective. He had shown real potential when he was hired a year ago. He'd charged head-first into his work right away, eager to prove himself as he took the lead in some high-profile cases. Now, Stacy saw a sloppy mess in a uniform who only wanted to do the bare minimum to get by.

She thought about the mistakes Payton had made with this case. Not only did he not verify Dr. Portsmyth's credentials, causing Kaitlyn to be kidnapped, but he also slowed the search for the ambulance so much that she had to cut him loose. Those weren't mistakes a seasoned officer should make.

Stacy only hoped she could protect Kaitlyn by stopping Brandon. She knew Brandon had at least one informant in the Portland PD; she just didn't know who it was. Besides her father, she didn't know who she could trust.

Stacy turned into the fast food joint just across the street from the station. She tried her father's direct line again, and again she only got his voicemail. She called his cell phone for about the fifth time, and still no answer there. She was starting to worry about her father. As Police Chief, he never stayed out of contact this long. Never.

Sitting in the car as she finished off some semi-edible chicken tenders, Stacy finally resolved to just take her chances and go over to the station to track down her father. Someone there would know where he was. She didn't have many options left, and she couldn't sit on it much longer. Kaitlyn depended on her.

She wadded up the brown paper sack and tossed it onto the back seat. As she opened the door to get out, she spotted Detective Payton coming out of the station's side door, followed by a couple tall guys in dark suits. One had a perfectly trimmed goatee, the other clean-shaven. She didn't recognize either one of them. She quickly got back into the car and watched the three men walk across the station's narrow parking lot. They got into a black Mercedes sedan, Payton in back and the two men up front, and the driver pulled away.

Stacy had no idea why Payton would be in Portland. She had left him back in Cannon Beach before meeting up with James and rescuing Kaitlyn. She watched the car leave the parking lot, then merged in behind it. The windows were tinted black, allowing no visibility into the vehicle. She memorized the license plate number as she drove, hoping she didn't lose it in the dark.

Stacy followed the Mercedes into the parking lot of a local restaurant and bar she used to wait tables at when she was in college. This bar was the reason she never had roommates after freshman year. The place was open twenty-four hours, was always packed, and tips were good. But the money wasn't the only reason she loved Dennigan's. Annie Clement, the owner, was like a second mother to her. It felt good to be on familiar ground.

She parked three cars down from the Mercedes and watched Payton and his comrades stride inside. Stacy knew the layout of Dennigan's like the back of her hand. Twelve booths against the far walls, fourteen bar stools—three of them torn—lined the front of the hand-carved mahogany bar, and six high tables filled in the middle around the pool table. Her old section started at the pool table and ended at the patio doors. She laid claim to that section after she earned seniority and kept it until she graduated. Famous for high tippers and low maintenance patrons, it was the prime real estate all waitresses coveted.

Stacy watched Payton and his comrades sit down at a high table, then she slipped into the kitchen. She found Annie working diligently on the computer in the small office. Stacy lightly knocked on the door.

"Yeah?" Annie said without looking up. Her readers were balanced on her nose, and she clamped a pen between her teeth. Her slightly aged skin glowed in the screen's blue light.

"Hi, Annie." For a moment, the years melted away, and Stacy felt as if she had never left the familiar noises of the bustling kitchen, the smell of the fryer thick in the humid air, and the rhythm that seemed to make it all tick.

"Oh my gosh!" Annie squealed. She jumped up from her chair and gathered Stacy into a tight hug. "To what do I owe this pleasure?"

Stacy knew she had very little time to explain, and with such an infant case, she didn't want to go into much detail.

"I need a huge favor. I can't really say why just yet, and it might be a little dangerous, so you can say no if you want to." Stacy wrung her hands tighter the more she talked.

"Nonsense," scoffed Annie. "I would never say no to the best employee I've ever had. I am at your service."

Stacy explained that she needed as much information about Payton and his companions as possible without making them suspicious. Annie listened carefully, nodding every now and then.

"So you want me to spy on my customers," she said when Stacy finished.

"Yes," Stacy said with a little cringe. "You can call it detective work if it makes it sound better." Stacy would rather do it herself, but Payton would spot her quickly. Under the circumstances, she felt lucky to have a trustworthy person like Annie there to help.

"Sounds good to me. Where are they sitting?" Annie dusted off her apron and walked over to the swinging doors between the dining room and the kitchen. She peered through the slit of a window in the door.

"They're in C-6." Stacy was surprised she still remembered the section layout perfectly.

"Got it." Annie pushed through the doors, grabbed a water pitcher, and headed over to the table.

***

As she approached the high table, Annie heard Payton making light jokes and laughing at his own punch lines. The two guys in suits had foreign accents. She tried to place them. Maybe it was German or Czech. No, maybe Russian?

"Hello, gentlemen. My name is Annie and I'll be taking care of you this evening. Can I start you off with a drink from the bar?" Annie stood with her hip slightly cocked so it brushed the leg of the man with the goatee. He didn't seem to mind.

Payton ordered a round of shots for the table.

"Coffee, black," the man with the goatee said in his thick accent.

"Coffee black it is," she said casually. "You haven't been in here before. Are you from out of town?"

"These are my good friends from Russia, so get them anything they want," Payton said as he clapped the two men on their backs. They were not impressed.

"Russia, huh? I've heard it's beautiful there," Annie said and then walked away to get their drinks.

She poked her head into the kitchen quickly to tell Stacy that they were Russian before hurrying to get the drinks. She didn't want them to talk much without her being able to listen. Balancing the tray on one hand, she headed back to the table, snatching up a rag with her free hand as she passed through the wait station.

As soon as Annie set down the shot glasses, Payton downed his. The Russians didn't touch theirs. The jovial mood among them died down, and Payton sat nervously, looking between the two men as Annie poured the coffee.

"Would you like to order something to eat?" she asked, looking from Payton to the goateed Russian and back again. The clean-shaven man sat silently, but she could tell he was in charge.

"Not now," Payton said quickly. Annie nodded, then turned to clear the table behind them. She hoped she was close enough to catch some of their conversation.

"How much?" asked the clean-shaven man.

Payton looked down into the empty shot glass in his hand. After a few seconds of silence, he replied, "Two hundred grand."

"You're crazy," the goateed guy said, leaning back in his chair. The tension increased between them.

"Considering the situation you're in, I think it's fair. Luckily for you, I risked everything by putting the GPS locator on Brandon's car. If he found out, I'd be a dead man. Without it, you don't stand a chance finding him before he finds the map." Payton looked up at the clean-shaven man. "Your only access to that information is through me."

"Give us a minute," said the man with the goatee.

Payton stood and sauntered over to the old juke box in the corner. Annie kept her head down as he passed. She slowly wiped down the table and chairs, keeping her attention on the Russians.

At the table, the two Russians whispered, but the volume slowly increased. The one with the goatee used his hands to talk, slicing the air with each stressed syllable. Annie tried to concentrate on what they were saying, but she couldn't understand a word. The whole conversation was in Russian.

A table in the next section opened up, so Annie moved quickly to bus it. Just as the Russians signaled for Payton to come back, a couple sat at the table Annie had just cleaned.

"Can we get some menus?" the woman asked, looking irritated.

"Sure, just one moment," Annie answered. She didn't want to miss the next part of the conversation, but she knew the couple would cause a distraction if she ignored them. She quickly finished wiping the table and hurried back to the wait station. After telling another waitress to take the new table, she now needed another reason to go back over to the Russians' table. Annie snatched up some chips and salsa and headed back out to the dining room.

"On the house," she said, setting down the chips and salsa. She let her blouse dip low to show some cleavage as she reached across the table. Payton nearly drooled trying to glimpse the lacy edge of her low-cut bra. Even at almost fifty years old, she found that her much younger waitresses still envied her body.

"We are strictly here for business," said the clean-shaven Russian. "I'm sure you can entertain this gentleman later." He nodded toward Payton.

"Don't worry, honey." Payton laughed. "I can come back after we finish our business. I'm about to get a little bonus, and I'd love to show you a good time." He tried to run his hand down Annie's arm, but she pulled away just out of reach. Cringing internally, she flashed a smile and turned to attend to other tables close by.

***

The goateed Russian looked at Payton. "We need more information than just GPS coordinates for that price. Where is the map?"

Payton picked at the chips and salsa, trying to act nonchalant. He thought about Brandon and Mettinger and the number of people they had already killed in their pursuit of the map. They wouldn't think twice about knocking him off, too. After the attitude Brandon had given him earlier, he wouldn't mind if these two got to the missing map piece first and gave Brandon a taste of his own medicine. He knew deep down that fate had introduced him to the ones who would pay more than Brandon. Who was he to mess with fate?

"It's in some storage unit, but they don't know where it is. I don't either, but I can track Brandon. Once he finds it, he'll lead us right to it."

The two Russians made eye contact. They didn't speak a word, but their gaze said plenty. Payton felt beads of sweat gathering on his forehead.

"I can also keep my partner off your tail as an added bonus. Stacy Logan. She's been poking around, and she's in deep with Kaitlyn and the Indian boy. I can feed her false info."

The goateed man dropped a fifty-dollar bill on the table and stood. "You get the cash when we get the map," he said, then directed Payton to follow the clean-shaven man.

***

Annie watched them walk toward the door. The early rising sun reflected off the cars in the parking lot, glinting through the windows. Payton followed the clean-shaven Russian through the door. The goateed man walked back to the table and tossed back the remaining two shots. He looked over at Annie.

"It looks like you might have to wait a while for lover boy, but I wouldn't hold my breath." He laughed, then disappeared through the front doors. Annie watched the black Mercedes leave the parking lot and head toward the interstate.

***

Back in Vallejo, California, James stood in the storage unit at the end of a pointed gun as a text message chimed on his cell phone.

"Give it here," ordered Mettinger, holding out his other hand. James slowly turned the phone over in his palm before reluctantly handing it over. He inched closer to where Daniel stood by Kaitlyn, and once Mettinger looked down to read the text, James leaned over and told Daniel what the message said.

Mettinger couldn't unlock the phone, but it didn't matter. The notification glowed bright against the locked screen. "Russians are tracking Brandon with GPS. Payton is with them. Call me ASAP."

Chapter 20

Beads of sweat rolled down Mettinger's temple from his short, dense silver hairline. Thick veins arose on the heavy hand currently gripping the handgun.

James slowly raised his left arm and protectively motioned for Daniel and Kaitlyn to gently take a step back. The room was silent, all eyes on Mettinger, unsure of how long the rage within could be contained.

Looking Brandon square in the eyes, Mettinger motioned with his head toward the door of the storage unit. "We need to talk. Now!" he barked, stuffing the phone into his jeans pocket.

Brandon gave him a confused look before focusing on the situation at hand. "Everyone move up against the back wall.

Quickly, people. Side by side. That's right, hands behind you," he ordered. "Except you!" Grabbing her elbow, he pulled Kaitlyn sharply toward him before pushing her out the door of the storage unit.

Mettinger backed out behind them, gun still pointed at the group. "I don't think I need to say what will happen should any of you try to be a hero today." He sneered at them as he pulled the door slowly shut.

The coolness of the corrugated wall was the only thing connecting them to each other. They stood in confused silence for a few seconds before James broke the trance. "We have to do something," he rasped quietly.

Chooli stepped out of line and tiptoed toward the table in the center of the unit. Carefully, he gathered the papers and constellation map, handing everything to James to hide underneath his shirt.

Taking one of the table legs, he motioned for the others to do the same. Flipping the table onto its back, Daniel stood on it while the others pulled the legs toward them. Old, rusty nails slowly gave way, and the wood crackled and splintered before finally snapping free. Daniel picked up the tabletop before making his way to stand behind the door of the unit.

***

"This better be important, Mettinger, or I'm going to—" Brandon stopped talking as Mettinger held the phone up in front of him.

Mouthing the words as he read them only made the blood surge from his feet to his head at breakneck speed. Anger coursed through him. Turning Kaitlyn around to face him, he released the safety on his gun and pushed the cool steel of the muzzle underneath her chin.

"Seems as though we may have some company soon," he spat in her face. "Trust me, Pumpkin, if you know what any of that meant in there, now is the time to speak up." His eyes bored into hers. Kaitlyn held his stare and pushed her hands into his chest, hopelessly trying to place some distance between them. The harder she pushed, the tighter he gripped the front of her jacket, pulling her so close he could feel her heart pounding in her chest.

Nose to nose, the only thing separating them was the gun.

Kaitlyn's eyes flickered with rage. Locking her knees, she pushed back. Her shoes slid on the concrete as she tried to break free.

Mettinger grabbed her from behind and held her still.

"I will get it out of you, one way or another, Katy," Brandon hissed.

Before she could answer, a harsh backhand slapped her across the face. She dropped to the floor, her hands covering her mouth and a trickle of blood running down her chin. She gagged slightly.

"Lock her in the car. I'll get the file and take care of the others. Oh, and send a text back to the lovely detective that it's all under control now, you'll contact her in a few days, and for her not to contact you under any circumstances!"

When Mettinger pulled Kaitlyn up by the hair, she winced at the pain and began to sob. His ape-like paw clasped her mouth shut. Grabbing her forearm, he marched her toward the car.

Brandon surveyed the storage facility. To the right, about ten doors down, an old couple slowly loaded bric-a-brac into their rusted red pickup truck. Engrossed with the jigsaw puzzle before them, they seemed unaware of Brandon and the others. Satisfied they wouldn't be trouble, he turned back toward the storage unit. Pausing outside the door, he pulled the nine-millimeter silencer from the holster beneath his jacket.

***

The black Mercedes sped down I-5. Detective Payton sat behind his Russian companions. American gangster rap had been blaring for hours. It seemed Russians listening to classical music was just something you saw in the movies. Payton grimaced, rubbing his temples as Tupac came on for the hundredth time. They still had a good five hours to go before reaching Brandon. Payton could see from the satellite tracking device that he was in Vallejo, California, and he had confirmed the exact coordinates were at a storage facility.

A gas station loomed in the distance, its red and blue sign throbbing against the dusty landscape surrounding them. Payton reached forward, tapping the men on the shoulders simultaneously. He could see Victor, the clean-shaven one, had his hand on his gun.

Reaching for the radio with his free hand, Victor slowly turned down the noise.

"Ah, just wanted to know if we could stop at the gas station. Really need a Coke and a cigarette." Payton tried to sound jovial.

The Russians stared back at each other. Turning forward, Victor reached for the stereo again, restoring the car to a boom box. Payton sighed and slumped back into the plush cream leather, biting the dry skin around his middle fingernail.

Money! Money! Money! he repeated over and over in his head. *Get the money and get the hell away from the Bratva brothers.* Victor and Vladimir—or Vlad, as he was known—were notorious in the Russian underworld. Men of few words, they preferred to shoot first and talk later. He had done some work for them many years ago when he was in Portland's North Precinct. Helped a few murder cases disappear. He should have known that when they came into the diner that day looking for Kaitlyn, they were also looking for him.

Spitting skin from his mouth, he rolled his eyes. *Maybe it wasn't such a coincidence after all. I should have known you never stop working for these guys, no matter how much time there was between drinks.*

The Mercedes downshifted. His eyes darted up from the cream carpet as the wheels skimmed over the sandy gravel, pulling up abruptly at the pump. Vlad waited until the dust cloud had washed over them before turning off the engine.

"You have five minutes." His eyes fixed on Payton's from

the rearview mirror.

Payton grabbed the handle, waiting for Vlad to push the unlock button.

***

Detective Stacy paced up and down the brown linoleum corridor of her precinct. Still unable to contact her father and with no word from James, she had come back to Cannon Beach to keep an eye on things and plan her next move, as well as to grab her ankle holster and make sure her pistol was loaded. She hoped she wouldn't need it, but she felt safer having it. Once she was geared up, she set her mind to the puzzling situation. One thing she knew for sure—Payton was corrupt. His meeting with the Russians at the diner, plus his incompetency with Kaitlyn's case, had proven just that.

What's in it for him? she wondered.

Her phone buzzed in her pocket. As she read the message, the pen in her other hand clicked a little quicker.

"Hmm." She paused for a few seconds before turning swiftly on her heel toward her office. She needed to map this out in front of her.

Pulling the whiteboard from behind the bookcase, she rummaged through her drawers for a marker when she noticed a small, faded picture in the bottom drawer. Bending to pick it up, she stared at the smiling girl's face in her father's arms. They stood on a rocky outcrop with a shimmering pink lake behind them. Flipping it over, she read, "Stacy, aged nine, Owens Lake."

How strange, she thought. Winding back her memory, she tried to recall if her parents had ever spoken of this trip. She couldn't remember them mentioning it, and for some reason, she didn't remember it herself. *Owens Lake... where is that?* She flipped on her computer and ran a quick Google search, gasping when she saw that the lake was in the Sierra Nevadas. The gears in her head began to turn. When Stacy was nine, Kaitlyn would have been about seven, when her parents had their accident, also in the Sierra Nevadas. The coincidences just stacked up, along with the questions.

Taking a deep breath and refocusing, she slid the photo into her back pocket.

Picking up the phone on her desk, she hastily entered the number of her father's cell once more. Ten rings later, she was just about to put the phone down when he picked up.

"Hey, Stacy." Her father coughed into the phone.

"Dad, where the hell are you? I've been worried."

He coughed again before continuing. "Your mother and I got a little lost on a hike and accidently left the phone in the RV. I know, rookie error." Her parents laughed in unison.

"Look, Dad, can you come straight here to Cannon Beach? I need your help with a case I'm working on. Have you ever heard of the Black Coyote project?"

Awkwardness lingered on the end of the phone; Stacy could hear her father's breathing had increased.

"I'll be there as soon as I can."

***

Brandon pushed the key into the lock with force. He was determined to get the information he needed out of someone in this room. His cell phone rang unexpectedly.

"Damnit!"

Leaving the key in the lock, he fetched the phone from his coat pocket, ready to press ignore. A single word pulsed on the screen.

OFFICE.

Brandon knew better than to ignore a call from the big boss.

"Yes? Yes, I'm here now." Brandon's mouth was desert-dry; he ran his tongue over his cracked lips, swallowing hard a few times. "Progress is a little slower than I anticipated. I should be back on track by the end of the day… Yes, I know I promised to have the location of the map by now. Trust me, I'm working on it, more than you know… You should also know the Bratvas are on the hunt as well, so you know what that means… Yes, I thought he was dead too, but obviously not. Gotcha. Will speak at 0600 tomorrow."

Brandon ended the call a little quicker than he'd intended. Cursing under his breath, he turned the phone to silent. He was done with interruptions today.

***

They heard the key turn once more in the lock. James nodded at Daniel as they stood gripping the chair legs a little tighter. Brandon stepped in and immediately noticed the line had become a lot thinner.

His knuckles turned white as he tightened his grip on the gun and crouched a little, jerking from side to side. James and Chooli pushed themselves off the wall with as much energy as they had, James coming in low from the side and whacking Brandon in the stomach. The force made Brandon choke for air, momentarily losing control of the gun. As he regained control, he fired off a shot, which ricocheted off the wall. Russ punched him in the jaw. Chooli took to his back. Three heavy slugs, and Brandon lay motionless on the floor. The others came in to help, pulling him farther into the darkest corner of the unit. They removed his shoes to use one of his socks as a gag. Chooli removed the leather thongs from around his own neck, pocketing the charms, and used the chords to bind Brandon's wrists and ankles.

"Is anyone hurt?" James inquired from the group. Everyone checked themselves. Luckily, no one had been hit by the wayward bullet.

James took control of the room, ordering the others to check Brandon's pockets for the keys to his truck and anything else they could find. They knew Mettinger could be back at any moment, so they needed to move quickly. Thomas pulled Brandon's keys as well as something large and dark from Brandon's jacket pocket and slipped them into his own, nodding to James that he had everything they needed.

One by one, they filed out of the unit. Russ took the lead with the gun, followed by the others, who still gripped their chair legs. Closing the door, Daniel locked the unit behind him. They looped around the back of the facility so they could get into the cars from behind.

As they approached the back of the sedan, Mettinger was nowhere in sight. James grabbed his cell phone off the top of the trunk, leaving behind a pack of menthols sitting beside it, then glanced through the rear window. Kaitlyn lay on the back seat, her matted hair covering the front of her face, polluted by traces of blood. With the doors locked, they used the chair legs to break the passenger's side glass. Kaitlyn barely roused as small shards of glass showered her.

James carried her to his truck and set her in the center seat up front, taking the passenger seat beside her. Kaitlyn moaned, touching the side of her jaw. Carefully, he smoothed her hair back to see the red and purple welt along her jawline. It took all his self-control not to take the gun from Russ and finish Brandon off once and for all. Kissing her forehead softly, he promised to never let her out of his sight again.

Chooli fired up James' truck, and the others jumped in the back. "I know somewhere safe we can go," he said, then put the truck into gear and thumped his foot on the gas

Chapter 21

It was only minutes to the storage unit now. The two Russian brothers and Detective Payton saw the facility coming into view on the edge of this particular patch of nowhere. The detective nervously shifted in the back of the Mercedes. He could not help but squirm like a helpless child. The Coke from the gas station had been cold, sweet, and refreshing, despite the fact that he really did not want the beverage until he had it. Now, he needed to use the bathroom, but he did not want to do anything to call attention to his presence in the back seat. He could try to kid himself all he wanted, but deep down, Victor and Vladimir terrified him. Even if only a tenth of the stories he had heard about them were true, it was enough to turn his stomach. At this point, Detective Payton felt more like a prisoner than a partner.

Vladimir sat in the front passenger seat, scratching at his goatee almost constantly when his hands were empty. He didn't realize he did it. It was just one of those subconscious gestures repeated so long it had become a reflex. As they neared the storage facility, he reached inside his jacket and pulled out his pistol.

As soon as he saw the gun come out, Payton sat straight up. He was in the most gruesome discomfort, and the last thing he wanted was to interact with the two brothers any more than the bare minimum. He felt like Vladimir's action warranted a break in the silence.

"Whoa, whoa," Detective Payton stammered. It was barely a whisper compared to the blaring rap music threatening to rupture the Mercedes' speakers. He tapped the headrest of Vladimir's seat, voicing his alarm. His words were swallowed up by relentless bass and aggressive vocals.

Vladimir turned down the volume of the radio after a few heartbeats of the detective's panicked reaction.

"What's that all about? You two remember the deal, don't you?" said Payton after the music was finally soft enough for him to speak over it.

Victor and Vladimir exchanged a few words in their native language before Vladimir responded. "Of course we remember the deal. Just better to be ready for anything. I'm sure you can agree. It never surprises how stupid people can get when there is only one of something and more than one who want it." A small laugh punctuated his words. He released the magazine from his pistol and checked the weapon. Once he was satisfied with the condition of his firearm, he reloaded it and chambered a round.

The detective noted that Vladimir left the safety of his weapon off as he returned it to the holster inside his jacket. Payton did not like the pulse of the atmosphere in the vehicle, but he nodded. At this point, all he wanted to do was try to maintain the peace. The last thing he wanted was anyone deciding to be stupid.

***

Victor made the turn onto the road where the storage unit was located. His body drove, but his mind had wandered. It often did. Much like his brother's compulsion with petting his facial hair, Victor was a daydreamer. His mind was not so much taken with fantasies, but rather reminiscing.

They say you never forget the first life you take. In his case, it was certainly true. Victor often thought about Uric whenever he was about to start a "job". It had nearly been two decades since Uric had died, but it still felt fresh. Victor could still smell the pungent scent of the man's pipe tobacco, recalling how dank the sauna had been. In the end, Uric's life and death had served as nothing more than an initiation for Victor into the good graces of his present employer. He didn't even know what the man's offense was, or even if he had committed one. At the time, as far as Victor knew, Uric was just a name on a piece of paper. Victor surmised that much of the initiation was not about the killing but about the killing of a total stranger. The lesson he'd taken from Uric was that if a man could kill someone without knowing them, he was capable of great things.

But a few matters about the demise of Uric had never fully come to rest with Victor. The thought digging at him most was whether or not his brother felt the same way. In this unique situation, Uric had also been the first person Vladimir killed. In fact, it was Vlad who fired the first shots. The two brothers debated to this day who had been the one to deliver the fatal bullet.

Victor's thoughts came to an abrupt end as the Mercedes finished pulling up to the storage unit. Victor shut off the engine and unbuckled his seatbelt. He drew his gun from its holster and checked it in the same fashion as his brother. Victor and Vladimir took note of some broken glass and tire marks on the pavement. Clearly, someone had left in a hurry after some sort of commotion.

***

After a moment, the three men got out of the vehicle and made their way through the facility. Detective Payton did everything in his power to keep from wetting his pants.

As they passed by one of the doors, a muffled sound drifted out, like someone screaming or shouting through a pillow. Victor and Vladimir paused to look at each other before stepping back to the door and pressing their ears up to it. Payton didn't know exactly what it was, but something about the men's exchanged glance screamed a warning. He pushed the thought aside while they leaned down and picked the lock, then followed them into the unit.

No one had expected to find the scene awaiting them. The room was empty save for a smashed table and Brandon, who was bound and gagged in the middle of the floor.

"What the hell!" Payton exclaimed as he regarded the restrained man.

Vladimir went to Brandon and removed his gag.

"Kaitlyn and her friends got out with everything. Mettinger must have run off. I don't know how long I was out, but I think we can catch up to them," Brandon blurted with heavy pants and gasps. He had exerted himself for some time screaming for help and fighting without progress in getting out of his bonds.

The two brothers looked at each other one more time and nodded.

"Well, untie me!" Brandon yelled.

"This is going to make it easier and harder," said Victor in amusement.

"What are you talking about?" Detective Payton asked.

Victor gave the briefest of grins before he pulled out his gun. He pointed it at Payton's chest; he didn't fire until he saw the terror and comprehension on the man's face. Victor let off one shot.

"What? No!" Brandon shouted.

Payton staggered back and leaned against the wall of the storage unit. Blood flowed down his shirt, and a large wet stain of a different sort had formed in the crotch of his pants.

Vladimir stood, drew his gun, and fired one shot into Payton's core as well.

The detective slumped to the ground. He breathed quick,

panicked, erratic breaths. All he could think was that his last meal had been a bottle of Coke and a package of Swiss rolls.

***

Victor and Vladimir loomed over the dying man and finished him off with a synchronized burst of gunfire.

After the guns fell silent and the last of the bullet casings had finished rolling on the ground, there was a disarming moment of calm. Brandon ended it with a mortified outburst.

"You! Are you crazy? We had a deal! Do you know who we're working for? You're dead! Dead men!" he shouted. Vladimir kicked him in the face, silencing him.

Victor knelt beside Brandon and waited for him to gather his wits again. "Yes, I know exactly who you're working for, but can you say the same about us? Do you think he can say that?" Victor said to Vladimir with a cruel smile.

"No, I don't think he can," Vladimir said with an equally sadistic grin.

"Well then, I think I shall have to tell him who we work for. Then we will tell you what the new deal is. But first, we are going to ask you some questions, and you will tell us everything we want to know," Victor continued, removing his jacket and rolling up his sleeves.

Chapter 22

Derrik Myers slid his phone back into the left inside pocket of his gray suit jacket and took a long sip of brandy from the clear crystal cup in his other hand. The night lights of the city below glinted off his cufflinks, and his suit was freshly pressed for the arrival of his much-unwanted visitor.

"There's been a problem with Brandon's team." Derrik's voiced grated against the silence of the darkened room. His penthouse overlooked the shining city of Seattle from above the Presidential suite of a Four Seasons on the water. Once, the sight would have captured his attention with wonder, but now it was just another place in another city, and the sights were well worn and a far cry from what he once had.

A fizz and sizzle accompanied the flame of a match, lit by a shadowed figure sitting on a couch nearby. The smell of wood-fueled smoke seeped into Derrik's senses, and the figure took a long drag from the slender cigarette between her white-gloved fingers. The woman brought the red, gleaming tip of the cigarette up and down two more times before speaking.

"Problem, Mr. Myers? What sort of problem might that be?" Her voice was clear and refined. It held the strength of authority behind it, and the way she asked the question made Derrik's fingers twitch with a desire to see her neck between them. He only hoped one day soon—perhaps very soon, if his newly hatched plans went accordingly—he would get his wish.

For now, though, Derrik counted to five in his head and let the impulse die. He gritted his teeth and pulled back an insult taut against his lips. Instead, he said, "The Russians are getting involved, and Brandon sounded... well, he sounded less than his usually-composed self."

"Need a hand, then?" Her voice concealed a chiding, mocking tone. It was a tone she never would have dared loose on him in the beginning, before he started allowing mistakes like Jacqueline Hart's death at the hands of Mettinger. Now it seemed that habit of mistakes had continued tonight with Brandon's mounting errors. That, Derrik mused, had been the beginning of what led him to the sorry state in which he now found his ambitions and honor.

"I've got it nearly wrapped up, but we might need to send another cleaning unit in if things get messy."

"Do your men at least have Daniel and his daughter yet?" The woman paused at Daniel's name for only a moment, but that moment had been long enough for Derrik to catch it.

Interesting. After all these years, she still cares for the man. I can use this. Derrik's mind churned with the new information. "They should have them both by now. The rest they'll handle in the usual way."

"Good. You know as well as I do that not all of us were comfortable with how things went with Daniel. It was your mistake that pushed our little group over the edge and caused all this strife to start with."

Derrik ignored the obvious baiting. He pulled his phone back out and sent a quick text to Brandon. *Change of plans. Bring the traitor and his daughter in. No plans for the rest.* Derrik would have to think more on how he could use Daniel against Minerva later, for now he needed to placate her enough that she'd leave for the evening.

"I just told Brandon to avoid the Russians if he can, but that we'll back him with a cleaning crew if needed." As a second thought, to reinforce the lie, Derrik added, "Can you get a fire team approved locally, just in case?"

"We don't have much in the area. That's why you and your team were trusted to do it despite your track record with the Harts. But"—Minerva smirked—"perhaps I can give you a little helping hand. Just this once now, am I clear?"

It was clear to Derrik—clear that Minerva suspected nothing and felt herself in control of him and his plans. Inwardly, he laughed loud and free as he nodded toward her and thanked her for the aid.

Minerva dropped her long cigarette on the white leather seat beside her. "At least you're no Mettinger." She sidestepped the coffee table and coldly caressed his chin. "You're as loyal as the original Black Coyote."

"How kind of you to say."

She smiled down at him. It was a blatant smirk this time, yet he caught a hint of nostalgia or possibly sadness in her eyes. She dropped the smirk and put on her usual emotionless mask. Her long, jade-painted nails dug in, the ring finger reopening a shaving cut from earlier that day.

He gasped. "Really now?"

She dropped her hand. Her bracelets clinked together as her wrist swung into her side. For a moment, he sweated in the belief that perhaps she desired to choke the life out of him just as greatly as he did her.

She walked away, her back defenseless and unassuming, and

picked her coat off the wall, draping the fur across her arm. "Let's just hope you don't get more of us killed," she said. "Ta."

Derrik slumped into his chair as soon as his front door shut with that woman on the other side. One thing was for certain; she had best die before he did, or there was no such thing as karma.

It had been some time since he had thought back to the beginning. He, Minerva, Mettinger, Daniel and Jackie, and Thomas—they'd each been given a piece of the puzzle and had been thoroughly warned by their predecessors not to share, but youth was cursed with curiosity.

Who could have known that Thomas would get all self-righteous and Daniel would agree, that Mettinger would sell his soul to the Russians for money that Derrik could have provided had he come to him first, and that he and Minerva... Well, they were still sticking to the same path his grandfather had, digging the same hole. It was the others who'd let themselves be swayed.

Derrik set his glass down on the coffee table. It missed its mark and landed on the polished wood inches away from the coaster. *Does it really matter?* Derrik asked himself. *If it stains the wood, I can buy another. I've plenty now, and more than enough is coming my way.*

Though his vision grew increasingly blurred from the drink, Derrik grabbed the empty glass and set it directly centered on the coaster. *Waste not want not, or however it goes.* He stripped off his collared shirt and kicked it against the wall in the hallway on his way to the bathroom. He swished a bit of mouthwash and squirmed out of his pants, which nearly tripped him. Funny, he hadn't thought he'd drunk nearly enough that night to be this out of it. His age must be showing. Or maybe it was karma.

Though logic told him his path was true, the actions he'd had to take along the way didn't sit well with him in the still and silent hours of the night.

Derrik sat on the edge of the tub and wrestled off the rest of his clothes and his shoes. He turned the faucet to scalding and let the heat crawl up his body at a hearse's pace. As a boy, he had been the sort to dip a toe in first, be it a cold public pool, a hot bath, or the journal his grandfather had left to him. He'd read a bit, then a bit more, and then there was no turning back. Some riddles could not be unread. Some projects could not be abandoned. Now, he was the sort to face the risks head-on, to jump into inky black waters, to let the heat purify him of doubt.

He lifted a leg, pushing the knob to turn off the water, and the room swelled with silence. The steam filled his head and distorted his senses. A scene played before him of Minerva stepping into his water, her body like porcelain. She curved downward until her lips brushed his cheek. She slipped her fingers into his hair. Though he knew them to be a figment, her fingers were so cold they left trails of fire across his scalp.

I shouldn't think like this, he warned himself. *It'll only make the solstice harder.*

"You're a snake, and you always will be." Minerva gouged her long nails behind his ears. Her glowing green eyes struck him with terror. The porcelain skin that fueled his foolish lust sprouted coarse, dark fur. Her nose stretched into a thick snout, and her newly fanged mouth lunged for his throat.

Derrik lurched forward, shattering the nightmare, but the fire remained. His head pounded hard, and his blood pulsed frantically beneath his skin. The light of the bathroom grew dimmer and dimmer, and the heat of the tub dissolved away into nothingness. He felt only pain. Pain in his head, and a stinging pain in his face. Shaking, Derrik touched his face and felt real heat radiating from the scrape across his chin. Fear blossomed heavily through his mind.

Minerva! The bitch. Poison, after all the years and all we've done. I thought she'd have the decency to look me in the eyes as she gutted me. His thoughts grew heavier with every passing moment of inaction. He had sent his bodyguard out to wait for and follow Minerva. No help would be coming for him. Not in time to save him, and Derrik knew it. Stumbling, he barely managed to pull himself out of the water and onto the floor. Each inch forward crawling to his bedroom was an eternity. Derrik felt the Reaper falling upon him, but he tore onward for life. He got as far as the hallway before his chest seized and his arm felt pinned to the floor in pain. Derrik tried to cry out vainly for aid, but only a hoarse moan came.

Forcing his fear away, he thought of his training—the same training he and the others had all received when they first joined the project. *Even then, Minerva had a talent for poison,* he thought. He forced the past from his mind as he clutched at his arm. Flailing wildly, he felt the smooth fabric of his suit coats to his left. He reached out and with fumbling fingers pulled his phone out of the suit's pocket. Mashing his finger on the touch pad, he dabbed at his contact list, searching for one name in particular. Finding the name he sought, he pressed call, and another phone rang far away in another city.

As his heart slowed to a faint but even pulse, one thought echoed through Derrik's mind. *Karma's a bitch, Minerva. As bad as you.*

Derrik faded into darkness above a shining city, happy in the knowledge that Minerva would never know his piece of the puzzle; his journal detailing its secret was long ago burned, engraved only in his dying mind.

***

Emerging from an alley several blocks away, Minerva pulled out a handkerchief to dab the blood off her nails. *Foolish of Derrik to send a thug after me,* she thought. Just as foolish as thinking she could ever forgive his role in the death of her dear friend Jackie.

Cabs and delivery trucks sloshed street water onto the sidewalk. There was more than one way to rip a secret from a stubborn man, many of which didn't require him to live. Though Derrik had been an ass about destroying all evidence except what he claimed to have memorized, Minerva had heard enough rumors corroborating each other to believe Derrik's predecessor had left a duplicate journal to someone else.

It was more of a risk than her own predecessor would ever have allowed, but it was her generation's time to define the project, and she'd prepare for the solstice on her own if that was what it would take.

Chapter 23

Chooli trotted out of the well-kept house, similar in size and color to the many others in the residential neighborhood. The place was absurdly peaceful for the group waiting in the truck after the tension and violence they'd experienced. Chooli signaled to them, and James was first out of the truck. He stopped to help Kaitlyn down. She'd been shedding quiet tears through much of the drive from Vallejo to Vacaville. James felt such relief at getting to look at her without being cranked around in the passenger's seat. An hour and a half of knowing she was distressed and being unable to comfort her had been agony.

She held onto his hand, and they climbed up the curb together, waiting for the others. Russ jumped down from the truck bed where he'd been riding and tucked the gun he'd taken into his waistband, covering it with his shirt. Daniel and Thomas exited the truck and joined them on a sidewalk covered in children's chalk doodles. Daniel searched Kaitlyn's face, frowning. His eyes landed on her hand, still clamped around James'. He gave James a half-hearted smile before his face morphed back into its ever-worried and efficient expression.

"Should we move the truck?" he asked as Chooli joined them.

Chooli nodded. "Russ, will you? There's an alley around back and a gravel driveway with a red Explorer on it. You can park next to that. Keys are in the ignition." Russ jogged to the truck, and Chooli turned back to the rest of the group. "Follow me."

On the drive, he'd explained that a good friend of his had offered Chooli a place to stay anytime he was in town. It was a trailer house that had been a mother-in-law home until the mother-in-law passed away. It was still furnished and often served as an impromptu guesthouse. He led them through a break in a hedgerow and across the spacious backyard a few days overdue for a mow. The trailer was nicely shaded by trees and couldn't be seen from the street.

The lights were already on for them, and they climbed the steps and piled inside. Chooli explored the small space while Daniel and Thomas pulled out the prize they'd taken from the trailer and laid the information out on the kitchen table. James led Kaitlyn over to the couch and they sat.

"How ya doing?" he asked. She shook her head, shrugging. He ran the back of his fingers gently across the purpling bruise on her cheekbone. She flinched but didn't pull away. Anger flooded his senses for a moment. "I'll see if there's ice for that."

Chooli had rejoined the men in the kitchen. James stomped up to the fridge, and they all turned to watch as he dug through the freezer's contents with manic energy, stopping only when he found a bag of corn. Daniel stood and handed him a dish towel to wrap around the bag. James reached for the towel and fixed Daniel with a hard stare, shocked by his own boldness.

"I still don't know what Black Coyote is," he said. "I don't know what's in that wretched journal, but I know it's not worth this." He gestured toward the couch where Kaitlyn had pulled her legs up and sat hugging them, staring ahead without seeing. "And whatever it is," he said, "you'd better start explaining, or I'm taking her and leaving."

The door opened with a clang, and Russ walked in, coming to a halt as he saw the tense faces in the kitchen. "What'd I miss?" he asked. James left without answering.

Kaitlyn blinked and looked up as James' weight landed on the couch beside her. She had been rubbing a spot under her chin where the muzzle of a gun had bruised her. She accepted the bag of corn and played it between her hands for a moment before holding it up to her face. She sucked in a breath as the cold hit her tender flesh.

"I'm okay, you know," she said. James raised an eyebrow. "I am. I just—I had a gun to my head today. So did you. And my father. Who, by the way, I thought was dead. All for something from my childhood I don't even remember and probably didn't understand."

James nodded. "I hate what you've gone through."

"You mean the fraud marriage, the multiple kidnappings, or getting beat on?"

James' jaw dropped. Kaitlyn shifted her makeshift ice pack to better see his face and laughed at his expression. The sound seemed to shake loose the tension in James' shoulders, and he laughed too.

Their laughter cut off as raised voices pulled their attention back to the kitchen.

"It's true, Daniel," Chooli said. "I've brought a good friend of mine into this. I'd never forgive myself if they found us here and something happened to him and his family. It's time for action. And it's not fair not to let everyone in on what they're facing. Especially now that the Russians are in play. Not questioning things isn't working anymore." He shot a glance over at James and Kaitlyn.

Daniel and Thomas exchanged an indefinable look. "It'll be easier to explain when I have my journal," Daniel said.

"Where is your journal?" Russ asked. His voice was not loud

but demanding.

"It's safe. With a friend. Just a phone call away."

"Well then," Chooli said, jerking his cell phone out of his pocket and slamming it onto the table in front of Daniel. "There's the phone."

***

Stacy Logan let out a sigh as she walked away from the counter where Maya had gone back to refilling salt shakers. She crossed the floor of the Bridle Café, returning to the table her father occupied. As she slid into the booth, she glanced back at the waitress, meeting her razor-sharp gaze. Stacy knew Maya didn't believe her. Which was smart, as she was lying. Guilt filled her chest and pulled her shoulders downward.

"What's wrong?" her father asked, setting down the fry he'd been about to eat. His phone vibrated on the table next to his plate, and he silenced it and placed it on the booth beside him without looking at the number. "Stacy, what's going on?"

She looked at her father, unsure how to begin. This was more than just a case with which she needed help. It was life and death. What's more, she'd felt connected to the case from the start, and what had seemed just a detective's natural drive to solve a mystery could be personal. Hadn't Owens Lake come up at some point with James or Kaitlyn?

She bit her bottom lip. She'd been kidnapped. She'd gone rogue, searching for Kaitlyn in plainclothes. How could she possibly tell her father—by-the-book, straight-laced, Chief of Police Lucas Logan—all of that?

She took a deep breath and reached into her back pocket. Pulling out the photo of the two of them at Owen's Lake, she pushed it across the table. He gave it only a brief glance before meeting her eyes again. "Does this have anything to do with the Black Coyote project?" she asked.

When she said the words, he lifted his head and scanned the booths on either side of theirs. One was occupied by a family

172

chatting together. The other was occupied by only a regular, Troy, who sat reading a newspaper.

"Yes," he said.

Stacy's eyes widened. "You're involved in this? *I* sure am!"

He cleared his throat. "I am, yes. I became involved during that trip," he said, nodding toward the photo on the table. He hung his head for a moment. "I never wanted you to get involved."

"Well, that's not true," she said. "You encouraged me to move here, to look into joining the police force *here*. Where Kaitlyn Hart lives. That wasn't an accident."

"Lower your voice," he said, again glancing at the tables around them quickly filling as the dinner rush picked up. When he looked back at her, he said, "Listen. We'll continue talking in the camper. We need to deliver something to a friend, and we need to hurry. If Black Coyote is resurfacing, he's going to be needing it. You head out, and I'll pay the bill. We'll come back for your mother's car later. If they know you're involved, they'll be looking for you."

Stacy nodded, picking up his brisk, efficient attitude. She pulled a few bills from her pocket to leave as a tip. With a quick glance at Maya, she pulled out a few more. Then she retrieved her purse and the photo and went to wait for her dad in the camper.

When her father joined her, he immediately started up the vehicle and pulled into traffic. Stacy caught a glimpse of the old man from the café watching them as they left, but her father was already issuing orders.

"We need to look up a phone number and address for Thomas Newell. He'll know how to get in touch with Daniel Bayers. Can you get on th—"

Stacy's gasped. "Daniel Bayers is alive?" At her father's nod, Stacy rubbed a hand across her face. "Gah! Dead people are coming back to life, a crazy woman turns out to be the only sane one, and my partner is in league with Russian thugs."

"Vlad and Victor? Payton is involved with them?" Lucas asked.

"Yes." Stacy's hands dropped limp into the seat on either

side of her. Her father knew so much more than she did.

"Okay, well, none of that matters. I have to get Daniel's journal to him. With the Russians in the mix, he's going to need it quick." He reached into the pocket of his shirt and frowned. "Damn. I left my phone at the diner."

"There's a place to turn around up ahead," Stacy offered with a gesture. "You can get back on—"

"Never mind. No time. Use your phone. Look up Thom—"

"I don't need to look up anybody," Stacey interrupted. "I've been working with his grandson, James. I helped him find Kaitlyn, and they went back to Reno and Thomas."

Lucas was silent for a moment, glancing back and forth from the road to his daughter. "You're deep in this, aren't you?"

She nodded.

"No chance of getting you to go visit your aunt for a bit, is there? That's where I sent your mother, to keep her safe until this is through."

"Not the slightest chance, Dad."

"Okay." He sighed. "Call James."

She took out her phone and brought up James' number from her contacts, pausing with her finger hovering over the green button. His last text had been odd. It hadn't sounded like him. Her gut turned and pulled. She knew she wouldn't be satisfied everything was right until she saw him and Kaitlyn.

"Stacy?"

"I don't want to call him. I want to go to him." She looked at her father, who met her gaze and nodded before turning back to the road. "I know his address in Reno."

"That's better, anyway," he said. "Better to do this in person."

In the diner, Lucas' phone vibrated for the third time and slid off the leather booth onto the floor.

***

James collapsed on the couch beside Kaitlyn once more. She reached for the TV remote and muted the late-night news. She hadn't been paying much attention to it anyway.

"Well, it's all set," James said. "I had to call in a favor, but my friend's going to bring Bullet here in the morning. I always feel safer having him with me. He'll come to the mine with us. It couldn't hurt."

Kaitlyn nodded. Her heart warmed a little when she thought of Bullet. She felt like she'd watched the pup grow up through James' letters, and she'd loved the way James behaved with the dog during the brief time they'd been in Reno—like they were friends.

James caught her watching him, so she quickly said, "I'm surprised they let you make a call." She swung her legs up across James' lap and he laid his hands on her knees.

"I doubt anyone is gonna trace my phone for one quick call any more than they would trace Chooli's. They've been calling and calling your dad's friend at every number they have for him. No luck." James glanced over to where Daniel was again dialing the telephone. He lowered his voice. "What did your dad say to you while I was away?"

Kaitlyn sighed. "He apologized. He's pretty horrified that Brandon *married* me to get to the map. He hates Brandon. Says he was never supposed to be a part of this. Says it was an accident." She shrugged. "I just want this to be over. I want to know what's so important in that journal and get my life back. Whatever's left of it." She leaned her head on the back of the couch and looked up at James.

"It'll take more than this to derail your life, Kaitlyn." He rubbed a hand back and forth over her shin. "You're amazing. You bounced back after the death of—well, apparent death of your parents. You'll bounce back again."

"You helped me with that, you know? The letters. The visits."

James smiled.

"I'm sorry you have to be involved in this, James. I can't

175

help but feel you're here mostly because of me. Because of our relationship."

He shook his head and lightly gripped her knee. "Our relationship is the only good thing about all this. I would've been pulled in anyway, with Grandpa's involvement. But I *want* to be here for you. I've always wanted you." Their eyes widened at the same time. James stuttered. "I've always wanted to be there for you, I mean." He looked up in time to see his grandfather lead Daniel out the trailer door.

"Let's walk for a bit, old friend," Thomas said. "We'll try again when we return."

As the door thudded behind them, James looked back at Kaitlyn to find her staring at him.

"You always *have* been there for me," she said. She smiled and glanced down the hallway toward the room they'd designated as hers. With a sigh, she said, "I wish I had the dreamcatcher you gave me. I think I'm going to need it."

"You still have it?"

"Of course," she said. "And every single letter."

James leaned toward Kaitlyn and slid his hand along her neck, holding the non-injured side of her face in his hand. She shivered and turned her head into the touch, his hand just a little rough against her cheek. He closed the distance between them and pressed his lips to hers.

For as long as the kiss lasted, they were lost to their current, unhappy reality. When they separated, Kaitlyn stayed cocooned in James' arms, her own hands gripping the back of his neck and his shoulder. They'd shifted so their bodies pressed together, but as they heard voices approaching the trailer door, they separated.

Russ and Chooli tromped up the short porch stairs, and Kaitlyn stood. She crossed the room and paused at the hallway. Turning, she said, "Goodnight, everyone."

A chorus of "goodnights" followed her down the hallway, but the only one she really heard was the hoarse one James had spoken.

***

The next morning, the Logans arrived at the home address James had given her and headed up the walk. Stacy jumped and nearly crashed into her father as a dog barked viciously. They hadn't even made it to the front door, but she was sure whoever was there would know they'd arrived. A car occupied the driveway, not the truck Stacy had expected.

"That's better than a doorbell," Lucas said.

He'd only just gotten the sentence out when the door opened and a woman with long dark hair stepped onto the porch. "Enough, Bullet," she said, giving the dog a hand signal that made him sit. "Can I help you?" she asked the Logans, glancing from them to their camper.

"We need to see James," Stacy said. "We're friends of his, and it's kind of an emergency."

Her father nodded beside her, his hand on her shoulder. "We're police officers," he offered. "My daughter has been helping him with a missing persons case."

The woman's skeptical look grew into understanding. "Right. Kaitlyn. Didn't you all find her, though?" She stepped forward through the door, releasing Bullet. He approached them calmly, sniffing at their shoes as the woman walked up and introduced herself. "You have good timing. I just came over to grab Bullet, but I'm on my way to take him to James now. Let me give him a call."

Stacy and her father shared a look of relief and happiness as the woman dialed on her cell.

***

In Vallejo, Brandon's face wrinkled in distress as he dialed his boss' number a fourth time. He glanced at the clock on the phone before putting it to the side of his bruised, bleeding face. 6:32 p.m. The call had been set for six. Derrik was never late.

The voice that answered wasn't Derrik's.

"I need to speak to Derrik immediately," he said with a nervous glance at the Russians. Vlad and Viktor watched from their mirrored positions, leaning against the two opposite walls of the storage unit with eerily similar, deadly eyes.

The person on the other end of the line fumbled. "I'm so sorry, sir," the woman said. "I'm his housekeeper. Uh… Mr. Myers passed away."

Brandon's eyes widened, and he let out a noise that sounded like he'd taken a gut punch. The brothers stood up straighter and watched.

"Sir?" the voice said. "The police are here. I'll let you speak to them."

Brandon hung up the phone and shut it off, his hand shaking.

"Well?" Victor asked. "I didn't hear you asking any questions to your boss."

Brandon swallowed hard, holding back the surge of bile threatening to choke him. "Ah… funny story, really. Derrik is…" He swallowed again, afraid of what they would say when they realized he was all but useless. "He's dead."

Tension hung thick in the air as the echo of his words faded to silence. Brandon's heart beat faster with each passing second until Vladimir shook his head, a thin smile revealing his disapproval.

Victor took a step forward, clicking his tongue. "What a shame." He raised his pistol to Brandon's forehead and cocked the hammer.

Chapter 24

Minerva inspected the jade polish on her nails. It had begun to chip around the edges, and she wondered if there would be time to get a fresh manicure today. The gel polish she had always applied typically lasted two weeks. But then again, she usually didn't coat her nails with poison and commit murder.

She ignored the waitress who deposited a steaming mug of coffee on the table. Her eyes instead studied the glass front door of The Eating Establishment in Portland, watching a burgundy sports car pull into the parking lot. It disappeared past the door, and Minerva took a long draught of the coffee. There was a smear of red lipstick on the mug when she placed it back on the table.

Her eyes never left the door.

Mettinger pushed open the front door. His hard eyes

surveyed the booths inside the diner before fixing on Minerva, and he wound his way over to her. He wore a pair of faded black jeans and a navy blue button-down shirt, worn but clean.

"You're late," Minerva said. She drummed her nails along the side of the mug.

He ignored her and removed a laminated menu from behind the napkin dispenser. He methodically examined the menu before ordering a Western Omelet and a coffee from the waitress. When the waitress finally walked back toward the kitchen, he turned his attention to Minerva.

"Why did you arrange this meeting?" Mettinger asked. "Our goals are very much opposite one another's."

Minerva inhaled and forced herself to relax. This was all part of the plan—getting Mettinger's cooperation to find the copy of the journal belonging to Derrik's grandfather, then getting possession of the stone ... and revenge for Jackie.

"Brandon is no longer a viable option for getting ahold of Daniel's journal," she said. "And while we were initially led to believe that Daniel's journal contains the most complete copy of the map and the puzzle pieces—and the only copy of some pieces, at that—it doesn't."

Mettinger leaned onto the table. "Explain."

She let a smug smile slip onto her face. A jade fingernail traced the mug's rim. "Derrik's grandfather included a copy of his map piece in *his* journal," she said. "From my conversations with Derrik, he was only missing half the map."

"Derrik destroyed his grandfather's journal," Mettinger said. He sat back against the seat.

"You and I both know it wasn't the only copy. Derrik's grandfather was a cautious man. He made duplicates of everything he ever wrote and kept them in a separate location from the originals."

"You know the location of his journal?"

"I do," she said. "It's with a Mr. Ronald Dwyer in Eugene, right here in Oregon. The only reason I haven't simply gotten it myself and gone to the Sierra Nevadas is because Dwyer isn't going to just hand over the journal. He doesn't trust me. He is going to require your special brand of persuasion."

Mettinger said nothing. He took a white mug of coffee from the waitress and gulped the steaming liquid.

Waiting for his response frustrated Minerva. But she couldn't afford to show impatience in front of Mettinger. She knew him, and she knew he would pounce at the first sign of weakness. So she curled her fingers around the coffee mug while studying the retired couple at the next table.

Mettinger's cell phone rang. He reached into his pocket and silenced it. "What do I get in return?"

She measured her next words carefully. That was the difference between Mettinger and Derrik; she never feared Derrik. He may have dreamed of killing her, but he didn't have it in him to carry out his plans. Mettinger would put a bullet in her brain between bites of his omelet. No hesitation.

"A copy of the journal," Minerva said. "Then we go our separate ways."

Except she didn't see things ending so smoothly. Mettinger would undoubtedly try to kill her as soon as he got his hands on the journal, and she could not allow that. Even if it meant killing him as soon as Dwyer handed over the journal. He wouldn't die as slowly as she had always imagined, but he would die all the same. For Jackie.

Then she would simply hop on a flight at the nearest airport and head to the Sierra Nevadas. Before sundown, if everything went according to plan.

If Mettinger agreed to help her.

He drained the last of the coffee and devoured the omelet. After wiping his hands on a paper napkin, he deposited it on the empty plate. "How long will it take to get there?" he asked.

"Two hours."

He checked his watch and nodded. "I need to make a phone call first."

***

James noticed that Bullet looked very much at home in the Logans' camper. The German Shepherd curled up on the captain's chair behind the front passenger seat, ears pointed in opposite directions and droopy eyelids flickering as he dreamed of chasing rabbits. At least he looked comfortable.

Chooli piloted the big camper down the highway while Russ sat in the passenger seat. James sat at the table with Kaitlyn beside him. Across the table were Daniel and Thomas, and Stacy and her father Lucas sat on the couch on the other side of the camper. The vehicle designed to be comfortable for two—maybe three—people was cramped with all eight of them and a dog stuffed inside.

It had surprised James that morning when he had heard Stacy and Lucas were on their way with Bullet to the trailer in Vacaville. He'd hoped Stacy had been able to get in contact with her father, but he'd never imagined the man was involved in the Black Coyote project too.

James watched Daniel gingerly open the weathered, leather-bound journal. Its pages were yellowed with age but didn't seem brittle. They flexed when his fingers turned them.

"Now that we're on the road, I think it's about time we got some answers," Stacy said. She leaned forward on the couch, resting her elbows on her thighs.

"I agree," James said. "It's time for someone to start talking."

Daniel met Kaitlyn's eyes across the table. His fingers curled around the faded blue baseball cap lying next to the journal.

"It's time," Thomas said.

"You're right, Thomas. You're right," Daniel said before taking a deep breath and addressing Stacy, Kaitlyn, and James. "You have heard of the Black Coyote project. It was founded in 1892 by Dr. Edward Phillips, after he heard an old Cherokee legend about an indestructible stone."

"Hold on." Stacy held up her hand. "Which Cherokee legend is this?"

"Legend says," Thomas interjected, "the Great Spirit

foretold of a magical stone that could be created during the winter solstice. The stone would draw its energy from the elements of earth, wind, fire, and water, powerful and indestructible."

"But the stone can only be created during the year of the solar eclipse, the great comet, and the alignment of the four stars," Daniel added. "Those events all occurred this year. Dr. Phillips started the Black Coyote project to learn whether the legend was true. He worked with a historian named Caroline Richards. The pair traveled all across the Southwest, interviewing Cherokee men and women who had relocated there. They spent years hiking all through the better part of the Sierra Nevadas. They created a map showing where the stone's creation will take place," he finished.

He flipped to the back of the journal and removed a folded piece of paper tucked against the cover. Unfolded, the page stretched across the table in front of them. It was comprised of four pieces, not all in the right shapes, with nicks and notches along all the edges. Although each piece was faded and worn, they were clearly added at different times. Even still, the pieces were taped together just right so the pictures all lined up flawlessly. Delicate black lines traced mountain ranges, twisted into rivers between the mountains, and formed a simple compass rose in the bottom left corner. The entire top right corner, however, was missing.

Kaitlyn leaned over the aged map. Her index finger hovered over a detailed sketch of a coyote on the top, and she brushed the lines of fur on the coyote's head. "This map shows the location of the stone?" she asked. Her eyes drilled into her father's.

"It should," he said. His fingers touched the top right edge, where the map lines ran off the page. "This section should show where the stone will be formed."

"And the missing piece… that's at Owens Lake?"

Daniel nodded. "That's what I believe. In the old silver mine. It's been so long, though, there's no telling whether it's even still there…" Thomas placed a hand on Daniel's shoulder.

"So that's it?" James asked. "We find the piece of the map in the silver mine, then follow the map to the place where the stone's going to form. What then? The stone's not going to be there yet."

"According to legend, there's a stone already in the mountains," Thomas said. "A seed around which the elements will converge."

"We just have to find that?" James added sarcastically. "Sounds easy."

Thomas gave him a warning look, but James paid him no attention. He settled back into the seat when Kaitlyn wrapped her fingers around his hand.

"What happens if... when... we find it?" Kaitlyn asked slowly.

Thomas and Daniel exchanged a quick glance. After a moment, Thomas answered. "We protect it. Getting to it first means keeping it out of the hands of those who seek nothing but power. If the seed stone gets too far from the place of convergence, there's no telling what will happen. It might not even form at all. But if they get it first..."

The road noise from the highway filled the silence inside the camper. A large semi-truck passed by on the left, the diesel engine rumbling as brown smoke billowed from the exhaust pipes. A bright yellow sports car tailgated the large truck, and it whizzed in front of the camper van as soon as its back bumper cleared the camper's front bumper. The camper lurched as Chooli slammed on the brakes, swearing loudly.

"What exactly happened in that silver mine?" Stacy asked. She turned to Lucas Logan. "And how did you get involved in this, Dad?"

Lucas ran his fingers through his silver hair. The wrinkles branching out from either side of his eyes looked like canyons in the camper's yellow ceiling lights.

"I can fill in certain details of the events," Lucas said. "But Daniel could give you a better idea of exactly what happened."

**

1997

184

Daniel paused on the side of the trail less than a hundred yards from the old silver mine. He removed his blue baseball cap and wiped his forehead with the sleeve of his shirt. The camera bounced against his chest with the movement. Water sloshed in the canteen at his hip.

According to his research at the county library, the old silver mine was parcel 435, originally owned by a Carlyle Wagner before the county took possession of it in 1978. He wasn't sure whether Wagner himself survived until the 1970s or if his descendants had held onto the property until handing it over to pay for back taxes. But Daniel did know that he'd already passed three "No Trespassing" signs. From the state of the trail, it looked like no person had traveled there in months, if not years.

He replaced his baseball cap and turned himself back toward the trail. "Onward and upward," he muttered. He hadn't taken two steps before he felt the cold steel of a gun muzzle on the back of his neck.

"I would remain very still if I were you," Victor said.

Daniel did as the Russian instructed. He held the dry desert air in his lungs as sweat beaded on his skin.

"You are going to show us to the mine," Victor said. "And then we are going to have a discussion about the location of the Black Coyote."

Daniel was silent.

"Understand?" Vlad chimed in.

Daniel nodded.

"Good," Victor said. "Lead the way."

Daniel did as he was told. He put one foot in front of the other as he picked his way up the uneven, barely-there trail. The only thing on his mind was his family—Jackie and Katy on the highway headed back home. He wondered how far Jackie had driven in the past four hours since they'd left.

He'd said goodbye to them both—said, "I love you," and hugged them tight. He'd kissed Jackie. But it wasn't enough of a goodbye. He knew, logically, that they knew how much he loved them. Yet he felt like he could have done more. Could have held onto his wife a bit longer. Could have whispered, "I love you," to Katy one more time.

A watery film coated his eyes, blurring the path in front of him. He caught his toe on a rock and stumbled.

The entrance to the silver mine opened wide like a yawning mouth. As soon as they passed into the shade, the temperature dropped, and Daniel shivered.

"That's far enough," Victor said. "Turn around."

Daniel turned around. He balled his hands into fists to keep them from shaking. If he hadn't known their voices, he wouldn't have recognized the Russian brothers in the darkness. Especially with the sun to their backs.

"Now, you know why we are here," Victor continued.

Daniel swallowed hard. "I haven't the faintest idea."

Vlad pulled the trigger, and Daniel felt a searing pain in his thigh. He let out a choked scream of pain before collapsing to the ground. His fingers searched his pant leg for the wound, only stopping when they felt a wet warmth.

"Let's try this again," Vlad said. "We want the map, and we want you to tell us where we can find the Black Coyote in this mine. Hand it over."

Daniel's hands were too busy clutching his leg, so Vlad bent toward the downed man and pulled the black notebook from Daniel's pocket. The two conversed in Russian for a moment. Daniel gave up trying to decipher the words and instead calculated his options.

He needed that journal back.

His leg wouldn't support him for long if he lunged at Vlad. Both men carried guns and would not hesitate to kill him. What he needed was a distraction. Something big enough to draw their attention for more than a few seconds.

And he got just that.

"Hands above your head," a voice said from the mouth of the mine. A shadow appeared at the entrance.

As Victor and Vlad whirled around, Daniel snatched his

chance. He scrambled to his feet and lunged for the Russians. His fingers curled around a fistful of shirt before his injured leg gave out from under him. Vlad came down on top of him.

He tried to wrench his journal from the Russian's hands, but Vlad was too strong. The man's fist plowed into Daniel's temple, and he blacked out.

Chapter 25

"How did you get the journal back from the Russians if you were unconscious?" Stacy asked Daniel. She was thankful to have something to talk about. The group was getting closer to Owens Lake, and they all felt the anxiety building as each mile melted away.

"As soon as Vlad hit me, your father shot him in the shoulder. He dropped the journal and, lucky for us, it toppled into a crevice about fifteen feet into the mine where it was hidden from view. Your father managed to subdue the Russians until backup arrived. Victor was taken into custody immediately, and Vlad was supposed to join his brother behind bars once he was released from the hospital. But he didn't make it there. Within hours after Vlad's surgery, they were both released." Daniel shook his head.

"What? How could they get away with that and not serve any time?" Stacy was appalled that the justice system she believed in had failed in such a reckless way.

"They have diplomatic immunity."

"They're the sons of a very popular Russian diplomat, so they walked," Thomas said. "The Russian Embassy bailed them out and sent them back to Russia for a little while. Not long enough, in my opinion. They've made millions in the Russian underworld, but ever since they found out about Black Coyote, they've stopped at nothing trying to get to it. Sometimes I wonder if even death would stop them."

"How did they even find out about Black Coyote?" Chooli asked from the driver's seat. "I mean, it's not necessarily public knowledge."

"Their father is very interested in Native American legends. He has studied our people for longer than you've been alive, Chooli. Anyone who studies the legends long enough can eventually put the pieces together. They'd have enough information to imagine how powerful Black Coyote is. Power will make people do unthinkable things. Even good people can turn on everything they know and everything they are when they're in pursuit of power."

The group fell silent, all thinking about the stone and what they would do if they had it.

"Their father began his quest long ago, but he is very old now. He can no longer search for the stone himself. Instead, his youthful sons now work to finish what he started." Thomas sighed, looking at those around him with worry in his dark eyes.

"How did you recover the journal?" Stacy asked, unable to bear the silence any longer.

"I was in no shape to crawl around in the dark mine, blindly grasping for the journal," Daniel continued. "So your father, hero that he is"—Daniel held his hand out to Lucas—"recovered it and saved it from being discovered by anyone else. His loyalty all these years has protected the stone from ending up in the wrong hands."

Lucas smiled back at his dearest friend. "Once we heard

Jackie had been killed in the car accident, we knew Kaitlyn would not be safe until she was as far from Black Coyote as possible. To save her, we needed to make Daniel disappear as well. That's when we reported him missing and helped arrange for Kaitlyn's care."

Daniel looked at Kaitlyn and reached out to her. His large hand easily covered hers. "I know you were made to believe both your parents were dead and that it hasn't been easy for you. But, sweetheart, I needed to protect you. You were all I had left, and I needed to keep you safe from exactly this situation we're in right now. Believe me, I would have done anything to keep you with me if I'd thought you would've been safe."

Kaitlyn jumped up and hugged her father, stumbling a little as the camper hit a pothole. "I know, Dad. I missed you and Mom so much, but I understand why you did it. I'm just glad to have you back."

"So, I hate to crush the mood here, but what happens now?" The group turned to look at Chooli in the driver's seat. "What happens when we find the rest of the map and the stone? You said we'd protect it, but what does that even mean?"

Thomas and Daniel made eye contact. "Just get us there, Chooli, and leave the rest to us," Thomas said.

Chapter 26

1983

A large, polished oak table stretched out like a monolith in the barren starkness of an empty room. The stained wood grain carved itself through the hard timber facade like a thousand flowing rivers. Not a single piece of ornamentation decorated the walls, nor was a hue of color visible other than the earthy variations of desolate tan throughout. A single lamp fashioned out of a hollowed log with a sheepskin shade sat in the center of the table, casting a sickly, yellow-tinted glow. Its reach struggled to illuminate beyond the edges of the massive table.

Six people sat around the table; four barely pushed thirty

years of age, another neared forty, and the last—a Native American—was easily in his sixties. Half cloaked in darkness, each person sat at an equal distance from the next. In the uncomfortable silence, the nervous guests looked about the room, their eyes meeting one another's occasionally, then darting in nervous anxiety to anywhere else. They measured each other and contemplated their situation. Were they all feeling the same way, or did someone in the room have an advantage and know something the rest did not? The antique chairs creaked under their nervous, shifting weights. The invitations they had received weeks earlier had promised them financial support in their respective fields in return for unquestioned participation in this secretive meeting. A joint venture of utmost importance, which held the fate of the world in its balance. After a three-hour drive into the desert, they found themselves in this unnerving situation. These six individuals wondered now what would be required of them for their participation in this gathering of strangers, let alone if they would even survive the night.

There came a slight creak as the door to the room opened slowly. It could have easily been the stealthy awakening of the undead from a coffin as much as an entrance to the room. From the blackness beyond the threshold, an elderly Native American gentleman appeared. His feet shuffled across the poorly-laid concrete floor. He entered, carrying a leather briefcase in his left hand, worn from decades of use, and an ornately carved wooden cane in the other. He took his place at the head of the table and seated himself in the only remaining empty spot. As he positioned himself, his joints groaned, even more so than the rickety chair into which he settled.

He flopped his briefcase onto the table and rested his cane across his lap. With shaky hands, he flipped open the two fasteners locking the case and opened the lid, revealing five manila envelopes. He retrieved the top four and left the fifth in its place. Each envelope was embossed with a symbol on its cover representing one of the four elements—earth, wind, fire, and water. The elderly gentleman pointed toward Thomas, the oldest of the group, and gestured for him to approach.

Thomas had been so intently focused on what the old man was going to pull from the case—thinking perhaps it was a weapon and they would have all been robbed or worse—that he didn't immediately realize he was being singled out. Thomas complied and made his way to the elder. He glanced across the table and made eye contact with two other guests who leaned near one another.

"Thomas, please hand out these envelopes." The elderly man handed over the stack of envelopes. They shook in his unsteady grip.

Thomas took up the stack. "Yes, of course… but they have no names," he replied.

"You don't know anyone else in this group anyway, so what does it matter?" responded the cryptic old man. "I trust the spirit of my people and yours will guide your hand." He gestured for Thomas to continue.

Thomas walked cautiously around the table, and examined each envelope closely. He rubbed his fingers over the raised symbols depicting each element. The paper felt warm and fibrous to his touch. A calm washed over him as he momentarily closed his eyes and let his fingers outline the minute ridges of the symbols. Upon awakening from his reverie, he found himself standing behind a beautiful young female.

"Miss, I give you water. I hope that's all right." Thomas placed the envelope on the table in front of her and shrugged, hesitant in his decision.

Minerva's face lit up. The envelope she received, although she had no clue what it meant in this context, hit close to home. She had studied the new applications of hydroelectric energy creation in college and was now actively pursuing its applied science in the field. She could only believe this was a positive sign and that she had indeed made the right decision to come here tonight. Then again, it could have been merely coincidence, but either way, she was hopeful. One of her perfectly painted nails began to tear into the envelope when she was interrupted by the elderly man.

"All in good time, my dear. All in good time."

Derrik was surprised by the envelope he received—the element of wind. His grandfather had built windmills for farmers back in the day, and he himself was always intrigued by the power of the wind, having spent those many afternoons watching his granddad erect the beautiful, functional pieces of art on the landscape. His father had taken it a step further and automated the process of fabricating uglier and cheaper versions for the small farmers popping up during his time. Business dried up as fast as it came, but he had been very successful. Derrik never considered following in his family's footsteps, but with his engineering degree and the millions bequeathed to him after his parents' death, he could see himself carrying the torch of the Myer tradition and making a bigger, better windmill. Possibly changing the world. A slight smirk of satisfaction crossed his face.

A well-built, broad chested man in his early forties sat next down the line. A scowl crossed his face as Thomas neared. With his arms folded across his chest, he didn't move when the envelope with the fire emblem was placed on the table before him. The stout man shifted his eyes to the envelope and scoffed.

"What the hell is all this cryptic nonsense?" he exclaimed. He glared intently at the old man sitting at the head of the table. "I thought we were here for some type of business proposal. I don't have time for this."

The elderly man shifted his weight and addressed him in a cordial fashion that only many years of a peaceful, tranquil temperament could have produced. "We are almost through, here. Be patient. I'm well aware of who you are, and you can rest assured... you will benefit greatly from tonight's meeting."

"Sir, there's only one more envelope and still two people sitting at the table. And myself, I might add," Thomas interjected, positioning himself behind the man and woman at the end who had now scooted in close enough to hold hands.

"They get the last envelope. They're married. They count as a single unit in this venture."

"What about myself?" questioned Thomas.

"You are done here. Please wait in the hall. You'll find a comfy chair in the corner." The old man pointed to the door.

Thomas set the final envelope down between the married couple. He shuffled back past the group of strangers and gave a gracious nod to the elderly man as he exited through the door. Thomas gave a last once-over glance to the strangers seated around the table as he shut the door. An uneasiness about a few of the guests came over him. Though he felt a calmness—a security— with the married couple, he wondered if he would ever see any of them again.

The elderly man gently closed his briefcase and pushed it to the side, out of the way. "I have brought you all here for an extremely important reason. That reason is written in a letter to each of you, written by your predecessors and given to me to deliver. That letter sits in front of you. You are to read your letter but not share its contents with anyone for any reason... ever. You are never to communicate with each other about what you will soon learn. Not at any point for as long as you are alive. With the exception of the married couple, of course. You are a single unit as far as I'm concerned, and you will be held responsible as such. Simply follow the stipulations, and each of you will be rewarded in ways you have never imagined. Now go. Remember to stay steadfast."

The group gathered their envelopes and proceeded toward the door. The room was quiet; no one had any idea what had transpired that night. Some were filled with hope, others with contentment, while still others didn't know what to make of it at all. They needed to talk but felt that, under the circumstances, it was better not to push their luck. Maybe the letters would answer some of the questions stirring in their heads.

Mettinger was the first out the door; he mumbled, visually agitated, then disappeared into the darkness.

Minerva and Derrik were the next to leave. Both smiled as they realized in their hearts that something wonderful was about to happen. Neither could explain it, nor were they allowed to try, but they looked at each other and smiled wider as they exited. They knew they would meet again and be the better for it.

Daniel and Jackie were the last to leave. Daniel took the envelope and ran his fingers gently over the raised symbol representing the last element—earth. How did the elderly man or his assistant, the Native American, know they were adventurers? They were indeed the offspring of two close families, each successful in the mining and drilling business, but they themselves barely made a decent living. They foraged in the most inhospitable places on Earth, looking for that which had been hidden from before time was time. They were not scholarly, nor business owners, nor wealthy. They wanted a simple life, full of fun and adventure and, God willing, a family to share it with. They did not know the stories of the strangers who sat across from them, but they left feeling their participation was a mistake.

Jackie glanced at Thomas, who sat quietly in a chair in the hallway. They acknowledged each other with a nod as she and Daniel left through the front door. Cars pulled away in succession. Only Thomas and the elderly man were left.

The elderly man was the last to exit the room. Thomas stood out of respect as he approached.

"Please help me to my car," pled the man.

"Yes, of course," Thomas replied. Together they walked to the double doors leading out into the night. The air was crisp and cool in the desert. It smelled of jasmine.

The elderly man stopped and turned, looking back in the direction he had just come. He sighed in discontent. "I forgot my briefcase on the table. I'm getting too forgetful these days and too tired to go back. Please fetch it for me."

Thomas released the old man's arm, who immediately propped himself on his cane for support. The younger man hurried back to that stark mysterious room. He grabbed the briefcase off the table and made his way immediately back down the short, narrow corridor. Then he stopped in confusion when he saw the elderly man no longer waited there. Thomas hurried outside to see if the man had made it to his car, but only his own vehicle sat in the small dirt parking lot. The elderly man was gone. Disappeared.

After a few short minutes of standing in disbelief, Thomas set the case on the nearby chair and opened it. He looked over his shoulders a few times, half expecting the elderly man to pop out of a secret door and catch him, but nothing stirred. He cautiously retrieved the one envelope remaining in the case—the only thing still inside. Not a pen nor a piece of scratch paper could be found— definitely nothing that would lend itself to answering any questions about who the old man was or where he was from, or even who he represented. On the envelope's cover was a picture of a pair of green, glowing eyes. They almost had a slight luminescence to them in the dim light of the hallway. Thomas opened the envelope, careful not to tear through anything but the envelope itself, and removed its contents. The first page was addressed to him.

Thomas,

Included in this stack of papers is a copy of each letter you handed out tonight. You are the bearer of this project in its entirety. You are the sole witness to its completion—or, should I say, its lack of completion. Its protection.

Fire - dynamic, masculine, passionate, heat
Water - nurturing, feminine, magnetic
Wind - movement, possibility, cooling
Earth - stability, support, strength

These are the elements you have been chosen to protect. Focus the energies of the others to achieve the goal. Each of the five has only a piece of the entire puzzle—one of five segments of a larger map, along with varied bits of information that complement each other but do not reveal the full magnitude of this important prospect on their own. They can never know what they are ultimately working against. This is imperative. Keep them on track. Keep them honest. The fate of the world rests in your capable hands.

Above all, my friend, remember to stay steadfast. Should any one person obtain the full map, especially with malicious intent, mankind would be doomed.

The following few papers were the letters each had received that night, explaining that each had the opportunity—the sole responsibility—to achieve harmony with the Earth through their life's work. If they stayed on that path, like the many before them, they would benefit greatly. But through dishonesty and greed they would, by the same account, die. The papers went on to explain everything in great detail. Thomas spent the next few hours sitting crosslegged on the floor with the papers scattered about him. As farfetched as it all sounded, he believed every word. He had been told stories about such things growing up, rooted in the teachings and history of his people. But of everything he read, one line of text scared him above all others.

The Black Coyote is not a "what" or a "when." It's not a "how" or a "why." It's a "who." The Black Coyote is you, Thomas.

Chapter 27

Victor picked up Brandon's phone and turned it over. He was about to put it into his pocket when it rang.

Vladimir, busy searching the pockets of the now-dead Brandon, looked up. "Who is it?"

"Mettinger."

"Why did you kill him so fast?" Vlad said suddenly.

Victor looked at his brother, shocked. In so many years of their career, never once had they disagreed on when to kill a man. In fact, they were known to do the deed at the same moment in most cases. "He spit into my face! He was asking for his death."

"Of course he was. And you didn't even think for a moment before giving it to him."

"Stop shouting at me! You shot Brandon not even a second after I did. If you couldn't bear him dead, what was that all about, huh?"

"I pulled the trigger because I have been doing that for years, or did you forget? Every time, it's the same thing. You make the decisions, you take all the first shots, and it's me who has to keep track of your signals and do whatever it is you deem correct. And killing Brandon? How was that an intelligent thing to do?"

"Are we going to take this call before it disconnects or not?" Victor interrupted impatiently and accepted the call, putting it on speaker.

"Hello? Brandon?" There was a brief pause. "Brandon, listen to me. I'm with Minerva. She's hinted that Derrik's out of the picture, and I can't get hold of him. She claims there's a physical copy of Derrick's information, and get this, the Russians are in play now too."

Victor could see what that meant, and he saw that Vladimir understood too. Mettinger knew that Brandon was getting nowhere, and when he got a call from Minerva, he'd decided to abandon Brandon and Derrik without a moment's hesitation. The question was, if he had the key to the journal, why was he calling Brandon now?

"If you're pissed at me for leaving you at the storage place, get over it," Mettinger began again. "You or Derrik would have done the same thing in my place, so let's not pretend to be good friends here. This time around, though, I have a better deal for you. A copy of Derrick's grandfather's journal exists, and Minerva somehow knows where it is. Something she never told Derrik despite all their claims of being on one team. She needs me to get it and plans on killing me after she has it. Not if I beat her to it. That woman doesn't realize she can get nowhere with half a map, no matter how much information the journal contains. That's why I'm calling you. Keep looking for Daniel's journal. With both sources combined, we'll have the whole map. After we get this stone, you get *all* Derrik's share. How's that?" After a pause, Mettinger asked, "Brandon? Are you listening?"

"Hey, Mettinger. Do you remember your old friends?" Victor said slowly.

There was finally a long pause on the other line.

"We had been such good friends, Mettinger. You, me, and my brother. We made a pretty good living nightmare. You shouldn't have left."

"You know why I left," Mettinger said, his voice low this time. "Don't pretend as if you don't. Anybody in my place would have done the same."

"Don't deem everybody to be as selfish and myopic as you are," Victor shouted into the phone.

"I don't have any more time. What did you do to Brandon?"

"Something I have always wanted to do to you... and will do very soon."

The call disconnected.

Victor laughed out loud as Vladimir looked at him incredulously. "Despite everything he claims to be, he is still afraid of us."

Vladimir flashed the device in his hand. "I traced the call. We have Mettinger's location and we can follow wherever his phone goes."

"Let him jump into whatever ditch he wants. I bet you anything Minerva's lying to him. There is no such journal. And even if a journal exists, it has far less information than Daniel's. We're going behind Daniel and his gang. Come on." Victor turned toward the door.

"How can you be sure Minerva's lying? Something tells me this is worth following. Daniel likes to riddle. He's smart. I don't expect him to lay everything plain and clear for anyone to see, even in his journal. And an incomplete but readable journal is far better than a complete one we can't understand."

"Once we get his journal, we'll find a way to read it. Now, hurry up!" Victor tapped his foot in impatience.

"Who's going to find a way to read it, huh? You, with your pea-sized brain? And stop ordering me around. You need to listen to me for once!" Vladimir paced around aggressively. "We don't have to choose which journal to follow. We can get both, if we split. I know we have worked together always, but I think it's essential for us now to work separately."

"I don't know what makes you think going after Minerva is a good idea. Obviously, you think it's worth fighting over with me," Victor said. "I can't convince you against it now. So go wherever you want. Only, if there is a journal, make sure you get it. And on my behalf, put an extra bullet in Mettinger."

***

Mettinger was still shaken up two hours after his conversation with Victor. He'd let his emotions get the best of him and had told the brothers everything. He wondered what the repercussions of this folly would be.

Minerva had picked him up in her car after he'd ended the call with the Russians. Mettinger could tell they were about to reach their destination, and he felt adrenaline pumping in his veins. He had decided to get rid of her even before they entered the house. Then he'd go inside and persuade the man to give up the journal. If everything went according to plan, he'd be on his way out of there after a couple hours.

Minerva parked outside a house looking like any other two-story house on the street—a small lawn, a picket fence, and a dog kennel. The street was completely empty and quiet.

Mettinger got out and drew his gun. Minerva walked around the car and would have walked straight past him into the house, but he trained his gun on her and ordered her to stop. She stopped in her tracks and turned to face him.

"You still need me," he said. "But I don't need you. Any reason I shouldn't get rid of you right now?" He brought the gun to her head and settled it on the center of her forehead.

"I knew you'd try a stunt like this"—Minerva smiled—"but I hadn't expected it so soon. What you don't realize, my dear friend, is that I know this man. What makes you think he would even open the gate for you? He knows he holds a lot of sensitive information, and I've seen his insane level of caution. There's no way he's letting you into his house without me by your side." She dug a fingernail into Mettinger's chest, just above the top button of his shirt, and a thin line of blood now welled above the skin.

Mettinger flicked her bloodied finger aside. "What are you trying to do, woman?" he shouted. Maybe he had acted too soon. After all, he had no knowledge of this man and the journal. There could be a lot Minerva still hadn't told him. "You walk first, and no funny business. I've got nothing to lose by shooting you. If the man doesn't open the door himself, I'm good at breaking in."

***

Having managed to get a flight at the last moment, Vladimir stepped out of the plane at Eugene airport and hurried out. He had to get to Mettinger before the journal was gone.

In the parking lot, he looked for a black Chevrolet. It was waiting for him just where he had been told it would be, and a thin, hardened Russian youngster waited inside. The boy stepped out when Vladimir approached, nodded, and left.

He got into the car and removed a parcel from under the passenger seat. He took out the gun and examined it quickly. It was not as good as his own, which he'd had to abandon outside airport security, but it would do the task. He clicked off the safety and accelerated away from the airport.

***

Minerva walked ahead while Mettinger trained the gun on her back. He kept it low, hidden by his own body, just in case the man was watching them from inside the house.

Mettinger used his free hand to ring the doorbell, and a white-haired, spectacled man of average build stepped onto the porch.

"Yes?" he demanded.

"Ronald, it's me. Minerva. We talked a few times last week, remember?"

"Oh, is that you? Really?" The man wiped his spectacles and stepped closer for another look. "Ah, I see. And who is this man with you?"

"This is Mettinger. He's a friend."

"A trustworthy friend, I assume?" Ronald looked at Mettinger's burly, expressionless figure with a measured degree of suspicion.

"Oh, yes. He's a fellow journalist. I've been working on your story since we last spoke, and I have a few more questions. Can we come in?"

"Yes, of course." Ronald opened the door and led Minerva and Mettinger inside.

"Is your daughter home?" Minerva asked once they were inside.

"No, it's only me here. I think I told you last time that these are her working hours."

"You're right." Minerva smiled at the old man. "Ronald, we wanted to know more about Frank. He was your father's friend, wasn't he? I know his grandson, Derrik."

"Ah yes, Frank! At one point in time, my father had begun to spend virtually all his time with that man. Of course, it bothered me. Dad had no time for family, no time for—"

"Let's just get to the point, now," Mettinger interrupted. He couldn't bear the old man's slow talk. "We need the journal he gave you."

Ronald's jaw fell open. "I don't know anything about any journal. Please leave my house. Minerva, I am sorry, but I don't feel comfortable in this man's presence."

"This is not about your comfort, old man." Mettinger wrapped one of his arms around Minerva's throat and pointed the gun at Ronald. "Tell me where the journal is."

"I-I…" Ronald stammered.

Before anyone could comprehend what happened, Mettinger fired a shot into Minerva's thigh and threw her aside. She let out a shrill scream. Mettinger pulled the old man by his t-shirt and threw him onto the floor. He straddled the man, trained the gun on his temple, and held him tightly by the jaw. "Now tell me, where is this journal? And be quick about it."

"I will… I will tell you. Just, please, don't hurt me." The old man began to cry.

"Quit crying."

Ronald seemed to calm down, and while he still appeared afraid, his hysteria had lessened. "You can't kill me. You need me to get the journal."

"You're right. I can't kill you. But I'll kill your daughter when she comes home, and I'll fill your last living moments with pain. And at some point, you'll tell me anyways. You'll tell me everything you know just to make the pain stop. The question is whether or not you're smart enough to do that sooner rather than later."

Tears clouded Ronald's eyes again, but when he spoke this time, it was in an amazingly clear voice. "The journal is not in this house. Let me up, and I'll lead you to it."

Mettinger tried to get off the old man, and finally succeeded after several attempts. He felt so dizzy he couldn't think. Just then, the door opened. Mettinger got one look at Vladimir, and he collapsed, the gun falling from his hand near Ronald's feet. His final thoughts as Minerva's poison drained the last of his life were to wonder why Vladimir was alone and where his brother was.

Chapter 28

With Mettinger dead at her feet and a bullet in her leg, Minerva obviously had difficulty moving away from Vlad as he quickly crossed the room. She scooted across the floor, reaching for Ronald. Vlad aimed the gun at Minerva, but he looked Ronald in the eyes as he spoke.

"The journal," he demanded, his hand extended.

"It's… it isn't here," Ronald stammered.

Vlad didn't believe him. Without missing a beat, he pulled the trigger and shot Minerva in the face. For a moment, he swam in the adrenaline rush of finally firing the first shot. Victor wasn't there to beat him to it, to take the credit, or to run the show. This was all Vlad, and he admitted to himself it felt even better than he had imagined it would.

"Try again," he said as he brought the gun forward and

trained it on Ronald.

Ronald stole glances at Minerva lying on the floor, her blood pooling on the edge of the Persian rug. He didn't look at her very long. "Okay, maybe it is here," he agreed, holding up his hands. "Wait right here. I'll go upstairs and look for it."

"You think I'm stupid?" Vlad leaned within inches of Ronald's face and shouted. "You think I'm going to let you out of my sight? We get it together, or you will join your friend here in the afterlife." Vlad shoved the gun into Ronald's chest, making him stumble backward.

Ronald's face fell. He must have realized there was no escaping. "Follow me," he said, slowly turning toward the stairs. The muzzle of Vlad's gun jabbed into his right kidney, and he flinched.

At the top of the stairs, Ronald headed down the short, narrow hall and stopped under the attic entry panel. Still holding up his hands, he turned to Vlad. "It's up there," he said, nodding toward the small square panel recessed in the ceiling.

"So what are you waiting for?" Vlad spat. He was losing his patience with the old man. He should have been out of this shitty house already and on his way back to Victor with the journal. He couldn't wait to finally prove to Victor that he was smart enough and could follow a lead successfully on his own. He couldn't wait to hear Victor's apology and the best phrase of all—*you were right*.

Ronald reached up and pulled down the ladder. He climbed up and disappeared into the dark attic above. Vlad heard scuffling and a loud scrape of what sounded like metal on wood. After a few minutes, he decided to see what the old man was doing.

Vlad climbed four of the seven steps up the ladder so his head and shoulders were just inside the attic. A thin sliver of light came from a tiny round window, illuminating boxes, furniture covered in sheets, and odds and ends scattered about. A narrow path had been paved through the junk, and when he followed the fresh footprints in the dust, his gaze landed on Ronald's silhouette. It looked misshapen in the dark.

Ronald moved, and Vlad saw a suitcase swinging in his direction. It struck a glancing blow against a low rafter first and barely grazed the Russian's thick skull. Vlad's roar reverberated off the rafters, followed shortly by the crack of the gun.

Vlad ran up the last few steps of the ladder and held the gun at arm's length, searching for movement among the shadows. His boots scraped loudly on the plywood flooring, and he stopped after every step to listen for Ronald's movements. He heard nothing. Again, he slid his boots, the wood scraped, and then he stopped. Nothing.

"Come out, old man, you little shit!" Vlad hollered. "Let's see you try again. Come on!" Still, there was only silence. He shuffled slowly toward the back corner of the attic—farthest from the little window but where he saw a small light—hoping to trap the old man and get a good shot. Vlad's boot hit a short box, and something scurried away. Flustered by the sudden noise, he swung his gun in the direction of the sound and fired. Nothing.

Vlad moved a little faster toward the lighted corner and found stacks of papers slightly askew, as if they'd been in the process of being sorted. The light came from a small kerosene lamp. He slowly lowered his gun and bent to see them closer.

Some of the papers were tax documents, mortgage receipts, and financial statements. Some were letters written in a sloppy scrawl, barely legible in the dim light. Vlad was almost ready to turn around and leave when he noticed a small bundle of papers in a stack, roughly bound on one edge. They were tied together at the center with a string, and Derrik's name was written on the front.

Vlad set down his gun so he could untie the bundle. He removed the string, lifted back the top paper, and saw the words *Black Coyote* written underneath. Holding his breath, he thumbed through the copy of the journal. He couldn't believe it. The rumor of the copy was true, and Minerva had not been lying. This would finally earn him some respect.

A piece of folded paper slipped from the bundle and fell to the floor. He picked it up and opened it, reading the carefully handwritten letter.

June 11, 1997

Ronald,

I know we swore we wouldn't share information anymore, especially now that it's out of our hands, but recent events have forced me to send you this. As always, I trust I have your utmost confidence. Mettinger has sold his information to the Bratva family. I hear Jackie's brother is involved as well, and there's no telling how much of her information he's garnered. Derrik panicked and burned the journal I gave him, including his map piece. That means this journal you have now is the only surviving copy, so keep it well.

As you know, I did not give you the copy of my map piece. I assure you it has nothing to do with my trust in you. It appears paranoia is creeping up on me in my old age. I originally had it stashed away at an old mine in California ... but the Russian boys were arrested near there just a week ago, and it leads me to believe they know the map is there. They were just too close.

I can feel it in these old bones. I don't have much time left. So I've moved it. It's in safety deposit box 106 at Umpqua Bank in Vallejo. They won't outright say they have deposit boxes, you have to ask specifically. I can't trust Derrik with this. His head hasn't quite been steady on his shoulders ever since he started communicating with that Minerva girl.

You are the only other soul who knows this, Ronald. Keep it safe until the next generation needs to know.

Forever in your debt,
Stanley Myers

Vlad gripped the papers tight and brought them to his nose. They smelled oddly like wood smoke mingled with dust. Before he could wonder why, he heard the unmistakable crackling of fire.

He turned and saw the haze of smoke filling the attic. Rushing out of the corner of the attic, he tried to make his way back toward the ladder. He held the copy of the journal under one arm and used the other to cover his face. As the fire grew, so did the light, and Vlad quickly spotted the way out.

As he approached the ladder, he realized he hadn't seen Ronald's body. He scanned the attic, trying to see through the thickening air. He would not go back to find Ronald. If he was already dead, good riddance. If he wasn't, he soon would be.

Vlad turned to where the ladder was but couldn't see the opening in the floor. Instead, he saw the ladder folded up tight against the panel. He pushed on the panel, trying to dislodge it, but it wouldn't budge. Something was wedged against it from underneath. Vlad kicked, jumped, and pounded on it; it was no use. That rotten old man must have gotten out and locked him inside. Just as that thought crossed his mind, the small window shattered.

Vlad tried to make his way across the attic to the only opening into fresh air. He shuffled quickly across the floorboards, but they broke beneath him, and Vlad plummeted into the blazing orange pit below. As he fell, the copy of the journal slipped from his hands. Sheet after sheet floated down like feathers into the consuming flames.

Chapter 29

The strong aroma of Chinese jasmine enveloped Kaitlyn with its intoxicating sweetness, pleasantly assaulting her nose, impoverishing all her other senses so her mind focused only on the scent. Her body barely registered the thin grass slightly penetrating her cotton top, which had become damp and cold from the bejeweling dew and slight frost. She did not perceive the fact that a vast body of water was nearby, accompanied by the faintest sound of trickling and, underneath that, harmonious vibrations of thrashing water against rock. The noise seemed so embedded into the location, it had become its pulse. In fact, she would have stayed in this catatonic state if it weren't for her father's voice cutting through the sweet fog clouding her mind.

"Now remember, Kaitlyn, these flowers need direct sunlight and can't deal with frost."

It was just a memory—a phrase she remembered her father saying when she'd first gotten her own potted Chinese jasmine. It provided enough clarity for her to open her eyes and unleash her other senses; at this time, she realized how impossible it was that she could smell the fragrance in the air.

Slowly rising onto her forearms, she noticed she was lying in a meadow bursting with the delicate, star-shaped flowers, so extensive in their quantity they almost looked like constellations in the night. The scene was wrong.

How could they grow here? The meadow basked in the shadows of the surrounding conifer forests, and the frost and lack of sunlight made the location inhabitable for such a plant. *They would be better off growing in the Sahara,* she mused.

Her clothes growing damper by the second, she decided to get up and try to figure out where she was. Standing and turning in every direction gave her no further clues; she could only see impossible flowers, trees, and a lake some distance away.

Despite the complete lack of knowledge of her location, she felt whole. Relaxed. Even placid. Something the last couple of days had robbed from her. Perhaps it was the presence of her favorite flowers that she had loved ever since she was a child, or because one could not be in such a location without feeling some sort of leisure. Whatever it was, it allowed her time to contemplate everything that had happened.

Walking to the edge of the tree line, where the flowers increased ten-fold, she tried to comprehend why this had happened to her. Why it was *her* dad who had supposedly died, leaving her to live her life alone. Why *she* had married a man, as it turned out, she barely knew. Why *she* had been drugged, punched, tied up, had a gun pointed at her, and all other manner of awful things that many never experienced in their lives. Why her, out of the billions of people in the world?

Before she could formulate even one answer, something in the depths of the forest distracted her. Glowing brighter than the white petals she had been stroking with her fingers were two green eyes, reminding her of the emeralds on her shark tooth necklace.

216

Adrenaline pummeled her body—a sensation that had become oddly familiar. When the eyes grew larger, their owner moving closer, she did not move. Instead, she remained still, her hand poised on a petal. Underneath the temporary adrenaline was the same calm she had experienced throughout her short time in the meadow.

So she let the creature come out of the tree line and into the attenuated shadows of the clearing. A beast with the silkiest black fur, ears standing rigid to catch the sound of the smallest footfall, a snout with the strongest of jaws, and gracefully treading paws came to stand before her.

"The black coyote," Kaitlyn whispered.

It looked at her for merely a second with a human-like expression—making Kaitlyn feel almost vulnerable—before running back into the cluster of tree trunks and darkness. Kaitlyn would never work out why she did what she did, but for some reason, she ran after it.

She chased the beast's tail, slalomed past trees. Never once did she look back at the meadow, and as before, her senses seemed to dull, focusing only on locating the animal. One thing she did note, though, was how the vibrations of water seemed to increase, creating a perpetual thud in time with her own pulse.

"*When you wish upon a star, the answer surely can't be far.*"

She slowed down as soon as she heard the words.

"*As the sun meets with the moon, what is missing uncovers soon.*"

She lost sight of the beast, looking now for the origin of the voice.

"*Plant your feet, relax your jaws, take a breath and take a pause.*"

It sounded like a man's voice, old and experienced.

"*When the earth and sky align, there you'll find this secret of...* 'mine.' Mine. Isn't that a funny word?"

The closer she moved to the voice, the more deafening the thump of the water. When the voice was so close it almost felt like he was whispering into her ear, she saw a cascading river, its currents so vigorous, sprays of water splashed upon the bank. Some of the water ended up by the feet of an elderly man.

Leaning on his cane, he turned to her, saying, "You're finally here. I've been waiting a long time."

She didn't know what to say but took in every inch of his appearance. His complexion suggested he was of Native American origin, which suited how he placed his feet and cane on the ground with a delicacy, as though one with the environment. Pulled back into a low ponytail, his hair was an onyx color matching his dark eyes, which were far from intimidating and held a warmth only darkness could create. Beyond this, there was something comforting about him Kaitlyn could not figure out.

"Nobody ever truly owns anything, so how can something be *mine*?" He smiled at her, like this sort of conversation was an everyday occurrence.

"Who are you?" It seemed almost rude how blunt she was, but she couldn't help it. Kaitlyn took a step tentatively toward him, somehow feeling she would get more answers from him than from anyone else in the past few days.

"It's an interesting little poem, isn't it? Have you figured it out yet?"

"Am I supposed to?" As soon as she said it, he bellowed, laughing like only an old man could.

"My dear child, are we ever supposed to figure things out, or do we just run into the answers?"

"I uh... I guess... look, can you tell me where I am?"

"Unfortunately, no." This disheartened her, but the man seemed not to notice—either that, or he ignored her and carried on. "But I will give you some advice." Raising his eyebrows up at her, he lifted his head to look directly at the sky. "Do you know what constellations are?"

Following suit, she looked up, surprised to find it was already night, the stars prevailing through the inky darkness. "Yeah, they're patterns made by stars."

"Wrong. That is not what they are."

Scrunching her eyebrows ever so slightly, she got the feeling she was being chastened.

"Constellations do not exist," he continued. "They are imaginary—"

"Constellations exist," she interrupted. "My dad used to study them all the time, I remember…" He moved his head so his eyes focused upon her again, and she grew silent, suddenly feeling embarrassed of her outburst.

"They are man-made by individuals looking at the night and drawing invisible links between stars millions of miles apart. Over the years, these links consolidate, as they are written down, sought out, and admired. So then people think these links, which only one person saw, become solid, like string in the sky. All done because they cannot be reached by a human touch… But the stars, they exist. And they, like yourself, know where the stone is."

"The stone? The all-mythical stone that seems to have wrecked my life? You know where it is?"

"Did I say that? I said *you* and *the stars* know where it is, not I."

They were both silent, only the thrashing water filling the silent void between them.

"Are you saying I discover this stone?"

Again, he laughed. "Who discovered America?"

"Christopher Columbus. Why?"

He ignored her question. "But was he the only one to know of the presence of America, or were the thousands of Natives also aware of its presence? Knowing and discovering something are not the same. One may know something before another, but they may not be credited with discovering it."

"Okay… so, I… me… a waitress who's done little, knows where this stone is, which people are ready to kill for? Because I can tell you right now, I have no idea where the bloody thing is!"

"Oh, Kaitlyn, my dear, you have no idea how special you are." Starting toward her with the lightest footsteps, he reached out and cupped her cheek. "You were born at the time when the sky and the earth really did align, and when the stars became more than burning gas and were—for a moment—joined with the rest of the galaxy… You are *so* important."

There was an intensity within his eyes, a disbelief, like he was a poor boy looking at a million gold coins. The moment was ephemeral, and he was off again to the bank, picking up the conversation, and Kaitlyn could barely keep track of it.

"Alignment is another word for perspective. Something becomes 'aligned' because you are standing in the right place, not because the object has moved. That is why the constellation maps are not working, Kaitlyn. They are not standing in the right place… but you are. Do you see why your father is desperate to go to the mine? He's looking for the key to this, the key that will get him the stone. Ironically, the key is with him right now."

"So, I… I have a perspective of what, exactly?"

Whispering with such an acuteness, he said, "Four stars… but I'm getting ahead of myself. We don't have much time, and I really should give you this advice."

Confused by the man's constant swapping from an austere personality to an old man giving sweets to kids, Kaitlyn burst out with, "What do you mean? If that… humble jumble wasn't the advice, then what is?"

He scoffed at her. "Humble jumble! Never have I been so insulted—that will become useful to you!" Muttering *humble jumble* under his breath, he turned to face the river, his cane close enough to nearly touch the water's edge. "The advice, if you don't think it's *humble jumble*, is…" His hand beckoned her to his side. "When the time comes, the river will lead you *there*."

"Wait… I thought perspective and the… the alignment of four stars will lead me to the stone."

"You need to wash your ears out. I said *there,* not the stone!"

"Okay, okay, we're not talking about the stone anymore, we're talking about… 'there', whatever that is. But a river, really? How many rivers are there? Is it this one?" She pointed to the swirling currents below.

"So many questions, and all of them the wrong ones. I do not talk of a physical river, but the one within the sky…" He leaned inward, building up an invisible tension that annoyed Kaitlyn. "Eridanus. I told you you are not supposed to discover the stone. That is a job destined for another... but you have a greater purpose. You have to ask the most important question of all. Who's good and who's bad?"

Flashing back to Brandon describing himself as 'not the bad guy', she looked up at the night, seeking the constellations of which he spoke. "I know who's good and who's bad." It was weak and feeble—a lie she had been silently telling herself for a while now.

"Do you? An indestructible stone is a powerful thing. If it were used by someone with dark deeds in their heart, there would be no hope. So, I repeat my advice. The river will lead you *there*, to the answer you need, because that is your destiny... the destiny to protect the stone. And Kaitlyn?"

"Yes?"

"I'm so sorry."

Before she could ask what for, he was gone, and she was alone in darkness.

***

"Kaitlyn, are you awake?"

It took her a couple seconds to shake away the grogginess and realize she wasn't in a forest but in the camper, James standing above her. "Yeah... yeah, what's up?" They were squished in the back, Kaitlyn lying on a built-in sofa for a nap before they reached Owens Lake.

"We're here. Everyone's waiting..." He looked everywhere but at her, reminding her of the kiss they'd shared and the awkwardness it had created between them.

"Okay... I'll, um... I'll be out in a sec."

He nodded but didn't leave, probably not wanting to end the conversation in such a stiff atmosphere. "Pretty flowers. They're your favorite, aren't they?"

She followed his gaze, which was fixed upon a shelf above her head. On top lay a potted Chinese jasmine. "Yes," she answered, but he had already left.

Delicately, her hand went to touch a petal. The dream came back to her, but she did not question its reality. She already knew. Earlier in the day, there had been no flower.

Chapter 30

Who was good? Who was bad? Was anyone entirely good or entirely bad? Kaitlyn couldn't help thinking about Brandon. If you weren't bad, and you weren't good, what were you? Did everything have to fall into either category, and if so, who decided? Apparently, now it would be her. Constellations came to mind. Man-made. Were *good* and *bad* also man-made? And if they were, did that make them any less real?

She looked at her hand, at the slightly paler bit of skin where her wedding band used to be. She couldn't remember getting rid of it, and maybe she hadn't; a lot had happened, and she could have easily lost it at any time without noticing. Maybe it had even been taken from her at some point. She wanted to think *good riddance*, but now she didn't know what to feel.

She sighed, and maybe it was too obvious, because her father placed a hand on her shoulder. They walked through the forest with the rest of the group, heading for the mine. They had parked as close as they could, but there were just too many trees, so they had a long walk ahead. It felt strange, to walk the same paths again after all these years.

"About Brandon…" he said. He slowed his pace without letting go of her, so she slowed down with him. It wasn't long before the group left them behind. She could still see them up ahead, but no one could hear them. Or at least, that's what her father seemed to think, because he kept talking. "I had heard about your marriage, but I didn't know who your husband would be. I was even sorry I missed the wedding. Well, in a way, I still am. I mean, you only marry for the first time once, but… I would have done anything to stop it if I'd known, Katy. Anything."

She grabbed his hand on her shoulder and gave it a squeeze. "A lot of things would have been different if you'd been here. But we've been over this. You can only choose based on what you know. I'm sure it wasn't easy for you to stay away, so—and I know this is weird, but—even when it didn't work out, I'm sort of grateful you cared enough to stay away."

Maybe this is fate, she thought. Maybe, if the dream was anything to go by—and she was convinced it was—whatever anyone did wouldn't matter. In the end, she would always be pulled into this, one way or another.

What she was pulled into, for now, was a hug, but it was quick. At this distance, they had to move, or they'd lose the group. They still held on fiercely to each other's hands, though, as if trying to make up for all the time spent apart.

"You have no idea how much you remind me of your mother. She used to talk like that."

Kaitlyn smiled, but what she said next had little to do with her mother. Or so she thought. "So you knew Brandon from before." It wasn't a question, so she didn't make it one. She knew this for a fact, ever since Brandon and Mettinger had stormed into Thomas' house.

"Yes," Daniel said, then stayed silent for so much time she

feared he wasn't going to say anything else. Just before she asked, he went on. "He was… He was your uncle. Sort of."

"Sort of?" she asked, confused and a little horrified. She didn't even want to consider the things *that* would imply.

"Yes. Your mother's stepbrother."

The relief was so strong it was almost physical. "How come I've never met him?"

"You did, but you were little. He wasn't here much. According to your mother, he was obsessed with spy movies as a child, and it wasn't long before he started grabbing novels. Tom Clancy, Ian Fleming. All very Cold War-ish."

And he never tired of it, she wanted to say, but didn't. He had been the one to introduce her to James Bond, and they had made a tradition of watching two movies a week until he had run her through all twenty-six of them. She felt a knot form at her throat. With everything that had happened, she hadn't had time to truly face the fact that the man she had fallen in love with had never existed. She had loved him with a passion she couldn't describe.

But then James came to mind. James, who—miles away— had been such a constant presence in her life. What did she feel for James? It wasn't the same she had felt for Brandon, that was for sure. It wasn't that burning passion that swept her off her feet, but it was still strong, and steady, and warm. It was something made up of thousands of tales shared, of words exchanged, of secrets entrusted. He felt safe. He felt like home. If that wasn't love too, she didn't know what was.

Her father's voice snapped her out of it. "It eventually evolved into a fascination for Russia, so much so that he said he wanted to learn the language. Your grandparents decided to pay for lessons. He did very well—he had always been a smart kid, got the best grades in school. He did so well, he got an opportunity from the Embassy and spent his high school years in Russia, as an exchange student. He came back when he was seventeen. You were seven at the time."

Seven, she thought. *The year of the accident.* It also meant he was a decade older than her and not five years as he'd told her. He certainly didn't look it, but uncovering yet another lie made it hurt even more. Never existed, indeed.

Daniel went on with the tale. "He found out about the Black Coyote project through Jackie. She thought she could trust him, but he became obsessed. He kept insisting on all the good that could be done with such power and couldn't believe we weren't trying to get more information, to force the others to share what they had. We tried to explain how dangerous it was, but he wouldn't budge. He said the benefits would be worth the risks and that we were acting like cowards.

"He was only here for the summer, though. He had done so well, he got a scholarship for college and went back to Russia after a couple months. If we had only known. He was so good with his studies, he got a job at the US Embassy as an interpreter. But your mother never knew about that. She was long gone by then.

"He came here on some diplomatic trip or other, and I'm assuming that's how he met Mr. Bratva. The man makes no secret of his hobby, so Brandon could have approached him about the legend only to find he already knew about it and was doing exactly what Brandon thought needed to be done. So they joined forces. Mettinger was already alongside the Bratvas, but then, he always was money-hungry. Brandon started working with him, I guess because he knew how to track you through your aunt."

"Your sister," she whispered.

"Yes. Our families met once or twice for holidays. He was very young, so she probably didn't remember him, but he knew where to start looking better than Bratva's men, I guess."

"Even if she had remembered…" she said, a dark thought occurring to her.

"What?" asked Daniel.

"I'm just thinking. We never visited while we were dating. And I never called Brandon anything other than Brandon. She passed a week after he proposed, and we were married two weeks later." Were they still married? She supposed so. "I never got around to introducing them. So all she ever knew was I was dating this guy named Brandon. He sent out the wedding invitations, so he probably never sent hers, and you saw these people… Anyone could have gotten to her computer or her cell phone to send me a reply. Who the hell checks their sent emails?"

"You can delete those too," her father added. "The recipient still gets them, but you don't see them anymore."

"I didn't know that," she mumbled, and fell silent. She felt the tears stinging in her eyes, filling up, and finally starting to fall. She started sobbing. "She always called. Always called about the important stuff. She couldn't have found out I was getting married and just *emailed* me her congratulations. She just wasn't that type of person. How didn't I notice? I was so… blinded. By Brandon and the wedding and everything…"

Her father let go of her hand, and a second later, she felt him rubbing her back as they walked. "Katy… It's okay, you couldn't have known."

"But I should have," she sobbed.

"And I should have been here. If you could forgive me for that, you sure as hell can forgive yourself for being too kind. You're like Jackie, always thinking the best of people."

"I was stupid."

"You were good, sweetheart. Never regret being good. There's very little left of it in the world." He grabbed her hand again.

She wiped away her tears, starting to calm down. The rest of the group had stopped at the entrance of the mine, waiting for them to catch up.

She looked at her father and tried to smile. She was good, he'd said. He sounded so sure.

You have to ask the most important question of all—who's good and who's bad?

She didn't know how to answer. But as she approached the gaping maw of the cave, she knew she'd be all right. She met James' eyes.

Her father trusted her.

James seemed to trust her.

She looked around. Thomas, James, Chooli, Russ, Stacy, Lucas ... her father. Some of them she barely knew, but somehow, she felt she could trust them. If fate had brought her here, to this place, with these people, then so be it. She wasn't afraid. She had a mission, and though she still didn't fully understand it, she was certain that when the moment came, she'd know what she had to do. She wasn't alone.

She ran the last steps and offered James the hand her father wasn't clutching. He took it, and Bullet poked his nose at their hands and licked her fingers.

No, she wasn't alone.

Chapter 31

Vlad sat quietly as the woman dressed his burns with clean cotton t-shirts and tights. The consistent twitch of the woman's hands irritated him, and his eyes bored into her. A sparkle of water threatened to spill from her eyes any moment while she focused heavily on what she was doing, regularly stealing glances at her young kids. She worked hard not to look at him, trying to block out the man who had forced his way into her home.

The smell of burnt wood and paint seeped into the air. Vlad knew he was far too close to the situation and risked being caught by the police now swarming in the street. Even he couldn't talk his way out of an arson charge when he looked like he'd just taken a bath in the flames.

The woman's children sat quietly in the two designated

chairs against the kitchen wall. He had no intention of hurting anyone but knew he would have no choice if it came to that. He chose not to speak much. The little he did say, he forced an American accent so as not to startle his audience further. His phone had taken a bit of a beating, but he carefully lifted the cover, wincing in pain, and managed to send a text through to Victor that simply read, *potrachennyy*.

They had long ago agreed on a word that, when sent, meant so much more than either could say. He hated to admit it, but he needed Victor's help. He didn't want to look at the burn damage covering half his face. The pain was excruciating enough, along with the limited use of his arms and the certainty that he had just hobbled on a broken leg. They had both found themselves in dire need of help over the years, but through pride—or maybe stupidity—neither had succumbed to using it. If Victor thought less of him, he conceded it was nothing new. He might be in a tight spot, but he knew something he hoped no other living person knew except for that old bumbling fool Ronald. He knew how to find the missing corner piece of the map.

***

Victor loved his brother. They had grown up in a place where men hugged and expressed their feelings, then tumbled into a world of power and greed that consumed their sense of family. He truly cared for Vlad's safety, but his obsession with the Black Coyote project and everything he had learned since had instilled a drive in him like no other. He thought about what his mother would think of all this. She used to tell wild tales, stories passed down from generations before. He believed she would have encouraged him to see this through. If such forces truly existed, he knew he had to be part of them.

After receiving that text, Victor called a number he had hoped to never use. He was connected to a private security firm named Sentinel that used an advanced tracking system to locate Vlad. The company would send an elite squad to extract him from any situation, whether dead or alive. Only after they recovered Vlad would he be informed how bad it was.

"Thank you for your patience, Mr. Bratva," said the woman on the other end of the line. "We'll phone you back as soon as your brother is in our custody. Is there anything else we can help you with today?"

"You know what? Yes. I have a phone number here... one moment..." He dug through his pockets and pulled out Brandon and Payton's cell phones; he'd taken them from their corpses before abandoning the bodies at the storage unit. Scrolling through Brandon's contact list, he found Kaitlyn's number. "I need a trace put on the girl's phone. Daniel won't be letting her out of his sight, so where she goes, he will be nearby." After giving them her number, he absently scrolled through Payton's contacts as well and saw the number for Detective Logan. "One more thing. I have another number. That detective, she's meddling too close. I need to keep track of her as well. For good measure."

After the call ended, Victor found a quiet, twenty-four-hour coffee shop and ordered a double espresso. Without minding who watched, he tossed the coffee into a larger mug he had asked for and topped off the drink with vodka he pulled from his jacket. He received some funny looks but didn't care. He was glad it was late in the evening, making him slightly less crazy than he was sure everyone assumed.

His phone vibrated with activity. Taking a breath, Victor answered. Sentinel had used their own system to patch a call through to him. The voice was his brother's. Victor smiled, allowing his relief to show, knowing his brother would never see it.

"Glad to hear your voice, brother," Victor said.

"Glad to be able to speak." Vlad coughed, and Victor could hear the strain in his throat. "I have great news. It makes this little... incident... worth all the trouble. I know where to find the map piece Daniel is looking for."

As Vlad explained, Victor shot up from his chair, taking in

every distorted word coming from his brother's mouth.

As if his mother were shining down on him, Victor said his silent thanks to the incredible fortune of finding himself in the middle of the city where the other piece of the map was. His only plan so far had been to locate the group in hopes of intercepting them once they had the final puzzle piece. But now he knew he could get to it before they could.

He left the table without thinking to pay for his drink, hearing the insult thrown at him from a distance but not looking back. He could taste victory on his tongue and only partially hoped Vlad could be there with him when he held the paper in his hands.

He smirked into his phone while he searched out the right man for the job. After the struggle so far, he couldn't believe how easy it would be to get a section of the map from a bank safety deposit box. He silently thanked the owner's recklessness for leaving it there. Both Victor and his brother used to pull this stunt back in Russia; it was one of the easiest jobs to pull off. All they had to do was quietly intimidate the manager by having someone watch his family, then hound him until he gave up everything.

Victor considered distancing himself from this job. He knew things were getting a bit heated and didn't want to draw attention to himself, but he just couldn't trust anyone with the contents of the box.

It was well past two in the morning when all the arrangements were finally made, so he waited outside the bank until five o'clock, when a car pulled up in the still-dark parking lot. A thin man strode quickly from the car to the bank door and unlocked it, glancing around nervously before entering. After waiting a few minutes, Victor sauntered into the bank, brushing past an unruly potted yucca plant, and confidently strode toward the private banking section, his eyes meeting with Mr. Reynolds'. The man's pasty skin covered in a nervous glint of sweat gave him away before his mousy features. Victor had seen the pictures of Reynolds' grown daughter entering her home late last night with his grandchild. She was striking in comparison to the old man before him, drowning in a brown suit more fitting in the 90s. On another day, he may have kept her for himself, regardless of the outcome, but Victor had become enchanted by the map and the prophecies it held. He had never been more focused.

Proud and confident after leaving the bank, he drove by Daniel's storage unit, parking a quarter of a mile down the road. Flashing lights at the entrance revealed that the local cops had found the dead bodies in the unit. Daniel and the others must have called the cops when they left.

Sitting in his car, he examined the map piece in the fresh morning light as the sun breached the horizon, wondering if it held enough information for him to go on without Daniel's map. He traced his finger along a pair of thin, parallel lines that looked like a railroad through what appeared to be piles and walls of rock. The lines split in many places, but in a small dead-end of the rocky maze, a large X had been drawn and circled.

Looking for any other sign of the location, he noted two small, faint pictures in the bottom left corner, where the railroad tracks began. The pictures were of a pickaxe and a cart piled with more rock. The pieces clicked in his mind.

"It's a mine," he said aloud, laughing at the irony. He and Vlad had followed Daniel to a mine years ago, trailing him as he searched for the final map piece he had been missing. The odds of the map alluding to Owens Lake were low; no one would hide the map in the same mine it described. The page didn't reveal where the right mine was located, though, so he contemplated his next move.

As if on cue, his phone rang.

"Good evening, Mr. Bratva. It's Sonya, from Sentinel. We have the trace on those numbers for you."

"Good. Where are they?"

"Well…" She paused. He could hear the clacking of keys on a keyboard. "It seems both phones are in the same area, within fifty yards of each other, in southern California. The exact location is around a lake called—"

"Owens Lake," he finished for her.

"Why yes. How did you know?"

He chuckled to himself. Daniel must have thought the piece was still down there. "I'm going to send a message to them. Keep track of their location and let me know when they get close to Vallejo. Oh, and Sonya… get in touch with my father. Tell him the stone is in a mine. I don't know which mine yet, or where, but it can't be far."

She assured him she would pass on the information, then ended the call.

Feeling jovial, he drew a small smiley face on the back of the map piece before holding it up to snap a picture in front of the sign for the storage unit. It was a very distinctive shape, which Daniel would be sure to recognize. Satisfied with the picture, he sent it to the detective's phone.

He was pretty sure they wouldn't know it was him, but either way, it didn't matter. They would allow him to be a part of this whether they liked it or not.

***

Absentmindedly scratching Bullet behind his ear, Stacy reached for her phone while sitting outside the cave, waiting for the others. She was glad they hadn't insisted she go with them; the last thing she wanted to reveal was her fear of unknown, tiny, dark spaces. She had always managed to delegate tasks which needed a certain level of bravery she just didn't have, and in this instance, acting as a lookout was clearly a smart thing to do. Especially with the German Shepherd by her side.

She had turned her cell off long ago, deciding it was best to save the battery, not knowing how far they would wander away from civilization. They had walked for hours, watching the dark night sky slowly fade to a deep blue before splashes of pale blue broke through.

Stacy always loved mornings and searched the sky for the translucent moon set to go into hiding.

Without thinking, her fingers swiftly went through the motions. She was surprised by a beep informing her of seven missed calls and three messages. She hadn't expected to have reception this far out but marveled at how far technology had come in recent years. She doubted anyone missed carrying around a brick of a phone with a retractable antenna.

Stacy rubbed her temple. Her mind had been working overtime, trying to make sense of everything she had heard to date. She didn't think much of old tribal legends. She knew very little about Natives and could only think of feathers and tepees when imagining them. There seemed to be a lot of blind faith going around, and that didn't sit well with her. She wanted to believe this solstice would happen—that the planets would align with an almighty bang and make a slab of stone enchanted. But she just didn't see it. Maybe her work over the years had stripped away anything magical left in the world ... or maybe she was the only one not enthralled by this crazy talk.

She had always aspired to be like her father; she used to watch the way he stood at the mirror and shaved against the grain with such precision. He would joke to her that a patient person who acted with sense and precision could achieve anything. She'd thought about that the day she was sworn into service, and she wore her uniform with pride, knowing she would always follow the logical path to help her make sound decisions.

Nothing felt logical about this, and she longed to again see the father who had winked at her in the mirror. His aged face, now stripped of all its youth, seemed void of its sureness. He looked weathered and tired, like he was truly afraid of what was to come. Perhaps he was more afraid of what wouldn't come—perhaps his belief in this folktale gave him hope and expectation his work had since consumed.

And Kaitlyn. Stacy had come to care about Kaitlyn and even considered they might become close friends once all the drama was over, but she questioned whether or not she had allowed herself to become involved in this for all the right reasons. Trying to channel her thoughts, she shook her head to dislodge all the fragmented pieces driving her crazy, instead focusing on her phone.

The first message was from John, with a time stamp from the night before. They had been exchanging texts for a while now, ever since she gave up her number one night after much persistence at the bar. He only ever became flirty after a drink or two, but those messages always made her smile.

The next message was from an unknown number just an hour or so ago. It simply read, *"Stacy?"* Her arms prickled as a sensation buzzed through her. She felt like it could be important but at the same time nothing.

She clicked onto the last message, which had been sent just fifteen minutes prior to turning on her phone. The image caused a pull in her stomach; she clenched her teeth and sighed heavily. It wasn't just the fact that she now knew they had been wasting their time coming here in the first place—it was more the fact that another piece of the puzzle existed, threatening the fact that this whole far-fetched, ridiculous journey could hold some truth.

She studied the picture closely. It was a torn piece of paper, shaped like what could only be the map piece they were searching for. Whoever sent the message thought they were being hilarious by turning it over so she could see nothing. They had drawn a tiny smiley face right in the center, annoying her further. She studied the image more closely, looking at everything around the paper. The person had held it up to the light, causing the sun to block out most of the background. She closed her eyes before looking once more, and her gut was right. She could just make out the outline of a prominent building in the background with a star-shaped silhouette beside it. Relieved, she now knew the person who had it was in a city, nowhere near the rural area surrounding Owens Lake. It also became perfectly clear that whoever held that fragment of paper needed them as much as they needed the fragment. The person had just brought their stack of chips to the table and made it clear they wanted in this next round.

She yelled to the others, hoping someone would hear her so she wouldn't have to wait hours for them to return empty-handed.

Her voice echoed down a long walkway heading deep into the cave, followed by a sharp bark from Bullet. The thought of following them caused a stir of nausea she was not willing to entertain, so she instead chose to sit with the dog at her side and watch the sunrise, resting before the trek back.

"I'm just tired, okay?" Kaitlyn marched out of the cave, swinging her arms about like she was creating a protective space around herself. The early morning sun already created hot spots through the trees, and Kaitlyn raised her hands to cover her eyes.

"We'll find it, we just have to keep looking." James' words were not angry or impatient. He seemed to really care for Kaitlyn. His eyes also strained in the light, not leaving hers once.

"About that…"

Both Kaitlyn and James snapped their heads to look at Detective Stacy as she painstakingly stretched each limb.

"What?" James asked.

"You said we'll find it. We—we already have, kind of. It's not here, so can you go get the others so we can get the hell out of here before we all collapse from exhaustion?"

"Where is it, then?" James asked anxiously. He and Kaitlyn had stepped toward her, wearing expressions of such hope and expectation.

"It's in a city. Someone texted me to let me know they have it, so we've wasted our time here."

Kaitlyn sank to her knees and sobbed. Stacy didn't blame her; between exhaustion and stress and reuniting with both James and her father, she probably felt stretched in many different directions.

Shaking off her hazy indifference from an impromptu nap, she knelt beside Kaitlyn, holding her as she cried. Stacy knew it would be wrong of her to share all her doubts with the others. She was one of the strong ones, able to push through and get the job done. With just a few words, she managed to calm Kaitlyn and debrief the rest of the group as they filtered out of the cave, frustrated. No matter how she felt about all this, she knew she would be there by Kaitlyn's side when the ray of sunshine filtered its way onto the stone.

Chapter 32

Stacy helped Kaitlyn to her feet and stood with an arm around her shoulders, both for physical and moral support. She faced the others, who took the news that someone else already had the missing piece of map with varying degrees of anger and disgust.

"Are you absolutely sure about this, Stacy? Let me see that picture," Daniel said in a no-nonsense tone that gave the clear message he was in charge.

Stacy handed him her phone without further discussion. He looked at the image in the same way Stacy had, turning it this way and that in order to see what was on the other side.

Finally, he sighed and gave her back her phone. "You're right. Not only is it far from here, but that's my storage center. Wishing Star Storage. It's right back in Vallejo where we *just* left yesterday."

A chorus of gasps and grunts rolled through the group.

"I'd like to know who sent that message," Daniel continued. "Whoever it is, he needs the rest of the map, and we need his corner piece. Apparently, he's willing to negotiate. We can only assume he's not a friend, or he would have identified himself. We have to be very careful. It could be a setup or an ambush. We know that originally, Minerva, Mettinger, and Derrik had pieces. There are also the Bratva brothers through their association with Mettinger and Brandon. One or both of them could be waiting for us back in Vallejo."

Kaitlyn's head snapped up. "It takes seven hours to get to Vallejo. You were going to explain everything once you had your journal, but you didn't tell us much. What haven't you said?"

Daniel sighed again. "Everything concerning the Black Coyote is escalating the closer we get to the big event on December twenty-first."

"That's when the great stone is supposed to be created?"

"Yes, but I'll answer all your questions on the way back to Vallejo," Daniel said. The others were almost out of sight on their way back to the van.

"I'll hold you to it," Kaitlyn said. "There's so much I want to know. I only have spotty memories of my childhood before the car crash, which don't help much."

Daniel, Stacy, and Kaitlyn made their way across the desert to the camper, which everyone else had already boarded. Chooli once again sat in the driver's seat, with Bullet occupying his spot in the captain's chair. Kaitlyn climbed into the seat beside James, who had saved a spot for her. Lucas, Stacy, and Russ sat on a padded bench at the end of the table under the rear window. Daniel sat beside Thomas across the table from Kaitlyn and wearily laid his head and shoulders back on his seat. James reached under his own seat and pulled out a cooler. He handed out bottled water to everyone.

Kaitlyn leaned forward, her elbows on the table. "Dad…" Daniel sat up reluctantly. She saw how tired he was. "Never mind.

It can wait. We have time for some rest."

She pulled some small pillows out of a storage locker under her seat and handed them around. Daniel put his pillow on the table and slumped forward onto it. He was asleep in minutes. Kaitlyn put her pillow up against James' chest and snuggled in.

***

James put his arm around Kaitlyn's shoulders, leaned his head against hers, and closed his eyes. This wasn't exactly how he hoped to sleep with the woman he loved so much, but he was willing to wait. He just hoped they both survived until that eventually happened.

After three hours on the road, Chooli pulled into a rest stop along the highway with a fast food restaurant, gas pumps, and restrooms. He parked the vehicle and got out to stretch. Sliding open the side door, he yelled inside.

"Get up, you lazy reprobates. Up and at 'em. We're going to take a little time-out. The camper needs fuel, and so do I. Russ, you're now the designated driver for the rest of the trip."

Chooli tossed the keys to his friend, who was half asleep and missed them entirely. Chooli laughed at Russ' cursing while he crawled around under the table to retrieve them.

James' entire right arm was numb where Kaitlyn had slept on it, but he didn't care. He had managed to sleep anyway with her in his arms.

***

The group spent an hour at the rest stop, filling up the van and their bellies. Just as they filed out of the restaurant, Daniel's phone chimed one short, loud ding. He scanned the screen, his brow drawing further and further down with each passing second.

"Dad?" Kaitlyn asked, concerned. Everyone turned to look at him.

Daniel shook his head and put his phone back in his pocket. "It was a text from an old friend. There's been an incident with the Russians. Or at least one of them." He glanced around. A few other restaurant patrons walked across the parking lot nearby. "I'll explain when we're back on the road."

When they were a few miles down the highway, Kaitlyn broached the subject of the Black Coyote project again. "Okay, so what was that text about? And while you're at it... you didn't explain why there seems to be more than one map floating around, and why a bunch of people are willing to kill to get their hands on enough pieces to find the stone. This whole project has been strictly hush-hush, but there seem to be a lot of people who know about it. Not to mention my own husband was willing to kidnap me and let Mettinger torture me to get information I didn't even have."

"I've known Mettinger for decades. He's one of the six people initially involved in this." Daniel went on to tell her everything he remembered from the meeting in 1983 that established him and Jackie as some of the key players. When he finished, Kaitlyn still had even questions.

"The Black Coyote project is a codename, right? What does it mean?"

"I don't know, honey. I never did," Daniel admitted.

"I know what it means." Reluctantly, Thomas spoke up. "The Black Coyote is me. I was charged with protecting the project." He then explained how he ended up with copies of all the letters.

Daniel's face flushed with anger, but he took a deep breath and managed not to yell at his friend. "Why didn't you tell me, Thomas? Does this mean you have copies of all the map pieces?"

Stacy's phone rang just then. She took the call, mouthing 'It's the station,' and moved from the group slightly. Thomas continued, answering Daniel's questions.

"I was sworn to secrecy, same as you, Daniel. I just have the letters. Each person had their own piece of the map. No one had a complete copy, not even me. You've worked so hard to assemble the full thing. You're only missing the corner now, and that's back at the storage unit with whoever sent Stacy that text. I couldn't tell you. To me, it was a sacred trust. It still is, but I recognize the need to tell those who are already deeply involved just what's going on. Their lives are in danger. They need to know why, and they need to know what's at stake too. When the time comes, everyone in this camper will be part of the legendary stone's creation—if we can find it, that is."

"I've been keeping an eye out for the three events," Daniel said. "This is the year they're all happening, so I've been on alert and watching over everyone. My own predecessor in the project is a man named Ronald Dwyer. We've been keeping in touch. He'd been friends with Derrik's grandfather, Stanley Myers, for years. They had researched the legend together, against their own predecessors' warnings not to speak to each other. That's why Derrik was chosen to become part of it all, because he already knew some of it from Stanley's journal.

"When it came time for them to pass down their secrets to the next generation... to us... they panicked and split their information apart again, swearing to suddenly follow the rules and protect the stone. But Stanley made a copy of his journal before he died and gave that copy to Ronald for safe keeping. All except the map piece. That, he said, he hid. Ronald said years ago that, in a passing comment, Stanley mentioned 'giving the map to Owen to keep with the rest of his dried-up silver.' Which is why we thought his piece was in the mine.

"Anyway, Ronald was the one who texted me back at the restaurant. One of the Russians was just at his house looking for the journal with Mettinger and Minerva, who are now both dead. He doesn't know what happened to the Russian, just that he was trapped in the attic when the house caught fire from a kerosene lamp."

Stacy broke in. "Speaking of panicking... I just got a call from the desk sergeant at our precinct in Cannon Beach. Your phone was found at the diner, Dad, and they can't reach you, so they called me. There's been a rash of unsolved murders here in the Pacific Midwest, and it's just a hunch, but I think they're all involved with the Black Coyote project in some way. The fire was mentioned, with a man and a woman found dead, but not a Russian, so he's probably alive somewhere. Derrik Myers' poisoned body was found in a hotel suite in Seattle. There were a few others that stood out, possibly collateral damage. Daniel, I have some very sad news for you. Your lawyer, Hugh McGraff, was found dead in his condo. Brandon was killed with Russian-made bullets in the storage unit in Vallejo. I'm sorry for your loss, Kaitlyn. I know you loved him once."

Kaitlyn sighed. She no longer loved him after all he had done to her, but she was sorry he was dead. "The Bratva brothers killed him, then," she said.

"Probably, and Detective Payton as well. He was found in the same storage unit. He was mixed up with the Russians too, apparently." Stacey shook her head. "I knew there was something off with him, but he didn't deserve to be murdered."

"That narrows things down as to who's probably waiting for us in Vallejo. Only Victor and Vlad are unaccounted for, assuming Vlad is still alive after the fire," Daniel commented.

After a moment of silence, everyone contemplating the new turn of events, James shook his head. "I don't understand, Grandpa. Why were all these people selected as guardians of the map when they did nothing but fight for the stone, taking every opportunity to kill each other?"

Thomas sighed. "Greed is a funny thing, *Ganodo*, as is curiosity. Both took over when we began to realize that the prophecy would come to fruition during our lifetimes. I don't think any of us could have foreseen that our lifetimes would be cut short because of it."

Another moment of silence followed, this one somber at the notion of death. Kaitlyn spoke up, steering the topic to something less dreadful. "I had a strange dream on the way to Owens Lake, Dad. It had a lot to do with your poem, and some other puzzles I don't know what to make of. I think it was meant to help me find this mysterious stone we're all looking for. I supposedly already know where it is, but I don't—not that I remember, anyway. Everything before I was seven is pretty blurry. Any way you can tell me what that poem's about?"

"That poem is only half mine. Parts of it were from me, and parts were riddles found in my letter. What was the dream?" Daniel asked.

Kaitlyn didn't think she would remember much of it, but as she talked, she discovered that she remembered it in minute detail. While she spoke, Thomas leaned forward and listened intently as soon as she mentioned the elderly Native American man.

"I wonder what river he's talking about," he mused. "Would you dig out that constellation map, please?"

Kaitlyn produced the constellation map and spread it out on the table, where everyone examined it, trying to make sense of it all. She took a red marker from her purse and traced the river constellation Eridanus with it. It grew into a game of connect-the-dots as they tried to line up four stars. Vallejo, California, was getting closer, and they still had no good idea how to find the stone.

Chapter 33

Victor counted roughly how many people he'd be up against and realized he needed to be prepared for anything. This job had seen so many twists and turns, he felt he needed to bring something more sizable to the inevitable final confrontation than a fine three-piece suit and a pistol with a few spare magazines. He had endured harder jobs with less gear in the past, but now he found himself in a position to avoid such a calamity should things go bad. He was not in the mood to take any chances, especially without Vladimir at his side.

He drove just out of town, about ten miles into the wide-open country, to an abandoned old aircraft hangar. It looked like it might have been a small local airport for crop dusters at one point, but the cobwebs and broken windows told him it had been out of commission for years.

As he cut the lock on the rolling door, Victor tried to remember the last time he'd been on an assignment without his brother. He could not come up with a single mental image of a time in his adult life he'd had to do something professionally without Vladimir.

The lights came on in the hangar as Victor stepped inside. He downed the last sip of his beverage, then let the paper cup fall to the floor. He kicked it aside with the toe of his finely polished, black leather shoe. He had not been inside the structure since he and Vlad had set it up upon arriving in Vallejo. The abandoned hangar was just the sort of place the brothers liked to use to establish as a safe house. Somewhere out of the way but accessible and—most of all—forgotten by the rest of the world. The Russian looked over the stockpile of tactical assets he and his brother had brought into the facility. Nothing had been disturbed as far as he could tell.

He quickly made his way to the small administrative office near the hangar's entrance. Slipping through the cracked glass door with peeling vinyl lettering, he went to the main desk at the far end of the cramped room. He moved the wobbly rolling chair away from the desk with such force it tipped over and skidded across the floor before stopping by the rear wall. Opening the largest of the three desk drawers, he pulled the squeaky drawer all the way out until it could move no farther.

Victor looked down at the assortment of colored wires, timer, and other contraptions attached to the blocks of plastic explosives inside the drawer. The digital timer—which had been going since Victor entered the hangar and tripped the alarm—displayed just under two minutes left. He stabbed at the keypad on the bomb with his index finger. After he entered in the five-digit code, the timer on the bomb stopped counting down. Victor gave a confident sigh and slicked back his hair before closing the desk drawer again.

Then he left the office and immediately stripped off his clothes. His jacket, shirt, and tie formed a crumpled trail as he moved to the bank of lockers near the office. Bare to the waist, he had kicked off his shoes by the time he opened the standup compartments where he had stored a change of clothes and some sturdy, steel-toed combat boots. While the clothes inside the locker were highly utilitarian and military in nature, they could still pass for civilian garb as long as nobody highly scrutinized him. Even the body armor was of slim design, and Victor could wear it underneath his new shirt. It only took a few moments to make the total transformation from sophisticated world traveler in a custom suit to a killer for hire in Kevlar. The clothes he wore now were heavier and not as soft as the denser labels in which he had just been outfitted, but they managed to offer him a sense of comfort. While his body no longer enjoyed the blissful touch of hand-tailored threads, Victor felt like what he wore now was an honest representation of who he really was.

He then set about loading up the black armored SUV with all manner of field equipment. He made his way to the hangar's cage, where compressed air and gas cylinders had once been stored. Victor and Vlad had repurposed the cage to serve as a small armory. He checked and loaded a couple larger assault weapons and a few small arms. He stowed most of the weapons and ammunition in a large black duffle bag and added a few small explosives before zipping up the bag and lugging it over to the SUV. At this point, he was confident he had everything he could possibly need for what was going to come next.

With the car packed and his clothes changed, he glanced at his watch. If the group had been at Owens Lake, he had at least five or six more hours before they'd be near Vallejo. As he stood in the center of the empty hangar with nothing more to do at that moment, his exhaustion caught up with him. He opened the door to his sedan, crawled into the back seat—lying out across the bench with his feet propped up in the open window—and fell into a much-needed sleep.

He awoke nearly six hours later to the ringing of the alarm he had set on his phone. Stretching widely, he took note of the mid-afternoon sun coming in through the broken windows lining the top of the walls. They should be getting close.

As Victor slid into the driver's seat of the armored vehicle, he felt his phone go off once more, this time from a call. He wondered if Sonya were calling him back already. He was pleasantly surprised to see it was his brother instead. Victor accepted the call. "Vlad," he said.

"Victor," came his brother's labored voice.

"What is going on? Are you safe?"

"Yes, I am well enough to move. Father has people coming to collect me and bring me home," Vlad said with an uncharacteristically comforting tone.

"That is good. I will see you soon. I am almost done here. I nearly have everything we were sent for," Victor responded, a measure of strength and confidence in his words.

"Are you at the hangar?"

"Yes."

"Good. Father is sending some of his men to aid Sentinel in helping you finish this."

Victor took a moment to process the information. He was not offended that his father had sent additional men. It was not a sign of lack of confidence so much as peace of mind due to the stakes being so high. He tried to think of something sentimental to say before ending the call, but his mind was empty of anything beyond the task at hand. "I will see you when I get home," he added in an attempt to be brotherly.

Before he ended the call, Vlad said, "Father has one last instruction for you."

"What is it?"

There was a lengthy pause. "He says to kill them all. I will see you soon, brother."

Victor put his phone away and turned the key in the ignition. He drove out of the hangar and did not look back. He was ready to be done with this job.

Within half an hour, he pulled up to the small café across the street from Wishing Star Storage. When the others arrived in Vallejo, that was where they would come. The police cars and ambulances had all left the storage unit, though yellow crime tape had been woven across the business' entrance. It wouldn't matter. They didn't need to enter the unit to hand over Daniel's journal, and he could shoot them just as easily outside the unit as he could anywhere else. He ordered a cup of coffee and made himself comfortable, smugly complimenting himself on his clever scheme.

Chapter 34

The camper sputtered to a stop a few yards before the "Welcome to Vallejo" sign. The crew piled out just as a mighty bang rang out from the engine. Thick, noxious fumes surged from under the hood.

Russ grabbed a pair of gloves from the back and propped open the hood. After a minute, he returned to the group, soot-soaked and disheartened. "It's not an easy fix. We should probably just get another vehicle."

Detective Logan pulled out her cell phone the fastest. "No bars," she said. "Anyone getting a better signal?"

The other three with phones shook their heads. Kaitlyn felt her pockets and discovered that, along with her wedding ring, her cell phone had also been misplaced at some point over the last few days.

"We're not that far out of Vallejo," said Chooli. "Russ and I will hike it, rent a van, and come back for you."

"Who's going to lease you a van at this hour on a Sunday?" asked Detective Logan. "We'd have better luck trying to flag someone down."

"And I suppose some nice, kind, non-murdering soul is going to pull over for us in the middle of nowhere?" said Russ, accepting a high-five from Chooli.

"We don't have time to waste," said Thomas. "We'll do both plans. Wake me up when something pans out." And with that he retreated inside the still-smoldering camper.

Chooli, Russ, and Lucas took off at a brisk pace westward toward Vallejo. Detective Logan clambered up to the roof of the camper to wave the emergency lights at any distant traveler, whether a weekend warrior returning home or a random helicopter eager to lend a hand.

Daniel took one look at his daughter and the young man holding her hand and announced he'd bide his time inside the camper with Thomas.

"Don't wander off too far, you two," he warned. "Or we'll leave without you."

"We'll stay close, sir," James said, then flushed. He looked as nervous as a prom date shaking his future father-in-law's hand for the first time. "She's safe with me," he called after Daniel.

The door of the camper creaked and snapped shut.

"Don't you think we should be helping in some way?" asked Kaitlyn.

"I don't think anyone could find someone to help better than Detective Logan up there." James and Kaitlyn shared a smile at Stacy sweeping the flashing emergency lights back and forth in a psychedelic arc over her head.

"Stacy, let me know if you want a break," Kaitlyn called up to her.

"I'm good," she called down, not wavering in her waving. "You two love birds take a walk or something."

Kaitlyn nearly protested but realized a bit of time with just James was exactly what she needed right now.

She'd thought her life was set. She had a job she was satisfied with, fun and caring coworkers, and what she thought was a kind and loving husband. She had a different life now with a father and a destiny to protect the stone. She had James.

James took her hand and led her away from the road. The hardened sand crumbled under their shoes. At times, they stretched their arms so they could keep holding hands and let a patch of tall brush pass between them.

"How come you never came to visit before?" Kaitlyn asked. It was a mean question of sorts, but her mind berated her with every manner of *what ifs*. What if she'd seen through Brandon? What if her father had taken her into hiding with him and told her bedtime stories about the Black Coyote project? What if James had swept into her life a year ago and not after everything fell apart?

"How come you never visited *me*?" he said jokingly, but there remained a darkness in his gaze—a small betrayal he seemed to want to hide.

The silence grew between them like a storm cloud of missed chances.

"My mom dying was bad," said Kaitlyn. James stumbled beside her in the sand but said nothing. "What's the tally up to now? Four of the six from the Black Coyote project, my husband, Detective Logan's partner, and who knows who else. Should I be checking up on my landlord, my boss, Maya? What stone could possibly be worth all this death?"

James caught Kaitlyn in his arms, and she relaxed. She sounded calm and even, surprised by her ability to almost completely hide all the rage beneath her words.

"It's no one's fault but the Bratvas."

Kaitlyn pulled away from him. "Isn't it our fault too?"

James stuck his hands in his pockets. "What do you mean?"

"This so-called magic stone isn't worth any of our time, let alone our lives. We should just burn our part of the map and walk away. Then all of this would just stop."

"But we've come so far," said James. "Don't you want to know what the stone can do?"

"Magic isn't real, James," said Kaitlyn. Her words echoed in her head. Through all this chaos and death, the light at the end of the tunnel had been a magic stone she had been chosen to protect. But she'd gone the last decade believing magic didn't exist, and that belief came rushing back, absolving her of any special duty or hope.

"Yes it is," he said.

Kaitlyn let out a stiff laugh and tears welled in her eyes. "No it's not."

James took a step closer and pressed his lips against her forehead. She let out a sob and clutched his torso tight, burying her face in his t-shirt. He kissed the top of her head, too. "Do you remember how I found you and rescued you from Brandon and Mettinger?"

"I'll never forget," said Kaitlyn, letting his warmth sink into her.

"That dream told me you were in danger. It led me to Detective Logan, who helped me get you out."

"Those are just dreams and coincidences," said Kaitlyn, though she was already beginning to believe again. "If magic is real, why doesn't anything magical ever happen?"

James lifted her chin and kissed her warmly. She felt her doubts and fears fall away as she melted into him.

The sun began its slow descent into early evening.

"We should get back to the others," said James.

"Yeah," said Kaitlyn. "Stacy's bound to need a break by now."

Hand in hand, they walked back to where the trailer ought to have been, only to find Detective Stacy Logan seething and slumped on the side of the road, flicking the emergency lights between rapid flash and SOS.

"What happened?" asked Kaitlyn.

"You tell me," said Stacy. "It was your father and grandfather in there."

"Take a breath," said James. "What exactly happened?"

"I was coming off the roof to get a drink of water, and Daniel and Thomas drove off with the camper!"

"Are you sure no one snuck into the camper first?" asked Kaitlyn.

"I'm a detective, kid. I would have noticed a break-and-enter right under my feet. Besides, Bullet never barked once."

"My dad wouldn't leave me behind," said Kaitlyn. The tears prepared to fall again.

"Sure," said Stacy. "Because he's never left you behind before."

"Look," interrupted James. "We don't know who or what happened to the camper. Last we knew, it wasn't even functional. All we can do right now is walk toward town."

They had trekked along for about five minutes when a white two-door sedan puttered by at ten under the limit. Stacy charged after it, brandishing her emergency lights.

"Ma'am, my name is Detective Logan." She flashed her badge. "My associates and I require a ride back into town."

"Oh my," said the magenta-clad businesswoman. "Well, hop in. It'll be a tight squeeze, but we'll get you sorted out in no time."

Kaitlyn lasted an entire five minutes of blues and country radio before her mood fell to pieces. She didn't dare ask their rescuer, Ms. Petridge, to change the channel, but the hope James had instilled in her was farther out the window with each verse about a truck.

"Can you take us to the nearest gas station or car rental, please?"

"Of course," the woman replied.

A gas station came up on the right after a few minutes, and for once, luck seemed to be on their side. Stacy pointed toward the small convenience store's entrance, where her father stood leaning against the wall, a soda in one hand and a plastic bag in the other. They slowed to a stop, and the three climbed out, waving ahead and calling to Lucas.

Stacy leaned down and looked through the open car window. "Thank you very much, Ms. Petridge." As the car drove off, she turned back to join the others.

Chapter 35

"Where does Russ think we're meeting him? I mean, where did you tell him to go?" Daniel asked.

Lost in thought, Thomas stared out the window of the camper, watching the bright afternoon sunlight bathe the landscape in golden yellow.

"Thomas!"

Thomas sucked in a breath and shook the distraction from his head. "Why does it matter?"

"Because I want to be sure to stay far away from wherever it is."

"But it's all right by you that he's still close to Kaitlyn and *Ganodo*? And Victor?"

"He was closer before!"

The camper swerved slightly toward the outer edge of the highway, the passenger-side tires rolling across the rumble strip once, then again as Daniel corrected his error. Thomas watched his old friend take a deep breath to calm himself.

"Well, wherever you told him to go, my plan got him away from them, at least for now. They'll get the message we left." Daniel nodded once with vigor, as if trying to convince himself. Still, something wild and broken stayed in his gaze.

Thomas glanced out the windshield at the thin trails of smoke still rising from the hood of the vehicle. "Vegetable oil," he said, shaking his head.

"On the exhaust manifold. And a little bit of clanking around on Russ' part. No one thought to question his word that it couldn't be fixed." A self-satisfied smile spread across Daniel's face.

"Yes, but how did you get him to agree to splitting up? How did you get him to believe that once he led the others to the gas station and abandoned them, we'd actually meet him?"

"He thinks he has something we need. The necklace."

"Kaitlyn's necklace? With the emeralds and the shark tooth?" Thomas let out a dry laugh. "He thinks *that's* the key to understanding the map and the chart?"

"It's plausible." Thomas admitted to himself that it was, but said nothing to encourage Daniel. "And," Daniel added, "when we don't show up to get him, without knowing where the others are, he'll have no choice but to go to the storage unit. With any luck, he and Victor will take care of each other."

"Russell was a good man once," Thomas said, anger boiling up in his throat. "We were all good once. Now, I don't know what we are."

"Yes, you do."

"I don't," Thomas insisted. "Russ is not the first person to be changed by the hunt for the stone. He's not the first one to become greedy and want it for himself. *I've* felt that lust before." Thomas cleared his throat and calmed the pounding of his heart so he could speak reasonably. "And instead of helping him overcome

260

it, we're sending him to the Russian. And it's naïve to think he'll take Victor with him. We've simply sentenced him to death."

"Yes, Thomas," Daniel said, narrowed eyes never straying from the road ahead. "For Kaitlyn? I would sacrifice a hundred men. Wouldn't you do the same for James?"

"It's not what they would want, Daniel. They're adults and good people. They would never agree to such a trade of their lives for another's."

"Maybe not," Daniel said. "That's why we didn't give them the opportunity to say no." He reached over and turned the dial on the radio. Voices blared from the speakers, growing louder until it was clear there would be no further conversation.

After a few minutes of driving away from the main streets of Vallejo, Daniel pulled over and turned off the engine. He went to the little pull-out table in the middle of the camper and spread the map across it, with the constellation chart on top of that. He double-checked each edge of the documents to ensure they matched up exactly. Satisfied, he reached into his jeans pocket and pulled out a shiny gold object.

Thomas lowered himself into a seat and looked up at Daniel. "Do you think Brandon actually cared for Kaitlyn?" he asked.

"No."

Thomas raised his brows as Daniel turned the object over and over between his fingers. "You don't think he intended to solve this mystery with her at his side?"

"No."

"Strange, then, that he put the key to deciphering the map around her finger." Thomas watched Daniel hold Kaitlyn's wedding ring above the star chart and click on a flashlight. He shone the light down through the stones on the ring, and four spots of light appeared on the map. He experimented with raising and lowering the ring until the points of light matched up to four stars in the Eridanus constellation.

"Get a pen," Daniel said.

With excitement and apprehension, they soon had the

information they needed. They took a fifteen-minute drive, cutting across Vallejo, then two right turns and one left. A few miles later, the camper pulled onto a wide gravel road that looked like it hadn't been serviced in quite some time. Daniel slowed down as he avoided potholes and large rocks in the road over the next two miles before pulling into a small convenience store parking lot and turning off the engine.

As he opened his door, he looked at Thomas. "I'm going to grab something to drink and hit the restroom. Want anything?"

"No, thank you. I'm going to rest for a few minutes."

Once Daniel had shut the camper door, Thomas stood and made his way back through the vehicle and into the sleeping area. He shut the door behind him and settled down onto the bed. Pulling a cell phone from his shirt pocket, he touched the screen. Kaitlyn and Brandon smiled from the background, an apparently happy couple laughing on their honeymoon.

Too many people had died for these stones—too many lives had been ruined. Kaitlyn and James might still have a chance at happiness. The detective and the police chief might still be able to go home as a family. But not if Daniel's plan somehow went wrong. He couldn't trust that Russ and Victor would leave the others alone. He couldn't trust that they would find the message or that nothing would happen to it before they reached it. He needed to make sure they got out of Vallejo.

The screen on the phone had darkened as he'd contemplated. He brushed his finger across it again and set about figuring out Kaitlyn's lock code.

***

Victor's phone rang just as he ordered another cup of coffee.

"Victor? It's Sonya again, from Sentinel," came the unmistakable voice of the Bratvas' contact.

"Yes? What do you have for me?"

"You asked for an update when the phones we tracked got closer to Vallejo."

"Excellent. Where are they?"

"Both phones are registering along the city limits, but they're no longer in the same location together."

Victor sat up straighter. The group had split up. Why?

"The detective's phone is showing up at a gas station just inside the county line to the east, along the main road. The girl's phone, however, is currently stationary at a convenience store approximately four miles northeast of town. It's along a little-used road that barely shows up on a map, and it comes to a dead-end at the Hastings Mine. We suspect they're headed there, as you said you were looking for a mine. I've taken the liberty of dispatching your father's men to secure the area. They're seven minutes out. I'll message you the precise location of the mine site."

"And Vladimir?"

"He's been collected and is safely on his way to Russia. I think we're finished, unless you need something else," Sonya said with a strangely alluring inflection.

"No, we are done. Thank you," Victor said flatly and ended the call.

He checked the GPS function on his phone and saw the new information had just been sent to him by Sentinel. He trusted that his father's men would apprehend the group when they secured the mine, and if he left now, he wouldn't be far behind.

"Damnit," he cursed into his coffee. He ignored the looks of disapproval from the next table over at the café. Daniel must have figured out how to find the stone without the piece Victor had obtained. On second thought, he mused, this saved him time. He knew his way through the mine thanks to the piece of map he had, and Daniel had inadvertently led him to the correct mine. He smiled. "Thank you, Daniel," he said aloud as he threw down the money for his order along with a generous tip.

Without waiting for his second cup of coffee to be brought to him, he left the café, speeding ten over the limit in a race to the mine. It was almost over.

***

Russ pulled the stolen Impala onto the road behind the black sedan and followed it at a safe distance. He had been watching Victor at the café for a few minutes now, ever since hearing him say "Vladimir" with his strong Russian accent. When he had said Daniel's name, it confirmed that he could only be Victor, the other Bratva brother.

Russ had originally planned on meeting Daniel at the storage unit, but when the Russian sped off like a reckless bat out of hell, he knew he had to follow him. A man didn't drive like that unless he had a purpose, and only one thing fueled everyone's thoughts these days—the stone.

***

In another time and place, Kaitlyn might have found the standoff between father and daughter amusing. Lucas Logan met his daughter's glare as she stood with fists on her hips, lecturing him about leaving a man behind.

"We have a ride waiting for us now, Stacy," he said. "How many more vehicles with seating for five do you think will show up here?" He gestured back toward the white van. Painted on the side was a church's logo with a cross and a red sunrise. The driver stood pleasantly beside the vehicle with her hands folded behind her as she looked off into the distance, pretending not to hear the argument.

"He's right. We should go," James agreed. His arm brushed against Kaitlyn's as he pointed at Chooli, who had been eerily quiet throughout the drama. "You don't think he's coming back, do you?"

Chooli shook his head and scuffed his boot angrily against the pavement.

When the first group had arrived at the gas station, Lucas had stepped inside to check a phonebook and use their landline, hoping to contact a cab company or a rental place that would drop off a car. Russ had gotten the key for the restroom, and Chooli had wandered off to a bush to relieve himself. When he came back, Lucas was still on the phone, and the door to the restroom was still locked.

Eventually, they'd gotten worried about Russ and knocked and called out to him. They got the station attendant to bring the spare key and discovered that Russ was gone. When Kaitlyn and the others had arrived fifteen minutes later, Chooli had been calling Russ' cell to no avail. Nearly half an hour had gone by, and Lucas still hadn't had any luck finding transport for eight people and a dog and held little hope of securing it for five—until the church van had pulled in to fuel up. The driver was traveling into Vallejo to pick up a musical group and was happy to drive them as far as her church, which was only a mile or two from the storage unit, according to the van's GPS.

They all piled into the van, grateful to sit for a while even if the music of a bell choir pouring from the van's speakers and the cheerful conversation of the driver grated on their nerves. Kaitlyn felt James' eyes on her and gave him a smile. He sat across from her, giving her space, which she desperately needed at the moment. Why had her father left without her?

She stared out the window as the lines of the rhyme Daniel had written rolled through her brain again.

Take a breath and take a pause.
When the earth and sky align,
There you'll find this secret of 'mine.'

The van slowed, and Kaitlyn blinked, craning to see out the window. Up ahead, a car had pulled to the side of the road, emergency flashers on. The driver approached a road construction sign in the ditch, weighted down with a sand bag. Tied to the sign was a German Shepherd.

"James!" Kaitlyn screeched. "It's Bullet!" Reaching for her seatbelt, she stood, calling, "Stop the car!" She leaped from the vehicle before it had come to a complete stop, her heart fluttering. She looked around frantically for any sign of the camper— wrecked or intact. James jogged past her, calling out to the driver, claiming Bullet as his. The dog's enthusiastic reaction was proof enough, and the man climbed back into his car.

As James freed Bullet, he pulled something from his collar—an envelope attached with string.

"It's addressed to you," James said, holding it out to her as Bullet's paws slammed into his chest. "From your father."

Kaitlyn's hands shook as she ripped open the envelope and unfolded the letter within.

Katy,

I love you so much. I've made a lot of mistakes, but these past few days—seeing what a wonderful woman you've become— have shown me one thing... I won't be making the mistake of endangering you any further.

Protecting the stone is no longer your burden to bear. I'll take care of it.

Stay away from Russ! Stay away from the storage unit!

Tell Lucas and Stacy to disappear for a while. And then, you and James need to disappear too. Start a new life and never think of the project again.

I'm so sorry.

Love always,
Dad

A tear dripped onto the page. Kaitlyn re-read the letter, only vaguely aware of the commotion around her. Stacy asked her what was wrong. Lucas and Chooli talked to the van driver, begging her to allow Bullet to ride with them, and James' phone beeped.

After the third read-through, she passed the letter wordlessly to Stacy and looked up to see James holding his phone out to her.

"I just got a text message from *you*," he said.

Kaitlyn wiped the tears away from her cheeks. "No, I, uh... I lost my phone." She frowned and reached out to take the cell. James stepped in close to look over her shoulder as she read the message.

'I pray you found Bullet and the letter. Stay away from Russ. Stay away from the storage unit. We have all we need. It's best if you stay out of this. I love you. Thomas.'

The others had approached and encircled James and Kaitlyn as they read, so she read the text aloud for everyone to hear. Chooli snatched the phone from her hand, and she gasped. James followed Chooli, demanding the phone back.

"The letter from Daniel said the same thing," Stacy told her father. "It said we need to disappear for a while and stay safe while they deal with the stone."

James returned, phone in hand, though Chooli took to kicking at the sandbag on the sign and cursing Russ. "We have to stop them."

"They're going after Victor on their own," Lucas said.

"No, they're not. They said they have all they need," Stacy pointed out. She paced along the ditch. "I saw Thomas pocketing something when they left the mine, but I didn't think anything of it. They must know how to find the stone."

"So they're going after the stone," Kaitlyn piped up. "That's not much better."

"We should go to the storage unit." Chooli returned to the group, his face flushed. "If we find Victor or Russ..." He paused as a shudder of anger passed over him. "We might be able to figure out where they went or how they're reading the map."

"No," James said. "That's too dangerous. They both said so." He shot Kaitlyn a look that was both protective and resigned.

Kaitlyn knew he could read the determination on her face. She'd been told it was her destiny to protect the stone, and whether or not she believed in such things, she did believe it was her responsibility to protect her father.

"We should call them." James' voice had lowered, as if he were speaking only to her, oblivious to the others around them. "I can convince my grandfather that—"

"No," Stacy interrupted. "If they even bother to answer, they'll lie. They clearly want you to run—to be safe. And as much as I want to know what's at the end of this mystery… running is starting to sound like a sane plan." Stacy glanced at her father, then shot Kaitlyn a pleading look.

Everyone stared at Kaitlyn, and the air seemed to thicken. It was hard to draw breath with the weight of such a decision on her chest. She turned away and stared at the city of Vallejo, so near now, and the mountains beyond.

Take a breath and take a pause.
When the earth and sky align,
There you'll find this secret of 'mine.'

"It *is* a mine," she mumbled.

"What?" Stacy asked.

"It has to be a mine." She turned back to the others. "The poem. The earth and sky aligning—that's however you read the map with the constellation chart. But 'this secret of mine.' It's a mine. That's where the stone is."

Stacy shook her head, a defeated expression on her weary face. "Then why come back here?" she asked. "We were at the silver mine. If they knew the stone was there, would they really drive all the way back here just to ditch us? Plus, they dumped Bullet *here*." She gestured around them. "They headed this way, and I doubt we missed them if they turned back toward Owens Lake."

"But that isn't the only mine in the state," Lucas said. "There's the old Hastings Mine and St. John's Mine. Both are within"—he shrugged—"maybe fifteen miles of Vallejo."

"How will we know which one, though?" Chooli asked. The group was quiet for a moment as they considered.

"Two old men in an abandoned mine," James said. He knelt and stroked Bullet's neck. "With Victor and Russ possibly still on their tails."

For a moment, panic filled Kaitlyn's chest, and she suddenly wanted to call her father and tell him to forget the stone—to run with her. Her hand brushed the back pocket of her jeans where she habitually kept her cell phone, and suddenly her heart stopped.

"My phone! We can track my cell phone! I have a locator app on it."

***

Thomas tucked Kaitlyn's cell phone under the pillow before leaving the small bedroom. He took a moment to breathe deep and look at the mountain range ahead. His conscience had lightened now that he'd made sure James and Kaitlyn got the message. Daniel climbed back up into the driver's seat as Thomas walked toward the front of the camper, and they continued their drive toward the mine.

***

Victor walked into the small convenience store and strode directly to the counter, greeting the attendant with a flashy false smile and a carefully planned lie. "Excuse me, sir, but I'm afraid I have been separated from the other vehicles in my party. We were traveling together. Have you seen a young woman with her father?" He gave a brief description of Daniel, recalling the way he looked back in the day.

"Sure, man, I saw a guy like that. No one else came inside, but you just missed them," the attendant said, leaning forward on the counter and pointing in the direction of the dead-end and the mine. "Drove an RV off to the left there. Just pulled away maybe two or three minutes ago."

Victor's smile grew wider and became quite real. "That's them! Thank you so much." As he sauntered back to his car, his excitement gave him a small skip in his step. He wasn't far behind now.

269

Chapter 36

Kaitlyn stood on the side of the road as Stacy and James struggled to download the phone locator app onto his cell without reliable service. A little ways off the shoulder, Chooli and Lucas stood next to the church bus, discussing something in low voices. They were too far away for Kaitlyn to hear exactly what was being said.

Overhead, a pair of black helicopters passed by, low to the ground. Most of the group gave them a quick glance before going back to their discussions, but Kaitlyn watched them for a few minutes until they reached a ridge not too far off. They seemed to hover before lowering down, and she wondered if perhaps they were military choppers landing at a nearby base. She watched until they were out of sight, then sighed and stretched her neck and shoulders.

Her gaze wandered to the flat desert stretching from one horizon to another. The beige landscape was broken by wisps of desert grass shivering in the wind and a gray road snaking its way toward the mountains in the distance. Nothing living seemed to move out there.

Bullet nudged her hand, and she rested it atop his smooth fur. "How much longer do you think it'll take them to figure that out?" she asked the dog, nodding to James and Stacy.

Bullet tensed beneath her hand. His fur pricked her fingers as it stood on end, and his body vibrated when he growled.

"What's wrong?"

She followed his gaze back into the desert. At first, it looked exactly the same as it had a moment ago, but then she spotted a large black dog slinking toward them. No, not a dog—a coyote.

"Easy, boy," she said. Her fingers slipped beneath Bullet's collar to keep him where he stood.

The coyote was closing fast—a hundred feet away, and then fifty feet, and then thirty feet. He came to a stop twenty-five feet from Kaitlyn and Bullet, his pink tongue lolling from his open mouth.

Kaitlyn had seen her fair share of coyotes, though mostly from a distance. Those coyotes weighed maybe forty pounds. The one staring her down right now was easily twice that and nearly as tall as Bullet.

His eyes were the same green as the stones on her old shark-tooth necklace. As they stared directly into hers, a shiver skipped down her spine. There was an intelligence in the coyote's eyes she had never seen in an animal.

The coyote held her gaze for a moment before taking off toward the horizon. He stopped about fifty feet away and craned his head to look back at her.

"Does he want us to follow?" she asked Bullet.

Bullet made the decision for her. He lunged, dislodging her fingers from his collar, and took off after the coyote.

"Bullet!" She bolted after him. It almost escaped her notice that the coyote started running again as soon as Bullet went after him.

Running had never been Kaitlyn's favorite activity, though she'd gone for runs two or three times a week to keep in shape. So while she couldn't match Bullet's headlong gallop, she kept a regular pace about fifteen feet behind him. The German Shepherd stayed another ten feet behind the coyote. His ears lay flat against his head, and his head dipped low with each stride.

Her foot landed on the edge of a hole rather than solid ground. She rolled her ankle and tumbled to the ground, rough desert grass scratching the bare skin of her arms and legs. Sand flew into her eyes. When she finally stopped rolling, she stayed where she was long enough for her world to stop spinning. Then she took stock of her limbs. Nothing seemed broken, but she could already feel the ache that would set into her muscles soon enough.

"Kaitlyn, are you okay?" James shouted.

She looked around to find James and Stacy jogging toward her. Lucas and Chooli weren't far behind.

"I think I'm okay," she replied. "Where's Bullet?" In response, the German Shepherd poked his wet nose into her neck. She rubbed his furry shoulder before grabbing for James' outstretched hand. "Did you see the coyote?" she asked.

"What coyote?" Stacy questioned. "We just saw you rushing after Bullet."

"It looked like he took off after a rabbit," James said. "And then you took off after him."

Kaitlyn brushed at her legs, removing the top layer of sand that had embedded itself into her skin. The tiny granules left matching pockmarks in her thighs and knees. Bright red scratches decorated her calves, and her movements smeared streaks of blood across her skin.

"You didn't see him? There was a black coyote that must've been as big as Bullet." She straightened up to look around, certain she'd spot the big black animal and point him out to the others. But he was nowhere to be seen. "He must've gone over the ridge."

Kaitlyn strode uphill toward the crest of the ridge with James and Stacy at her heels. She reached the top only to realize that the downward side was more of a straight drop to the ground fifty feet below than a gentle slope toward level ground. The height made her head spin just a fraction, and she was grateful when James grabbed her arm to pull her back from the edge.

A valley lay at their feet. It spread wide and beige and mostly empty, and the two black helicopters from earlier sat beside a brown road snaking across the sand. The road began on the left side of the valley, twisting and rolling around the bumps in the landscape until it came to the choppers, which obscured the road's final destination. A few men moved between the choppers and whatever lay beyond them.

"Did we miss the signs for a military base?" Stacy asked, voicing the same thought that had run through Kaitlyn's mind.

"There should have been fencing and razor wire if it was a military base," James said.

"The only bases in this part of California are at the coast," Lucas supplied as he and Chooli joined them on the ridge. "There's nothing on this side of Vallejo."

"Then what's going on down there?" Chooli asked.

Kaitlyn took a step back from the edge and hugged herself tight against a sudden chill. Something about those men sparked a fragment of a memory from when she had first come face to face with Mettinger. Even at a distance, she could recognize the danger rolling off them.

"Wait," she said. "Wait. James, did you get that app downloaded onto your phone?"

"I did," he said and retrieved his phone from his pocket. "Do you think that's the mine?"

"I don't like the look of those men," Kaitlyn said.

Before James could open the app, the men in the valley rushed around, one of them waving their arms as if directing the others, then they lined up along the road like a barricade. Kaitlyn's eyes followed the road in the direction they faced. There was no mistaking the camper, kicking up a cloud of dust in its wake.

"Thomas and Daniel," Lucas muttered. "Have you lost your

minds?"

"Dad?" Stacy questioned. "What's going on?"

Lucas ran his hand through his hair. The lines on his face seemed to deepen in the harsh desert sunlight. "The Russians must've called in backup, and I wouldn't be surprised if Victor and Vladimir found another copy of the map," he said.

"You're telling us there was another copy?" Chooli demanded.

"Not a full copy, no. But Daniel and Thomas always thought it had been destroyed," Lucas said, "or that it was lost for good."

Kaitlyn's heart sank to the very bottom of her stomach. The cold that had settled upon her skin now burrowed beneath it. They'd failed. And now the stone and the Black Coyote project were in the hands of the Russians.

She watched in silence as the men in the valley stopped the camper at gunpoint. One of them remained in front of the big vehicle, his gun trained at the windshield, while the other went around to the door on the passenger's side. He yanked it open before dragging Daniel from inside. The other man kept his gun pointed at Thomas in the driver's seat as he walked around the front of the camper and pulled the older man from where he sat.

The dust cloud created by the camper settled, and a second vehicle was revealed—a black sedan that veered off-road to park beside the choppers. A tall man in all black stepped out, opened his back door, and grabbed a backpack, slinging it over his shoulder as he walked up to the men who had Thomas and Daniel. A few words were exchanged, though Kaitlyn and the others couldn't hear what was said.

"That man," Lucas said, not tearing his gaze from the scene below. "He's one of the Russians for sure."

The man extended his arm to slap Daniel across the face. Then the armed men turned their prisoners around and marched Thomas and Daniel between the choppers toward the mouth of the Hastings Mine.

"It's over," Stacy said in disbelief. "It can't be over."

"It isn't over," Kaitlyn replied. Her heart stuttered when she saw him—the black coyote with emerald-green eyes. He stood just behind the camper and stared up at her with an intensity that made her pulse race. Then he took off at a trot toward the mine. "Follow me," she said.

And without waiting for a response, she took off along the edge of the cliff. The others might have shouted at her, but she didn't hear them. She was too focused on keeping her balance on the razor-thin edge between stable ground and sand that would disappear beneath her feet and send her tumbling down into the valley.

She skirted the curve of the cliff before coming to a point where the ground began a slow descent. A part of her expected to hear gunshots and shouts. And an anxiety welling up behind her ribs made her keep looking up from where she placed her feet on the unstable sand to confirm that the coyote still waited at the mouth of the mine.

Air escaped her lungs in trembling breaths by the time she made it to the camper. All the muscles she could name in her legs—and a number she couldn't—yowled in pain. Even the muscles running parallel to her spine tightly contracted.

But none of that stopped her. Only a hand on her shoulder finally dragged her to a halt.

Kaitlyn spun around, furious. "What are you doing?" she hissed at James.

"I should be asking you the same question!" Sweat glistened on his flushed face, and he panted. "We can't just go running in there."

"My dad is in there," she said. "And so is Thomas."

"I think what James means to say is that we can't go in there without a plan." Breathing deeply, Stacy came to a stop beside him.

"We don't have time for a plan," Kaitlyn protested.

"We have to make time," Stacy said. "If we aren't careful going in there, we could very easily get ourselves killed."

"Stacy's right," James said.

Kaitlyn checked that the coyote was still there before turning to face the others. Chooli and Lucas were just bringing up the rear, panting hard and struggling to move at more than a walk.

Lucas leaned against the camper for a moment before reaching for his ankle and withdrawing a revolver from a holster nestled into the top of his boot. "Stacy, do you have yours?"

Stacy nodded and pulled a pistol from her own ankle holster. "Grabbed it from the office before I left to meet up with you at the diner."

"Good," he said. "Good. Now, we don't have enough bullets to storm the mine or to keep them in there until they surrender. We're going to have to sneak inside and surprise them."

"There are two helicopters out here," Stacy pointed out. "*Helicopters.* Say even just six armed men for each one—that's twelve people, plus the Russian. It's going to be tough to surprise that many people. There's a lot that could go wrong."

"Unfortunately, we don't have time to plan for every possible scenario," he said. "We just have to go in and hope for the best." Lucas looked to the big German Shepherd sitting at his feet. "Chooli, go back to the road and take Bullet with you. If the van or the car are still there, see if they'll drive you somewhere with a cell phone signal, then call the police. They'll get here too late to be of much help. But it'd be nice to know the cavalry will show up eventually."

Chooli gnawed on his lip. He opened his mouth as if to say something but closed it and nodded instead. He grabbed Bullet's collar and jogged with the dog back the way they'd come.

Kaitlyn glanced over her shoulder. The coyote still waited for them.

"Ready?" Lucas asked.

"Ready," she said.

***

Thomas opened his eyes to see a pair of emerald-green ones looking back at him. The black coyote sat in the shadows behind Victor in the mine, silent and otherwise unnoticed. Thomas held

277

back a sigh. He knew the situation must be grim if he was seeing the coyote, and he knew Kaitlyn must be close.

"Let us start over," Victor said. His heavy combat boots thudded against the dirt floor. "Explain to me why you will not retrieve the stone."

"It is not a matter of *will not*," Thomas said. "I *cannot* retrieve the stone."

"Ha!" Victor sneered. "You don't believe the ridiculous rumor of the stone burning flesh?"

It took all Thomas' concentration to ignore the coyote's green eyes staring at him and to look only at Victor. "It's true. If you or I or anyone else were to try to touch it, the stone would melt the skin from our hands."

"You're lying," Victor spat. He motioned toward Daniel, who lay bloodied on the ground. "You saw what I did to Daniel when he lied to me. I will do the same thing to you if you do not tell me the truth. No… no, I will make it far more painful."

Thomas dragged his eyes away from Daniel only after telling himself that he saw his friend's chest move. Even if he wanted to tell Victor the truth, he couldn't. He was the Black Coyote, after all. The trickster.

But he knew the truth well enough. He was not lying when he said neither he nor Victor could move the stone without being burned. However, he left out the fact that one small, easy-to-miss passage of the legend told of a rare few who could touch it without coming to harm. A child of the alignment. Kaitlyn.

Thomas had opened his mouth to speak, to weave another half-truth that might buy him and Daniel a bit more time, when gunshots rang out inside the mine.

Chapter 37

Lucas led the way into the mine, followed closely by Stacy. They took cover behind stone formations jutting out from the scarred sides of the mine. Slowly, they crept along the side wall until some of Victor's men came into view.

"There are only four," Stacy whispered. Lucas shook his head and pointed out two other shadows on the wall by the small sconces lining the tunnel. As quickly as they could, they shot six of the bulky Russians guarding the entrance, making sure to keep them alive but incapacitated. The return fire ricocheted off the walls but never found its intended targets.

Now that their presence was known, they hurried around fallen bodies and descended deeper into the mine, looking for Daniel and Thomas. Kaitlyn and James crouched along behind

Lucas and Stacy, trying to stay out of sight. Kaitlyn held onto the back of James' shirt as they made their way through the twisting tunnels; he used his body as her shield.

Within minutes, Lucas came to a wide opening in the tunnel and saw Victor with his gun aimed at Thomas. At first, he couldn't see Daniel, but finally his eyes settled on the pale body of his friend on the ground. Lucas couldn't tell if Daniel was still alive. He just had to pray that he was.

"I wasn't expecting company so soon," Victor called out, startling Lucas. "But since you're here, you may as well come out and join the party." He held the gun to Thomas' head and motioned for the others to come closer.

Lucas straightened and slowly walked toward Victor. Stacy held her gun ready at arm's length as she followed in her father's footsteps. James looked back at Kaitlyn and pressed his finger to his lips. They quietly hung back inside the narrow tunnel to avoid being seen.

"Drop your guns, or I will make sure the old man never sees daylight again." Victor cocked the pistol in his hand to show he wasn't kidding. Lucas glanced back at his daughter and reluctantly laid down his gun. He nodded to her, and Stacy's gun clattered to the ground next to her father's, sending echoes like ripples through the tunnels.

***

With Lucas and Stacy disarmed, James feared they might not find the stone before it was too late. He grasped Kaitlyn's hand in his and tried to think of a way out. He knew Victor was armed, probably with more than one gun. If they were only up against Victor now, he thought they would have a better chance of making it out alive, possibly even with the stone.

As plans for escape formulated in his mind, James felt Kaitlyn's grip tighten in his hand. He turned to see if she was all right, but instead of seeing her beautiful face, he saw the barrel of a gun. When his eyes finally focused, James saw Russ at the other end of the gun, his hand over Kaitlyn's mouth. Anger ignited inside James, but he didn't fight back when Russ forced them out into the open.

"You better tell me how to get the stone, old man, or you will watch these two eat some lead," Victor said, just before Russ pushed James and Kaitlyn into the open cavern. Their shadows danced on the rounded surface of the tunnel, and light reflected here and there off rock embedded in the walls. Russ shoved Kaitlyn to the ground, and she saw her father's beaten body lying limp in a shallow pool of blood. Her cry echoed through the tunnels, and fresh tears flowed down her cheeks. She grasped at his neck, but Russ kicked her away from Daniel and sent her sailing breathless against a side wall.

Victor wheeled around and turned his gun on Russ. "You!" he shouted but wasn't able to say another word. Without warning, Russ raised his gun and fired two shots, striking Victor in the chest and neck. The stunned look on Victor's face made Russ laugh—a creepy sound bouncing repeatedly between the floor and ceiling like a rubber bouncy ball. To James, time seemed to have stopped as Victor fell in slow motion to the dirt.

James shook his head and peeled himself from the ground. As he got to his knees, he felt the hot steel of Russ' gun press into the side of his head. He froze in place and waited for the sound of the trigger.

Instead of a gunshot, James heard Russ order Kaitlyn. "Get up!" he shouted. She struggled to get to her feet, managing only to come to her knees. Russ shouted again, emphasizing his words with jabs to James' skull. "I said get up, or else your boyfriend here is dead!"

Kaitlyn used the tunnel wall to steady herself and finally made it to her feet. She looked at James, her bloodshot eyes filled with fear.

***

Russ kept his gun pressed to James' head, but he turned and

281

spoke to Thomas next. "I know there is only one person here who can handle the stone before the solstice," he began. "I also know she is that person." He looked at Kaitlyn.

Kaitlyn shook her head in disbelief. How could she possibly be the only one who could handle the stone? She looked at Thomas for answers but saw defeat in his eyes instead. He broke her gaze and hung his head.

Kaitlyn stepped back and pressed herself against the rough dirt wall. She suddenly felt as hollow inside as the main shaft of the mine. She leaned her head back and looked to the heavens for answers. She didn't see any angels, but what she did see was a thin beam of sunlight reaching through a moon-shaped crevice. It cut through the darkness like a knife and stabbed into the rock-embedded surface behind her. Following the light, Kaitlyn's eyes landed on a small black stone partially visible in the surrounding soil. On the surface of the black stone were green flecks the color of the black coyote's eyes, and they glinted in the light.

She slid her body in front of the stone and picked it loose from the wall with her fingernails when James shouted at Thomas.

"How could you not tell me she was the only one who could even handle the stone?" James was still on his knees and helpless against Russ. He rolled his eyes in anger, and they stopped on Victor's gun lying on the ground only ten feet from him. Kaitlyn wondered if he could move fast enough to grab it before Russ could stop him … if he had a distraction.

She felt heat from the black stone pulsing through her fingertips as it came free from the wall. Mesmerized by the energy it contained, she brought it out from behind her back and held it up to the thin beam of light. *This can't be it*, she thought. *It's much too small to hold such legendary power.*

Russ turned his eyes back toward Kaitlyn. The black stone shone like a beacon in the bright light. He gasped, and for just a moment, time stood still. Even the echoes hushed and fell silent. Realization hit Russ and James in the same instant, and once again, the hands of time ticked. As Russ poised to dive for the stone and James for the gun, a black coyote darted out in front of them. Russ tried to shoot it as it ran. The shot was straight-on, but the bullet seemed to dissolve into the creature. The black coyote snatched the stone from Kaitlyn's hand and disappeared into the darkness.

A scream ricocheted through the mine, and Kaitlyn realized it came from Russ. Anger distorted his face as he turned his gun on her and pulled the trigger. Kaitlyn squeezed her eyes shut, anticipating the impact of the bullet. Instead of feeling the searing-hot pain she expected, she heard a soft thud instead. She opened her eyes to see Chooli falling to the ground in front of her.

Russ was momentarily stunned by Chooli's sudden appearance and dive in front of Kaitlyn. James took the opportunity to tackle Russ to the ground and, with Lucas' help, wrestled the gun from his hands and handcuffed him. Stacy and Kaitlyn rushed to Chooli's side. Within moments, it was clear Chooli had given his all to fulfill his mission of protecting Kaitlyn.

Looking down the mineshaft in the direction the coyote had taken, Kaitlyn didn't know what to think. *Magic is truly real. Everyone else saw that, right? The black coyote just—*

Movement from the shadows of the shaft cut her thought short. She could make out a large black silhouette, then Bullet came trotting into the light, his tongue hanging to the side playfully. She held her hand out to him, and he approached her, licking her wrist and setting his paws up onto her thighs. Could it have been Bullet? She checked his mouth for the stone but only found drool. She checked his shoulders and stomach where Russ' bullet had gone through the coyote, but he was unharmed. Furrowing her brow, she sighed loudly.

James placed an arm around her shoulders. Pushing the stone and the coyote out of her mind, she turned into his embrace and melted into him, finally safe.

***

It was three days before the Vallejo police had all the statements they needed. The group had relived the entire ordeal over and over again through their statements until finally the police were willing to accept that their stories, as crazy as they sounded, were not going to change. The Portland and Cannon Beach Police Departments corroborated their statements, and Lucas and Stacy's police credentials added some credibility as well. But with so many shots fired, six Russian mercenaries severely wounded, and the medical status of multiple others still up in the air, they were each suspended from their respective precincts pending further investigation of the scene.

For now, finally, they were free to go.

Kaitlyn sat on a bench outside the police station, drenched in the warmth of the California sun while she waited for James to finish some paperwork. She was relieved the ordeal was over, but she didn't know what to do next. Her husband was dead. Her father was gravely injured and would be in the hospital for weeks, possibly months. She still had no word on Thomas' condition, but he had not looked well the last time she saw him. Lost in her thoughts as James approached, she felt the bench seat sag a little more when he sat down.

"Penny for your thoughts," he said and put his arm around her.

She leaned her head on his shoulder. "Just wondering how your grandfather's doing."

"He's better." James smiled. "He still claims he can't remember anything that happened inside the mine. I even asked him if he remembered you finding the stone, and he just shook his head. I think he's hiding something. There's more to it than just this memory lapse."

"He's old, James." Kaitlyn turned to face him. "And that was quite the ordeal."

"Yes, but I know my grandfather. This has something to do with the ancient secrets, I know it. We will need to keep a close eye on him for a while."

"So what's next for us?" She looked down at her knees and gently pulled at a thread on her pants.

"That's simple," he said. "We'll get your father moved to Reno, where we can make sure he gets all the treatment and support he needs to recover."

"Why Reno?" Kaitlyn asked with a hint of sarcasm in her voice.

"You're moving in with me, of course. After all this, did you really think I could live being so far from you again?" James winked at her. "Besides, you can't go back to living in Cannon Beach with all those traumatic memories waiting for you there."

Kaitlyn's quick smile turned into a wince. She hadn't thought of any of that. She couldn't stay at her old apartment; she'd be haunted by the memories of late nights watching spy movies with Brandon, curled up on the couch in his arms. Or at their house, remembering sunny days spent lounging about in the bedroom, stealing kisses between conversations. Even the café, envisioning Brandon walking through the door for the first time and how the very first thing he ever said to her was, "I thought I was coming in here for coffee, but now I think fate led me here for you." Every happy memory would be a knife to her heart. She hated that he had used her and lied to her, but more so, she hated that on her end, the emotions had been real.

No, James was right. She couldn't go back to that.

She looked up into his soft brown eyes. At least with James, she knew it was real for him too. "Okay. I'd like that."

James smiled and took her soft hands in his own, squeezing them gently. She leaned forward and pressed her lips to his. He hungrily devoured her kiss, both of them oblivious to those witnessing their intimate moment.

***

Kaitlyn looked at herself in the mirror for the thousandth time. She pulled a strand of hair back and held it a moment before letting it fall to hang along her cheek again.

"You look stunning," Stacy said, fluffing the train on her dress once more. She stood and, stretching her arms wide, allowed a deep yawn to escape.

"You must be exhausted," Kaitlyn said through a

sympathetic yawn. She turned back to the mirror, twisting the lone lock of hair around her finger to enhance the curl. "It's been a wild year, hasn't it?"

Stacy nodded and picked up the styling supplies scattered over the counter.

Over the past ten months, Kaitlyn had signed all the paperwork to untie her from Brandon's name, cleared out her apartment and her house, moved to Reno, and had settled into her new life with James. During late spring, he had gotten down on one knee, proclaiming his life-long love in front of their friends and families. He even presented her with a flawless Chinese jasmine in the center of a crystal ball, locked in eternal bloom. Stacy had jumped at the chance to be the maid of honor, and Kaitlyn's father—despite having needed a few surgeries early on in the year—had made a fantastic recovery and was now waiting to walk her down the aisle.

The only thing that had not quite gotten back to normal was James' grandfather, Thomas. His amnesia had remained after the incident in the mine. Kaitlyn and James took care of him in his home in Reno, but he had disappeared after their engagement. They had looked everywhere for him and had even considered calling the police until one of the tribe's elders stopped them.

"Let him go and finish his business with this life, James," the old man had said. When he saw that James didn't understand what he was referring to, the old man continued. "All Native Americans have a spirit animal," he said. James had nodded, then. "Mine is an eagle, my son's is a bison, and your grandfather's is a black coyote. There comes a time when all men need to go become one with their spirit animal. Let your grandfather do this in peace."

James had told Kaitlyn about his conversation with the tribal elder later that night. At first, she'd disagreed and demanded they call the police, but in time, she saw the sacred process was important to the tribe and finally agreed to let things be. She was at peace with the decision now, but she still missed Thomas terribly.

A knock at the door interrupted her thoughts.

"I think it's just about time," Stacy said as she crossed the room. She cracked open the door and looked up and down the hallway. There wasn't anyone there, but a small leather pouch lay on the floor. She picked it up and handed it to Kaitlyn.

Kaitlyn opened the pouch. Inside were two rings and a note.

Dearest Granddaughter,

The Great Spirit smiles down on you and James. Destiny has placed you in each other's lives, and as you say your vows, know that you are joining not only your hearts, but your spirits as well.

And rightfully so. You and James share a spirit animal—the golden jackal. It is much like its coyote cousin but inherently better. They are exponentially stronger when working together, and they make skillful scavengers and loyal partners. Should you ever find yourselves lost or apart, remember the way of the jackal. Plant your feet, relax your jaws, take a breath, and take a pause. Your spirits will each howl for the other, and you will always find one another.

Take these rings and make sure the two of you wear them always. They will protect you, and the strength of your union will ignite their power and unlock the mysteries within.

All my love,
Thomas

Stacy leaned down next to her to get a closer look. Kaitlyn laid the note in her lap and picked up the rings. They were both inlaid with a polished black stone. When she held them up in the light, green flecks sparkled like the eyes of the black coyote, and she knew that the mystery had not ended—that it would be with her and James for their whole lives and beyond.

A sharp rap at the door and a cheery call of, "Ready for you!" and the marriage ceremony was about to begin.

And so was the bloodline for the guardians of the stones.

THE END

Next Time
By
M.E. Anders

"You sure you're going to be okay on your own, Jordan?"

"Sure. Don't worry about it," he rasped. "I just plan to heat up a can of soup and stay on the couch all day."

Catherine gave him a sympathetic smile. "I could come home for my lunch hour if you want. Bring you some soup from work?" Years of marriage had already taught her how badly he handled even a mild cold.

"If all goes according to plan, I'll be fast asleep by lunchtime." His chuckle degenerated into a dry wheeze. "That reminds me, could you find me the cough syrup? I looked, but I'm afraid I wasn't up to your *organizational system* this morning."

"Hopeless," she said with a laugh and her customary eye-roll. As she left the room, she gave him a gentle push toward the living room.

He waited until she was out of sight before he dashed to the foyer. The stained glass surrounding the front door glowed in the morning sun and mimicked the wash of autumn colors outside. The pile of shoes that always accumulated next to the entryway blocked his path, so he picked through them gingerly, careful not to scuff a single sparkling tennis shoe or steel-toed boot on his way to the window. Two daughters and a wife, and none of them could put their shoes in the closet where they belonged.

When he got close enough, Jordan put his face up to the window and surveyed the neighborhood. The colored glass framed the scenes of everyday life unfolding on suburban streets all over the country. A man stopped mowing his lawn and wiped his brow through a curtain of gold. The mom who always wore yoga pants pushed a jogging stroller from a red square to a blue diamond as she made her way down the sidewalk. Somewhere to his left, a garbage truck rumbled to a stop, and its mechanical arm groaned as it reached for the trashcan. It was the normal rhythm of a happy neighborhood, and it was achingly dull.

No matter how far he strained his eyes in both directions, there was no sign of his quarry. Now that he'd determined he didn't miss his chance, he swallowed his flash of panic with a sigh. This whole sick-day charade would be wasted if he couldn't go through with it. When he heard the clack of Catherine's high heels on the kitchen floor, he stepped away from the window and tried his best to look pathetic.

"Oh! There you are." She handed him the bottle of cough syrup with a wry smile. "This doesn't look like the couch."

"Well, I… just wanted to say goodbye." He leaned in for a kiss, and she gave him her cheek.

"I don't want to catch what you've got, babe. Someone has to stay functional around here."

"Sure." His lips brushed her cheekbone, and he stepped away. She could pretend their distance was because of germs if that made her feel better, but he couldn't ignore how long it had been since there was any heat in their embrace.

"The girls both get home around four, but it's not our turn for carpool, so you don't have to do anything except order pizza later. I'll be working late." Catherine shrugged into her black wool coat and yanked on her driving gloves before opening the door. As she hopped off the bottom step, she called over her shoulder, "Feel better."

"Have a good day," he replied with a wave.

He reached into his robe and pulled out his phone. A slight tremor of excitement ruined his first attempt at the passcode, but on the second try, the screen flashed to life. There were only ten minutes to spare, so he bounded up the stairs to get ready to go outside.

In a few strides, he made his way to the bedroom, eyes carefully averted from the gallery of family photos arranged on the wall. It'd taken him hours to decide on the right combination of clothes to make him look both casual and appealing, but he'd eventually settled on a black shirt and a pair of artfully torn jeans, courtesy of his oldest and her endless quest to help her parents "fit into this millennium."

Jordan glanced at the time again as he slipped his phone into his pocket. Still a few minutes left, but he couldn't help but hurry back down to the first floor. If he missed her now, there was no telling when he'd have his next opportunity to talk to her. It had taken days to build up his courage, and he wouldn't let them go to waste.

His heart thundered as he slipped out the side door and into the garage. He slammed his hand into the button, and the garage door rattled to life. The sunlight crept across the floor as the door slid up its tracks, illuminating the pile of gardening equipment he never seemed to get around to putting away. Cobwebs coated the trowel and stuck to his fingers. He grimaced at whatever scuttled underneath the jumble of terra cotta flowerpots and grabbed the coil of hose and a shovel.

As he dragged his supplies into the yard, he congratulated himself on his careful planning and attention to detail. If he was working in the garden, he'd have the perfect excuse to be outside for hours, and he'd be sure to catch her even if she ran late. After the time he'd spent thinking about this moment, it had better be a good plan.

The man across the street stopped mowing his lawn and raised his arm in a friendly greeting. Jordan froze for a moment, afraid to show too much interest in case the neighbor decided this was a good time to chat. He shouted a noncommittal greeting, and the man pointed at the bulbous headphones that protected him from the sound of the engine and shrugged. Jordan dipped his chin in recognition and turned gratefully back to setting up his gardening props.

The automatic sprinkler system provided the shrubs and flowers with all the watering they could need, but he turned on the faucet anyway. His feet crunched through the scatter of leaves as he paced the yard, the sweet smell of decomposition rising in a cloud around him. A pinprick hole in the hose threw up a mist and left dew drops clinging to his bare arms, leaving him shivering in the cool morning air.

Then he heard it—the tell-tale jingle of the collar. Every morning for the past two weeks, the dog-walker had passed his house, ear buds in place and a soft, cooing melody on her lips. Her big, shaggy dog took the lead, snuffling along the pavement as they rounded the corner and lending a counterpoint to the rhythm of her determined footfalls.

She wore black today—athletic clothes that clung to her curves and complemented the dark hair she had slicked into a tight tail against her skull. Her sunglasses were flashier, a white dazzle of rhinestones flaring wide before coming to catlike points on the corners. The lenses were too dark to see through, but he was sure that, if could just see her eyes, he could know if this was a silly distraction or something bigger—something to pursue.

She was only four houses away. The timing had to be perfect.

The garbage truck clattered up to the next house and blocked his line of sight. Unconsciously, he counted down the seconds, waiting for her to emerge. The moments stretched, and he felt his throat tighten with concern, but then the dog's wide face popped into view, followed by his owner a moment later.

Jordan snapped his eyes away before she could notice and scanned his driveway for the next piece of his plan. The newspaper lay in a nest of oak leaves near the sidewalk, and for once he was thankful the delivery guy didn't bother to bring it all the way up to the house. She was two houses away now. Time to go.

His heart pumped so much blood through his body, it was hard to keep his steps slow and aloof, but somehow he managed to retrieve his paper with an easy bend of the waist. The white of her sneakers flashed in the corner of his eye, and he willed himself to stand slowly.

With his best neighborly smile, he turned his shoulder slightly to narrow the path. The dog-walker pressed her lips into a straight line and made no sign of stopping. His distorted face stared back at him from her dark lenses, and his courage wavered. The lines he'd been practicing weighed down his tongue like lead, and for a moment, he could only stand with the smile wilting from his face.

A sudden, cool dampness on his palm grabbed his attention, and he looked down at his hand. The dog bumped him with his wet nose again, then slid his massive snout under Jordan's fingers to encourage scratching. Never much of a dog fan before now, he stroked the smooth head and silently thanked his furry wingman for his ingenuity. After a few seconds, Jordan lifted his eyes to the walker's face again, the ghost of a smile pulling at the corners of her mouth as she nodded hello. Not much to go on, but he'd worked with less.

"What's his name?" Jordan asked as he ruffled the fur of the dog's neck.

The walker grabbed a cord and pulled one of her earphones out. "Sorry?" A pale imitation of her music wafted from where the tiny speaker hung near her waist.

"I was asking what you call this big guy." His fingers moved down the dog's shoulder, and the animal leaned its heavy body even harder against his hand.

Her smile widened a little, and she shifted her weight to her back foot, content to stop a moment or two. "Rufus."

All the things he'd planned to say evaporated at the sight of that smile. He felt like he had to say something smart but could only manage a lame splutter. "Rufus, huh?"

"Yeah," she said, giving the dog an affectionate pat. As she leaned forward, he caught sight of the freckles on her nose for the first time. "That's what it sounds like when he barks."

Jordan laughed a little too loudly. "I bet. Dog that big must pack a big bark."

"Sure does." She leaned out slightly to check if the sidewalk behind him was clear. Of course she wanted to finish her walk, but he couldn't let her go yet.

"You're new around here?" he blurted.

"Yeah," she responded idly. Jordan worried she would leave it at that, but she gave a small, nervous laugh and continued. "Moved in over on Maple, oh, two weeks ago now?"

"Just you and Rufus?"

The figure in black knelt and took the dog's shaggy head in her hands. Rufus luxuriated in her touch, and his long pink tongue lolled out of his mouth. "Yep, just me and this guy."

Jordan's mouth went dry. It was too good to be true. She wasn't married, didn't have any kids. His own family was pushed from his mind as he pictured himself snuggled on a different sofa with a big black dog at his feet.

"Well." She stood, shattering his happy portrait. "I've got to get going."

"Of course." He took a step back, opening the way again. "I guess I'll see you around?"

She peered at him over the top of her sunglasses, her eyes an unexpected and radiant blue. "Sounds like it. See you next time." One more smile, and off she went.

He stood dumbly and watched her go, the muscles in his shoulders shedding the tension he hadn't even realized was there. A grin split his face as he turned to put away the garden supplies.

Though he still didn't have her name, he did get her eyes, and even better, the promise of a next time.

***

Once she'd passed the next house, Jess pulled Rufus to a stop and let out a string of low curses. She pulled her cell out of her thick windbreaker and tapped in a familiar phone number. It rang only once before someone on the other end answered.

"You shouldn't be calling me," the voice said. "You're on a job."

"I know, but it's about the job," the dog walker replied in an urgent whisper. Rufus strained against his leash, eager to check out a particularly enticing bush, and they started moving again.

"What's the problem?"

"We can't go through with it."

The dog had tugged her past another whole yard before the voice on the other end spoke again. "And why, pray tell, would that be?"

She took a deep breath. "The husband at 1401 is home for some reason." A quick look over her shoulder told her he was still putzing around in the front yard. "He should be at work. I was sure the house would be empty. But he's home."

"How can you be certain?"

"You're not going to like this, but he just stopped me on the street for a nice little chat."

"You said no one noticed you!" the voice answered in exasperation.

Jess cringed. "I know. I didn't think anybody had seen me. It's not like anyone's ever talked to me before. And then today, of all days, he decides to be friendly."

"Are you seriously telling me that you just wasted two whole weeks scoping out this house and now we have to scrap the whole thing?"

"It's not like I can break in while he's home!" She checked her volume and continued. "You know that."

"Dammit, Jess. Now the whole neighborhood is shot. If we hit anyone else on the whole block, he can still I.D. you."

"It's not my fault!"

They'd reached the end of the block, and Jess checked for traffic before she crossed. After two weeks of walking this route every day, learning the pattern of the neighborhood, which people worked from home and which ones left their mansions empty, she would be sorry to leave it behind. It was inevitable—there was no way to keep coming around and snooping before someone realized she didn't really live there—but she'd gotten used to the wide lawns and happy bursts of flowers.

"Just come back in," the voice said, laced with disappointment.

A few more choice words come to mind, but she kept herself from voicing them. "I'll do better. I promise," she pleaded.

"I know. It wasn't your fault." The voice sighed. "Just come in."

"Really?" she cried in relief. Her head swiveled back down the way she'd come in case anyone had pulled out of their driveway and she caught a final glance of the idiot who'd spoiled all her plans.

"Yes, really," said the voice. "When you get in, we'll talk about the next job."

"Thank you!" Jess cried in relief. "I promise this won't happen again. I'll see you soon."

She ended the call and gave Rufus the command to go. As they crossed the street, 1401 gave her a final wave. With a sad smile, she returned the gesture and headed for her car. The job was botched and the boss wasn't happy, but at least there was going to be a next time.

Esyld's Awakening
Chapter 1

Esyld stood at the threshold, gazing out at the night. The new moon left the woods shrouded in a darkness as thick as black ink. If she'd had eyes, they'd be useless, even if her face wasn't hidden beneath the shroud. She smiled to herself—her other senses were at their peak, causing her body to tingle from head to toe. Leaving the old wooden door open, Esyld went back inside and gathered her things into a satchel. Pulling the strap over her head, she then stood in front of the broken shard of mirror hanging on the wall by the door. She lifted the shroud from the bottom edges gently brushing against her waist and raised it up over her bald head. She didn't gaze so much as sense her reflection. Esyld, though lacking eyes, saw everything through her mind's eye. It worked just as well, if not better than the eyes of mortals; it opened when she needed to see and closed when she didn't. Her mind's eye opened now as she took a rare look at herself.

Her features were less than conventional, with a lack of eyes, small slits with the tiniest bump of cartilage for a nose, and spiraled cartilage on either side of her head functioning as ears. The only aspect of her features considered normal was her mouth, with her full rose-coloured lips and two rows of tiny white teeth. Esyld lowered the shroud back over her face with a sigh. Even though she was well hidden in the woods, she preferred to hide herself, partly because she was worried that one day, her peace may be disrupted. But she also found the darkness sharpened her senses, allowing her to see the world not only as it was, but to also see the intruders lurking the earth from other realms.

Walking briskly out the door, she dragged it closed behind her. Esyld paused for a moment; the air had changed during the brief time she had been inside. There was a sense of urgency about the night now, and she felt that if she waited much longer, her opportunity would pass.

She hurried off along the path, worn by her many trips over the decades. The absence of any woodland noises disturbed her and made the sound of her footsteps on the stones beneath her feet all the louder. As she felt the incline of the ground beneath her feet, Esyld knew she was near the sacred well. With hands outstretched, she touched the cool, rough stone. She ran her hands reverently along the curve in front of her and took a deep breath. With a shaking hand, she reached into her satchel and withdrew the athame, careful to grasp it by the crystal-encrusted hilt. It was even older than she was, passed on from woman to woman down the family line. Esyld was all that was left.

Holding her wrist out over the deep darkness of the well itself, with a quick flick of the blade, she made a small cut across her flesh. She ignored the sting as she placed the athame on the well's ledge and overturned her injured wrist, allowing her blood to spill. When she felt the ground beneath her vibrate, she raised both arms towards the night sky. The ancient chant almost soundlessly spilled from her lips. As the vibrations intensified, she leaned against the well's edge. As her chanting increased in pace, Esyld shifted her weight farther forward until her feet lifted up off the ground and her torso hovered over the dark hole. With the chant at an end, she leaned farther still, allowing herself to fall head-first into the depths.

She hated the sensation of falling, but after a few seconds, her body felt weightless, as though she hovered or floated, though she knew from experience she was still descending. She willed her mind's eye to remain closed, not wanting to see what reached out for her from the darkness. Esyld had no concept of how much time had elapsed when she felt her feet softly land on plush grass. Its fragrant smell after her descent made her dizzy. Forcing herself to inhale deeply, she let her mind's eye open wide, and her surroundings appeared to her.

She stood in the sacred grove—a place hidden from all but her family line. The trees surrounding her grew thick and tall, their tops beyond her sight. A circle of the night sky was visible directly above her, the stars creating swirls as the ground beneath them spun. Standing out from the rest of the trees was an enormous oak tree, its long branches stretching out in all directions. From the lowest branch, still out of her reach and wider than she was, hung three pieces of rope. A rectangular glass cage hung from each length, every one containing a face.

Esyld walked towards them until she stood before the first.

The Maiden's hair was long and flaxen, floating freely around her face before gathering like waves across the bottom of the cage. A small wreath of delicate flowers adorned her head, and her heart-shaped face was flawless with its long lashes and rosebud lips. As much as Esyld felt pulled toward the beauty of the Maiden, she knew her innocence and purity would be of no use—not for what was coming. She moved along to the next cage.

While still beautiful, the Mother's face had the first traces of lines around her eyes and mouth and across her brow. Her hair had darkened with age and was pulled back from her face in intricate braids. Esyld understood that the Mother's energy was more worldly than the Maiden's, and while the Mother could be nurturing, she could also be fierce. The question was, would ferocity be enough? She moved on to the next cage, gazing up at the final face.

The Crone was heavily lined and radiated a wisdom beyond longevity. Esyld admired the wispy white hair framing the Crone's face, only just on this side of wild. By taking on the Crone, she would take on the compassion, transformation, and healing— as well as an understanding of death. Esyld nodded. Yes. The Crone would give her the strength to succeed.

As if in acceptance, the door to the cage swung open, and the Crone's eyes opened. They looked left, then right, as though trying to gather their bearing. When they came to rest on Esyld, she pondered what a strange sight she must be, hiding behind her shroud. With an unexpected nervousness, she lifted the shroud and revealed herself. Not even the slightest hint of surprise or disgust swept across the Crone's face as Esyld stood before her. Instead, the face hovered out of the cage, its hair cascading as it fell out into the open. Esyld let her own vision darken as the face neared, feeling its proximity decrease. As the Crone's wrapped itself around her head, she felt abuzz with everything the Crone had known and experienced, the knowledge permeating her every cell. Opening her eyes—real eyes, now—she noted how heavy it felt to blink but enjoyed the sensation.

The joy was short-lived as she felt a jolt in her solar plexus—an urgent pull from her own realm. She knew she must hurry as her surroundings disintegrated around her. First the leaves fell from the trees, disappearing before having the chance to reach the ground below. The branches and trunks of the trees crumbled away like ash, and the ground dropped away as though a sinkhole had opened up, encircling the grove. As the circumference of the ground on which she stood grew smaller and smaller, Esyld closed her eyes, hoping she could depart before it was too late. She felt herself lift briefly before the sensation of falling took over, and she squeezed her eyes shut as she pushed down the panic threatening to overwhelm her.

Taking a deep breath, she immediately coughed, feeling the cold water expel from her mouth. Gasping for air, she realized she was no longer falling but floating in darkness. Disoriented, Esyld splashed around as she tried to get her bearings. Looking up, the circle of night sky above confused her until she realized she was back in the well. She swam ahead until her hand hit the stone wall. Then, using all the strength she could muster, she climbed upwards. Relieved, she felt the top of the well wall and hoisted herself up and over it, tumbling to the ground. Esyld pushed the wet hair back from her face as she took a moment to catch her breath. As her heartbeat settled down, her hearing sharpened. She sat up with a start, looking at the trees surrounding her. Movement came through the woods, and she strained her ears to make out the cause.

Humans.

She froze, panic immobilizing her as her imagination flooded with what they might do to her when they found her there. As a wind picked up, blowing her damp hair across her eyes, she raised her hands and touched her face. After everything, she had forgotten her appearance was now that of a mortal. Of the Crone.

As Esyld saw the first hints of torchlight pierce the darkness, she got to her feet. Leaning against the well, she felt every bit the old crone. Before she had the chance to prepare herself, men ran out of the trees and up the hill towards her. Two fell to their knees before her, a third draped between them. As they looked up at her expectantly, she realized the man on the ground was severely injured. The Crone's instincts kicked in, and she bent to her knees in front of him. As Esyld struggled to determine where one wound ended and the next started, she looked up to find him alert and staring at her. His mouth moved, but she couldn't hear him. She gestured to one of the men beside him to make room for her as she moved nearer. Esyld lowered her head and held her breath as he whispered in her ear.

"They're coming!"

Esyld's Awakening is CWC's Sixth novel and is set to be published in 2017. Look out for the official release date and excerpts from the ongoing story on the CWC website and Facebook page.

ABOUT CW PUBLISHING HOUSE

CWPH was founded in 2015, dedicated to publishing CWC novels. Due to numerous requests, we have opened our doors to submissions from completed collaborative novels and will work exclusively with collaborative novels written by two or more authors. CWPH has also arranged a number of Anthologies, with more to come. To learn more about our books and our authors, please visit: www.cwpublishinghouse.com

ABOUT OUR PUBLISHING HOUSE

www.ingramcontent.com/pod-product-compliance
Lightning Source LLC
Chambersburg PA
CBHW060536180626
46817CB00002B/600